Dragon OVERLORD

AIR DRAGONS BOOK 4

CHARLENE HARTNADY

DEDICATION

To the humble hyena.
More specifically the spotted hyena is my inspiration for this book.

The spotted hyena (Crocuta crocuta), also known as the laughing hyena, is a hyena species, currently classed as the sole extant member of the genus Crocuta, native to sub-Saharan Africa.

PROLOGUE

AMY MANAGED TO SLIDE A hand between the elevator doors just before they closed. She was panting hard as she walked inside, hitting the button for the fourth floor repeatedly.

"Come on! Come on!" she chanted, as if saying the words would make the doors shut quicker.

After what felt like an age, they finally slid closed, and the elevator lurched upward. Amy pulled some damp hair behind her ear.

If anything happened to Lisa or her nephew, she would never forgive herself. Amy ran from the elevator before the doors were fully open, almost running into a doctor.

"Sorry!" she yelled.

"Hey!" The guy in the white coat stepped back, lifting both his arms.

"Amy!" someone called to her from down the hallway.

It was Sean. He was smiling. Sean was smiling. Not just smiling, the man was positively beaming. It made her heart rate slow, and her breathing come easier.

"Where is she?" Amy jogged towards him. "Is Lisa okay? What about the baby?"

"They're fine." He laughed. "I'm a dad. I can't believe it. Can you believe it?"

"And Lisa? I thought it was an emergency." Amy realized that her voice was raised. She forced herself to calm down.

"It was. The baby's heartbeat started dipping with every contraction. They performed an emergency C-section. The cord was wrapped around little Christopher's neck."

"Holy shit!"

One of the nurses at the station shushed her.

"Sorry," she mumbled in that direction before locking eyes with Sean. "I'm so sorry I couldn't be here sooner." She'd been presenting a project to a client. Her phone was on silent. She'd missed 23 calls and seven messages.

"Ingrid and Jen just left about five minutes ago."

Amy nodded. Their older sisters would have been there in a flash. It gave her some comfort to know that Lisa wasn't alone through her ordeal.

"I'm meeting your mom in the hospital restaurant. Lisa doesn't like hospital food. I'm ordering something from there for her. You go on in. Go meet your nephew."

"Congratulations." Amy smiled.

Sean smiled back like his face might split in half. "Thank you." They hugged. "You too, Amy. You're an aunty."

Again. This wasn't her first rodeo. Amy had three nieces and two nephews now that Christopher was there.

"Can I get you anything to eat?" Sean asked as he pulled away.

Amy shook her head, feeling guilty. "No, thanks. I can't stay too long." She had to be at an installation with a new client. It was important for her to be there. That she didn't drop the ball. James was still being handed the best clients on a silver platter. One of these days, the management at Trivector wouldn't be able to overlook her any longer. They just wouldn't be able to.

"See you soon." Sean gave her a quick hug.

"Definitely." She smiled, watching her brother-in-law walk to the elevator.

She sucked in a big breath, walking down the hall in the opposite direction. According to the numbers next to the doors, her sister's room was the next one. She stopped outside the closed door. There was this weird feeling inside her. She couldn't quite put a finger on what that feeling was.

Then she gave a soft knock on the door and entered. Amy found herself having to paste a smile on her face. Why? What was wrong with her?

Her sister was lying in the bed with the backrest slightly inclined. Her eyes were bloodshot. She looked exhausted but happy.

"You poor thing," Amy said, going over and gently hugging Lisa. "I'm so sorry I missed it."

"You didn't miss anything. No one was allowed in once those alarms started going off. They only let Sean stay. You would've had to wait down the hall like everyone else. I know how busy you are."

"Not too busy for my little sister." She sank down on the bed next to Lisa. "Not for you." She clasped her sister's hand, her eyes suddenly welling with tears.

"Hey, Ames. I'm fine. Christopher is fine too."

"I'm glad." She pushed out a huge breath.

"I'm so in love with him already." Lisa's red-rimmed eyes lit up. "He's perfect." She looked past Amy.

Amy twisted so that she could look into the little bassinet next to the bed. Christopher was swaddled in a white blanket. He was sleeping. His cheeks were rosy. He had the cutest button nose. Amy swallowed down the lump in her throat.

"You're right; he's perfect, Lisa."

Her sister sighed. "He's everything I ever wanted. We're a little family now."

"I'm so happy for you." Amy smiled, even though her eyes were stinging and her nose was threatening to run. She sniffed.

Amy was incredibly happy for her sister. Her *baby* sister. It wasn't supposed to happen this way. That funny feeling inside her, it was longing… longing for this. For a family?

No!

Couldn't be!

Amy had always put her career first. It had been years since she'd had a boyfriend. Forever since she'd been on a date, even. Where was this coming from?

Amy heard a loud ticking sound. She looked up at the walls around them, searching for a clock, suddenly realizing that the sound wasn't a sound at all. That it was a feeling… and it was coming from inside her.

Her clock was ticking. Not just that, she was lonely. Had she been reaching for the wrong thing all along?

No! She loved her job. She enjoyed the thrill of the close. Of working with people. She loved the installations and the operations side of it just as much. In the industry she was in, she couldn't have both. Most careers wouldn't allow for a family. Amy needed to choose.

"He's beautiful," she told Lisa. "I'm so proud of you. I'll see you on the weekend?" Amy said as she rose to her feet. "I've got to go."

"Of course." Lisa smiled. "Our big career girl. We're proud of you." The compliment didn't warm her. Amy felt hollow inside. She shoved the feeling away. There was no time for feeling sorry for herself.

CHAPTER 1

Two and a half months later...

AMY SAT UP STRAIGHTER IN her chair. "How much did you just say the deal would be worth?" she asked, unable to believe what she had just heard. She looked at Ray skeptically, cocking her head and narrowing her eyes.

"It would be a two-million-dollar deal if we secured the business." Their boss slapped his hand on the sleek table, beaming from ear to ear. "Two. Million!" he added, giving a holler.

"Holy fucking shit!" she blurted before she could stop herself. They were in the middle of a board meeting. Their CEO, Ronald Taylor, raised his brows disapprovingly. Amy widened her eyes. *Oops!* "My apologies for the outburst." She cleared her throat, turning back to Ray, who was still beaming.

"Holy fucking shit is right!" He slapped his hand on the long, gleaming table, hitting it harder this time. "If we secure this business, it would be the deal of the year. Trivector needs this to turn things around."

"Who is this company? Who requires an installation of that magnitude? I can't recall you saying," she asked.

"That's because I didn't mention it." Ray sat back down, shuffling through some papers on his desk. "They wish to remain anonymous at this stage."

Weird!

"Anonymous?" That made no sense. She sat back in her chair and folded her arms.

"Does seem strange." Her biggest rival, James Oliver, leaned forward, putting his elbows on the table. "What type of security systems are we pitching them if we don't know who we're pitching to?"

Ray ignored James, even though his point was valid.

"How do we even know they are legitimate?" Mr. Taylor asked, lacing his fingers together. His bushy gray eyebrows drew together, and he pursed his lips. "Have there been any developments since we spoke yesterday?"

"Oh, they're legit alright, Ron. I didn't get a chance to tell you, but they sent all the details this morning, including travel tickets to some obscure town called…" he started rifling through the papers, "Dalton Springs," he said.

"That still doesn't mean anything. Their terms are… odd, to say the least. What we need is something concrete. Did they disclose any further information?" Mr. Taylor's tone was no-nonsense.

"They deposited fifty thousand in the company account an hour ago as a down payment if we agree to meet them on their terms." The CEO's eyes doubled in size. Then again, so did Amy's. "We would be expected to conduct a full assessment and then to present our solution to their board. We'd have three days to survey and then two to put a presentation together. Should they decide not to go with us, we keep the 50K regardless. It's a no-brainer." Ray shrugged.

"Did you get a chance to chat to HR about that one particular requirement?" Mr. Taylor looked unsure, looking down at the table and chewing on his lip. "I don't like it, Raymond."

"I have a better solution. Once this meeting is concluded, we can talk through the finer details. You can advise on the way forward and whether or not you would like any changes made to the schedule and plans."

"Sounds good." Mr. Taylor rubbed his smooth chin. His eyes were clouded in thought.

"Who is getting the account?" The million… make that two-million-dollar question, and dammit, James beat me to it.

"That will be one of the finer details up for discussion," Ray commented.

"Can we pitch for it?" James added, looking smug. *Asshole!*

"No." Ray shook his head.

"My figures speak for themselves." James leaned back in his chair like he didn't have a care in the world. His small paunch caused the buttons on his shirt to strain. "I've been with Trivector Security Systems for 12 years now. I—"

"I said that pitching for the business wasn't necessary. Mr. Taylor and I will pick the candidate we feel is best suited for this particular assignment." Ray's voice was clipped. He removed his glasses and rubbed his eyes, looking tired now that the excitement had died down.

"Noted." James nodded, a smile toying with his lips. The bastard was assuming that he already had the account, which he more than likely did.

Amy bit down on her tongue to keep herself from putting in a similar pitch. She'd only been with Trivector for three years. Her first year hadn't been great. Thankfully, they'd given her a chance to learn the ropes before pulling the plug on her. Sales was a cutthroat game. Bring in the figures, or you were out the door. She'd worked harder than anyone on the team. Perhaps her figures weren't quite as high as James Oliver's when you looked at the gross amount, but her new business numbers beat everyone out, including James *I'm-so-smug* Oliver.

She looked to the side, seeing Mr. Taylor give her rival a small nod of the head.

Fucking hell! This really was a good ole boys' club. She was the only female on the team. She was sure the only reason she'd been hired in the first place was that she was cute.

Cute!

Argh! She hated the word. She hated how certain doors had opened for her as a result. Hated even more how many had closed… because if you were pretty, you didn't have a brain. At least, that was the general consensus. For once, she wished she could sprout a dick and grow an Adam's apple. Then she knew without a doubt that she would get this business. That Mr. Taylor would be giving her a nod. But because of her lack of cock and balls, and her nice perky set of boobs, she would be overlooked… again. It was frustrating. Irritating as hell! Her mind wandered to her brand-new nephew. To tiny Christopher. To his gummy little smile and chubby little hands.

"Moving on," Ray said. "Let's discuss new business installations scheduled for the coming week."

Moving swiftly along…? *Yep!* Ray was right. There was nothing else she could do except work hard and prove herself even more than she had already. There would be more opportunities, and not just at Trivector. Perhaps it was time to start looking for another position. In fact, that's what she was going to do. It was time for a change. Life had become boring and predictable. Since her work was her life… something needed to give. There was this feeling of restlessness that had unfurled in her. The feeling wouldn't let go.

There was a light knock on the door.

"Come in," she said, sounding bored. Amy *was* bored. The more she thought about it, the more she agreed with her decision earlier today. It was time for a change. There was no way she was ever going to see any real growth or recognition in this company. Not without a dick to swing around.

She almost groaned out loud when James sauntered in. From the swagger in his step, she guessed he was there to brag.

"Hello, hello, little lady."

Little lady? Little lady, her ass. "What do you want, James?" She projected as much venom as possible into her voice.

"I got it!" He plonked himself on top of her desk. *Asshole!*

"Got what?" She decided to play dumb. Of course, he got the client. He was the one with the dick.

"I leave tomorrow to go and survey the site. Ten percent of two million dollars would mean an early retirement for me."

Oh, so there was a silver lining. *Whoop-di-doo!* At least she wouldn't have to look at his ugly mug every day. Or hear him call her 'little lady' again.

"Congrats! I'm sure you'll do fantastically well. You're definitely the right man for the job." It was a pity that the right *person* wasn't going. Namely her! She wasn't going to give him the satisfaction of letting him gloat. James loved to gloat even more than he loved to brag. Infinitely more.

"Thing is," he scratched his thinning hair, his shirt buttons straining a little more now that lunch had come and gone, "there is a second ticket. I can take an assistant. Someone to—"

"I know what an assistant is." There was just no way he was going to invite her along. No freaking way. He would want *all* the glory.

"I could invite you… um… if…" He stopped there, looking decidedly uncomfortable. James started picking on his thumbnail.

"If…?" She raised her brows, trying to move him along. With any luck right out the door. He was irritating her.

"Okay, I'm going to lay this out for you…" He shifted, scrunching some of her documents under his ass. Irritating the heck out of her.

"Okay." She nodded. "Lay it out for me, then." Today!

"So, the person who comes with me will get a

percentage of the royalties. I'm not sure how much yet. That's something they still have to figure out upstairs. It'll be significant, not to mention the… the… prestige that comes along with helping me put this together and to close the deal."

"Are you afraid of going in alone? Do you need me to go with you, James?" She snort-laughed. She didn't want to play second fiddle. Not to someone like James. It would be hell.

"No!" he half yelled. "That's not it at all. I thought you might like to learn from the best. To grow. Don't you want to improve, little lady?"

Screw him and the rock he crawled out from under.

"Please don't call me that. You know I don't like it. Thank you for the offer…" She leaned back in her chair, about to add a "but," when James intervened.

His whole face brightened up. "Great! So, you're interested. I mean, of course, you are." He chuckled. Then he turned serious, his cheeks turning red. "I'll take you with me if you suck my dick right here and right now," he blurted. "There it's out." He smiled.

Amy was too flabbergasted to say anything or to do anything. She just sat there, slack-jawed, like an idiot.

"I'm going to take your silence as interest. You're clearly thinking it over." This man clearly had screws loose. "To sweeten the deal, I would agree to fucking while we're over there. I'll petition for a higher percentage for you."

"What about your wife… your kids… your family?" she finally managed to get a few words out. The nerve of this asshole!

"My kids are in college. My wife has needlepoint. She loves needlepoint."

Needlepoint? Holy fucking hell. She wanted someone to kill her if she ever became any kind of a version of James Oliver's missus. Killed as in dead and buried together with her needlepoint.

"Anyhow, the blowjob right now is non-negotiable. We can talk about the sex on our flight over there. Maybe join the mile-high club." He winked at her, seriously thinking he was in with a chance.

"Why don't you ask your wife to put her needlepoint to one side and to give you a blowjob? I'm sure she—"

James shook his head so hard she was sure he might put out a vertebra. "My missus doesn't like sucking cock… doesn't like fucking much, for that matter." While he was talking, James was opening his belt. "Nope. Not at all. Not for years." Unzipping and taking out his cock, which was in a semi-erect state. He started rubbing on it, making bile rise in her throat. It went from semi to fully erect in half a second. Although calling what he had fully erect was a stretch. "I'm seriously turned on. Wouldn't take much, Ames."

Ames?

What the hell!

Amy burst out laughing. She laughed so loud she had to clutch a hand over her mouth to keep the noise down.

"You call that a dick, James?" she asked.

"Hey…" He stopped whacking himself off. *Thank heavens.* "That's mean." He looked flustered, using a hand to cover his junk. He didn't even need his whole hand. It was that freaking small.

"Mean? Hah! Not hardly. Calling that a pencil dick would be mean. Then again…" She laughed louder. "I couldn't call that a pencil dick because that would refer to length. You have no length to speak of. In fact, if I had a husband with a little dick like that, I would take up needlework, crochet, and knitting. I'd buy myself the biggest dildo and have sex with that. No wonder you don't get any, little man."

His face turned a bright shade of red as he stuffed his tiny dick back in his pants. Did Ray and Mr. Taylor know that James had nothing to swing? That her little lady dick was about the same freaking size.

Assholes!

"Go away, James. Take your little dick with you. Don't bother me again."

"I won't! I'll be too busy bringing in wads of money. I'll have women lined up to suck this dick." He pointed at his pants.

"That's if they can find it."

"Stop it!" he whisper-yelled at her. "Don't you… dare talk like that to me."

"Or what, James? Will you notify HR? That would be great. It would save me the trouble of reporting you myself."

"You wouldn't!"

"Go away!" She *would* report him if she thought it would help. Unfortunately, she doubted anyone would believe her. They'd think she was upset about losing the business.

James made a noise of frustration, finally leaving her office and slamming the door as he did.

Bastard!

At least she wouldn't have to look at his face for the next couple of days. Amy couldn't wait to get her resumé out there. Trivector could suck her lady dick!

CHAPTER 2

S TORM SAT ACROSS FROM HIM at the table. Vortex sat perched on the edge of his seat, listening to what the prince had to say. His eyes felt like they were growing wider with every word. Vortex's mouth dropped open as he sat back in the comfortable leather seat. It squeaked as his skin rubbed against the leather of the backrest.

After a few moments of silence, Storm said, "Say something." His eyes narrowed on Vortex. "Anything," he added.

Instead of answering, Vortex opened and closed his mouth a few times, like a gigantic loser. If he didn't say something soon, perhaps the prince would retract his offer. He wouldn't blame him, but this was big. This was huge. Fucking gigantic!

By claw.

By scale.

By all that was dragon!

"I… I'm a little dumbstruck, my Lord." He shook his head slowly, still unable to believe that Storm had picked him.

"Either you're happy and accepting the position, or you're worried and thinking of turning it down," Storm tried. "This is a huge opportunity. Speak to me. Tell me what you're thinking."

"I was sure that Ice would get the position. I never in my wildest…" *Shut your mouth, Vortex!* "I'm shocked, that's all and happy. Don't get me wrong." Vortex ran a hand through his hair, roughing it up a whole lot. "Back to the part about being shocked." He really needed to shut the hell up.

"Ice's mate has a whelp on the way. We're in troubled times. He… he isn't the right candidate right now. His mind is not in the right place."

Ah! So, they'd offered the position to Ice first, and the male had turned it down.

"I value your ability to follow orders," Storm said, "To think on your feet. To ultimately get the job done. You lead by example. I firmly believe that you're the right person for the job. You shouldn't think that Thunder and I didn't notice how you missed out on many Stag run weekends, choosing to work instead. How you haven't taken a mate yet, even though you are eligible. We have… *I* have noticed. You're a force to be reckoned with, Vortex. We need you now more than ever. You get along with Cyclone better than most. You're our people's best hope against what might be coming. What I believe is coming. The only question is *when* and not *if* war is coming. It is!"

Everything in him tightened at the thought of the threat to his people. Of war. "Thank you. I appreciate that you've noticed my efforts… my commitment to the Air tribe. My position on this team means everything to me. My career is all-important, especially now with all of the unrest. Between the goblins and the cave dragons, we need to be ready." He felt his scales rub and clenched his jaw.

"I take it you're accepting, then?" Storm smiled.

"Of course," he pushed out, grinning. This was all he had ever wanted. All he had ever worked for. Even from when he was a whelp, barely out of diapers. An Overlord. *Holy fucking scales!* This was amazing. There were only two of them. Cyclone and Wind. The latter of whom had recently retired. An opening like this didn't come along very often. Never! This was it. His chance. Best he not blow it.

Storm grinned back but soon sobered. "Don't let me down."

Yep! There it was. A warning, and rightly so. Why? Because this was fucking gigantic. Especially during periods of unrest.

"I won't! I swear. This is what I've been working towards my whole life." It's what all dragon males wanted to be when they grew up. An Overlord. *Fucking hell!*

"I know." Storm nodded. His whole stance relaxed. "I'm sure you've heard that we have stopped all Stag runs for the foreseeable future. We currently have 32 humans in our lair – most of whom are females. No more will be permitted entry at this stage. All petitions to test compatibility have been put on hold indefinitely."

"That makes sense."

"There are a further 19 children and two pregnant females, including Azure and a human. Protecting the innocent is our top priority."

Vortex nodded curtly. "Of course."

"Thunder, Cyclone, Wind, and I hold daily morning meetings. Going forward, you will take the place of Wind. His retirement is already in effect. You're taking over, effective immediately."

"Of course."

"A decision has been taken to upgrade our security systems as a matter of urgency. We've selected a company we feel will be able to provide us with all of our requirements. Speak to my PA. She'll get you up to speed. I'm giving this important task to you. A…" Storm opened a file; his eyes moved as he scanned the top document, "James Oliver will be arriving tomorrow. He is Trivector's top Sales Executive. The male has vast knowledge of the industry and will be able to provide us with the best solution for all of our requirements. We can't have any of those fuckers sneaking up on us. I want the best systems in place. We need eyes everywhere. No expense should be spared."

With all the patrols they had going out at present, it was hardly a possibility, but one could never be too sure or too arrogant. Lives were at stake. "Of course, my Lord."

"Also, all the secrecy last week was because Thunder, Cyclone, and I met with an arms dealer. The arms and ammo arrive the day after tomorrow and will be kept under lock and key in the storage bunker. Tornado is handling that side of our defense strategy. It will mean extensive training in the handling of such weapons. As I said, speak to my PA about getting all of the minutes for the last couple of weeks' worth of meetings. I want you up to speed ASAP."

"No problem. Forgive me, Sire, but arms and ammunition?" He raised his brows. *Holy fuck!* Since when did dragons fight with human weapons? Never, they'd always preferred tooth and claw.

His prince obviously sensed his hesitancy because he added, "Yes." The male nodded. "We have purchased human weapons. We're not taking any chances. If we have to blast the fuckers with silver bullets and shrapnel, then so be it."

"Understood."

"Weapons would obviously be a last resort. One we more than likely will never have to choose, but I want us ready. Not just ready; over-prepared, even. Those goblins are wily bastards. They're also aggressive, with very few scruples. We'll do whatever it takes to win."

"That makes sense," he said. He was going to read all fucking night to get abreast of the situation.

"James Oliver is due to arrive at 11:30 tomorrow morning." Storm must have caught his quizzical look. "The male from the security company," he reminded him.

"Oh, right." He really needed to get up to speed, and fast. *Fuck!* "I'll meet him on the platform and get him everything he needs to be able to advise us."

Storm nodded, standing. "I want you to personally escort the male to all areas that require surveillance. Inform him of everything he needs to know."

Handholding. It had never been his favorite pastime, but Vortex would do what it took to keep his lair safe. He stood as well.

"Congratulations." Storm smiled, giving him a light tap on his back.

"Thank you." He felt himself light up from the inside out. Overlord. He was an Overlord.

"Oh, one last thing," Storm said, clasping his hands behind his back. "There is a three-month probationary period."

Vortex frowned. This was new.

"Technically, a probationary period has never existed before… not officially, at any rate. It's something new we've taken on board."

He nodded once, even though he felt disappointed.

"Three months will go by in the blink of an eye. You have nothing to worry about."

"I'm not worried." Vortex was mildly annoyed, but it was true; he wasn't worried at all.

"That's the kind of talk I like to hear. Don't fuck this up. It's my rep that's on the line. Thunder wanted Avalanche to get the position. I fought hard for you. The male disobeyed a direct order when he went down into those caves. I won't stand for insolence like that."

"Understood. Thank you, Sire! You made the right choice, my Lord."

"I know I did," Storm said as he walked towards the door, opening it. "Come to me if you have any questions… any concerns. I'm here."

"Thank you, Sire."

"You've got this."

He inclined his head before leaving. No pressure! War or no war. He was an Overlord. Nothing was going to stop him from keeping this position. Nothing!

CHAPTER 3

The next day…

WHERE ARE THEY?

Vortex scanned the horizon, using his hand to shield his eyes from the harsh midday sun.

Nothing! Not a damned thing.

It was already after noon, and there was no sign of the human from the security company. No sign of a dragon anywhere. At least, none that flew in formation from the southeast. None carrying a human. He spotted the odd patrol or lone dragon. That was it.

They were over half an hour late. He hadn't heard anything from any of the patrols about any strange sightings or goblin activity. What the hell was going on? Perhaps he should send a team to go and check. He'd give it 10 more minutes.

"Hey," he heard someone say from behind him. "Vortex… good to see you."

Vortex turned and smiled when he saw who it was. "Good to see you." He and Ice clasped wrists in a quick shake.

"I thought I'd come and congratulate you on your new position. Storm told me the good news."

"Thank you." He felt pride suffuse him, and warmth flooded him. "I'm happy, to say the least. I believe I have you to thank for getting the position in the first place."

Ice folded his arms. "So, Storm told you I turned down the offer."

"Not in so many words, but yes."

"I'm a little older… a little more seasoned. I don't take shit from Cyclone, either. I'm sure those are the main reasons that Storm picked me first." The male sighed. "There's a reason I left the guard and became a hunter. Even more reason now that Azure and I have a whelp on the way. Nope," he shook his head, "you're the better dragon for the job. You're focused and determined. I just want to feed the tribe and to be a good mate." He shrugged. "You're by far the better candidate. You've earned it."

"Thank you." Ice wasn't one for blowing hot air up a male's ass. "I saw Azure the other day. She's getting…" He started to make a round motion in the vicinity of his belly.

"Don't say it!" Ice widened his eyes and shook his head. "I know…" he whispered as if his female might magically appear or hear him talking about her from the other side of the lair, "she's getting well-rounded in that area, even though she still has a month to go. I made the mistake of teasing her about it. Let me put it this way… I won't make the same mistake again." He winced like he was in pain.

Vortex laughed.

"Thing is, I think she looks fucking amazing. There's something about a female ripe with child. Everything blossoms." Ice's whole face softened. The male got this goofy look.

"It looks like being mated suits you."

"That it does. I can't wait to be a father." Ice beamed. He got a faraway expression. Yeah, the male was not the right candidate for Overlord. It took a certain type. A mate, a family… nope, that wouldn't work. Vortex was glad that he had stayed the path. Once this war was over, there'd be plenty of time for a female and a family. Until then, focus was needed.

There was a screech in the distance. Vortex whipped his head to the southeast. Yep. It was the formation. They were coming in fast. *Fucking finally!* Then again, considering they were carrying human cargo, they seemed to be moving a little too fast. Vortex narrowed his eyes to try to see better, but they were still too far away.

"I'd best be going. The rest of my team are here," Ice said, pointing to a small group milling close by. They said their goodbyes, and Vortex watched the male walk away.

He turned back to the formation, his hands on the guardrail. It didn't take long for him to see that there was no human with them.

What the fuck!

Why not?

His first assignment and it was already a fuck up. Vortex forced himself to stand still. Not to fidget or to pace. All a waste of energy.

Five minutes later and the team landed, all still in formation. Great wings pulled back as they shifted in a series of cracking sounds. One of the males strode to him. He bowed his head for a second, acknowledging the fact that Vortex was an Overlord.

"Where is the human?" he barked.

"My apologies, Overlord."

There were a few gasps from around them. Vortex had yet to be officially named as the new Overlord. This male had obviously been briefed about the fact. It felt so fucking good to see those around them bow their heads in recognition, too. His years of hard work and sacrifice were finally paying off.

"Um… the human didn't react well when he found out what we are." The side of the male's mouth twitched.

"Go on."

"Ahhh… he was fearful, to say the least." The male clasped his hands behind his back.

The others were laughing as they dressed a little way off.

"I can't believe he pissed himself," one of them said.

They all laughed.

Vortex raised his brows.

"Um… I'm afraid it's true." The male before him smiled for a few seconds before schooling his emotions. He cleared his throat. "We met with James Oliver. Spoke for about half an hour. The human signed a non-disclosure agreement. We briefed him before carefully explaining to him what we are. The human – James – he wouldn't believe me, so I had Sleet over there shift…" He sucked in a deep breath. "It all went pear-shaped from there." His mouth twitched again.

The group of males started laughing loudly this time.

"It wasn't pretty. He screamed and cried. I don't think I've ever seen a grown male cry like that before. There was nothing I could say or do to placate him."

"Wet his pants…" Vortex heard one of the others snigger. "Pussy…" he heard another add.

"It quickly became apparent that there was no calming him, that he wasn't going to agree to come with us. In the end, I reminded him of the document he signed, and we left." The head guard shook his head. "I don't think he heard a thing I said since he was still bawling like a whelp."

Vortex could well imagine. "I will have our legal department send an electronic copy of the agreement and remind Mr. Oliver of the ramifications should he open his mouth."

"That would be a good idea, Overlord… Sir."

"I'll be in touch. We will need to find a replacement stat." That was putting it mildly. "I'm hoping as soon as tomorrow."

"Understood, Overlord. I am at your service." The male bowed his head again. "I will await further instructions."

Vortex turned and strode away. He would need to contact the Trivector management and have them send him a better candidate. Someone with balls this time!

The next morning…

H ER DESK PHONE RANG.

Amy stopped typing. The orange flashing light told her that it was an internal call. She sighed. At this rate, she wasn't going to be properly prepared for her 10 o'clock.

"Yes?" she said as she put the phone to her ear.

"Come to my office. Now."

Shit!

It was her boss, Ray, and he didn't sound happy.

"Sure." She put the phone down and grabbed her jacket, pulling it on as she walked.

Two minutes later, she was walking into his spacious corner office. This had better not take too long. There were so many things she needed to get done, including fitting job-hunting in with everything else. She'd updated her resumé last night. After her morning meeting, she was sending that bad boy out into the world.

"Take a seat." Ray scrubbed a hand over his face. Was it just her imagination, or did he have bigger bags under his eyes than normal? His hair also looked thinner and grayer than it had been yesterday. "This is a royal fuck up," he muttered.

"What happened?" She leaned back in the chair.

"I look like a complete idiot, is what happened. Fuck!" He ran a hand through his wispy hair. "I told him to send you. I insisted, but nooooo." He shook his head. His shirt looked disheveled. Come to think of it, the garment looked the same as the one he had been wearing yesterday. What the heck was going on?

Amy stayed where she was. She didn't move or speak. It was best to wait it out when Ray got like this.

He muttered to himself some more. She was sure she caught the word "balls" once or twice.

He finally leveled a look at her. "You got the account. The two mil one. It's yours, but you have to leave today."

"What happened to James?" She frowned. "Is he sick or something?" She could imagine him conducting the site survey half dead. James wouldn't just drop a client like this. Not one this lucrative. "Is he in the hospital?" It had to be something along those lines.

"Nothing like that. He didn't want it."

"What? Why?" This wasn't making any sense. This was unlike James.

"I'm not sure. All I know is that you need to be willing to travel… on your own. You need to be ready to work harder than you ever have over the next couple of days and make executive decisions where needed. Can you do that?"

"On my own?" She lifted her brows.

"That's what I said," Ray snapped, looking irritated as he removed his glasses to rub his eyes.

She frowned even harder. "I thought that James was permitted to take an assistant. Wait a minute, didn't he go with anyone?" *What the hell was going on here?*

"What does that have to do with anything, Amy? Either you want this, or you don't." He put his glasses back on and glared at her.

Touchy much? She had a right to know what the hell was going on.

"Of course, I want it, but I was under the impression that two people would be going."

"No! It's a solo gig. We were hopeful the client would allow me to tag along, but they were clear… one salesperson and no more."

"Okay. When did James find out about this? He mentioned something to me about an assistant going with him."

"For fuck's sake, Amy. Since when did you need someone to hold your hand?"

"Since never, but I would still appreciate it if you could answer the question." She folded her arms.

"As I said, I was hopeful in yesterday's meeting, but it soon became apparent that it would just be him traveling. I briefed him after my meeting with Ron."

The bastard!

It was bad enough to try to solicit a blowjob. To make matters worse, the creepy asshole had lied to her. It had all been a scam. She felt her blood boiling in her veins. He had assumed she would suck his dick in the hopes of being in on the deal, knowing full well that he was going alone. She'd kill him if he wasn't dead or dying already. Then again, the guy had to be dying to drop a two-mil account. *Good!*

"Rest assured that I will handle your accounts over the next few days. I'm—"

"I'm not understanding. Why doesn't James want this business?" She could smell a rat. A big one. "This sounds all wrong. Something funky is going on." Were they trying to set her up? Had Ray gotten wind that she was looking for another position? Couldn't be. She hadn't had a chance to do more than update her resumé.

Ray sighed. "I have no idea." He shook his head. "He had to sign a non-disclosure, so he can't say anything either way. He came back looking... not himself. Do you want this business, yes or no?"

"Yes."

"Good!" Ray said. "You need to be willing to sign a non-disclosure as well. You will also have to travel away from home for five days, a week at most, and then..." He locked his lips, looking distinctly uncomfortable for a moment or two. "Are you prepared to lie?"

What?

This was bizarre.

"Lie?" She wasn't sure she had heard him correctly.

"Yes, Amy. Lie! Are you willing to tell a teeny-tiny white lie in order to pick up this client?"

"I'm listening." She didn't like this. Not one bit! Funky was the right word. This whole thing stank to high heaven.

An hour later…

T HERE WAS A KNOCK AT her door. Amy ignored it. She was busy organizing her life so that she would be able to hand over her work to Ray in an hour. Make that less than an hour. *Shit!* She was already behind.

Then there was Jake, her parrot. Poor Jake would be lonely without her. Who would he yell at? Who would he squawk profanities to? She needed to arrange for one of her sisters to pop by her house while she was gone. Jake would need to be fed, and her plants would need watering. This little excursion was proving to her that she didn't get out enough. It was always work, work, work. She couldn't even remember the last time she'd gone out with her friends. When last had any of them even invited her? Then again, she always said no. Both of them were married with kids. Sarah had another bun in the oven… or had the baby been born? Come to think of it, Sarah and Lisa had been due at the same time, and Christopher was already two months old. *Shit!* Her sister and her best friend, both brand-new mothers and she'd barely been around for either of them. She was a lousy sister and an even lousier friend. It sometimes felt like the whole world moved forward. While she was stuck. It had to change! Amy would be fixing it when she got back.

There was another knock, and then whoever it was entered, anyway.

"James?" She cocked her head, her voice unsure, even

though she could see that it was him. Somehow, she'd truly believed that he had to be in the hospital or... something worse to have let this shiny new client slip through his fingers.

James had dark smudges under his eyes, which were bloodshot.

"Don't t-take i-it!" he stammered.

"Don't take what?" It was obvious to her after speaking with Ray that he was talking about the new account. She was playing dumb in the hopes of getting some new information.

"You know what I'm talking about." He looked around them like he was afraid someone might overhear. "You'll regret it if you—"

The door to her office opened, and Ray walked in. "There you are."

"Um... I was... I..."

It looked like James may have had some sort of breakdown. His creepy mental state seemed perfectly intact two days ago when he'd propositioned and lied to her. Right now... he looked terrible. Completely disheveled. Worse than Ray, and that was saying something.

"Come this way, James. I think you need a couple of days off. You were talking about taking a boating vacation," Ray ushered James away, "or a cruise, or something."

"Mmmmm... the missus would love a cruise," James muttered. He turned back to her just as they reached the door. "Don't do it. Don't take the account!" he half-yelled. His eyes were wide, and... Was that fear? Probably fear of her doing a better job than he had. *Jerk!*

"Now, now, James... that's enough," Ray murmured.

The asshole couldn't have the business, and so he didn't want her getting it either.

"They'll tear you to pieces," he muttered.

Ray laughed. "Careful, James. More like tear your bank balance to pieces if you disclose anything. Or your kids' college tuition, if you say anything more. You signed an NDA, bud." He shoved James out of her office. "Go wait for me at your desk."

"I don't want the business. Some clients are not worth having." James sounded more like himself, which worried her. What was wrong with this client? When something was too good to be true, it normally was.

Ray closed the door. "Poor guy has lost it," he said to Amy, using a soft tone while twirling a finger around in the vicinity of his temple. "There is nothing wrong with this client. It's James who we should be worried about. I need to get him evaluated." Ray looked genuinely worried.

"Shit!" She pushed out a breath, sitting on the edge of her desk. "He looks and sounds like he's having some kind of a breakdown."

Ray nodded a whole bunch of times. "We'll take care of James. Don't worry. You secure us the business. Are you all set to leave soon?" He looked at his watch.

James might be having some kind of a breakdown, but he was still ultimately a prick. Amy wasn't worried about the guy at all.

She nodded.

"Good!" Her boss cocked his head. "You've got your story straight, like we discussed?"

"The company credit card is in my purse. I'll go past a jewelry store on my way home to pack."

"Good." He got this hard look. "Don't come back unless you have the business."

She choked out a laugh, but Ray didn't move so much as a muscle.

"You're serious," she finally said.

"I am, Amy. Trivector needs this account. Times have been tough. Companies are cutting back left, right, and center. My job is on the line, which means that your job is on the line." He pointed at her, his bloodshot eyes narrowed.

"I'll get the business. You don't have to threaten me."

His shoulders sagged. "Sorry, Ames. It's a fucking shitshow! I know you've got this. You should know that the board wanted one of the others."

Someone with balls, no doubt. She bit back any comments.

"I pushed for you. I went out on a limb. I—"

"Because you know I'm fucking good at what I do." Her voice was cutting. She'd had enough of the old boys' club here at Trivector. Security was a man's world for sure, but this company took it a couple of steps too far. Pissed her the hell off. Amy was bringing home the business. Cashing in her commission check, and then she was putting her resumé out there.

Screw these assholes!

"I know you're good, Amy. You're the best. That's why I stuck my neck out. Point being, the pressure is on." He rubbed his chin, the stubble catching.

Amy wanted to tell him to go home and catch a shower. Instead, she nodded once.

"I've got this." Then she sat back down, wishing she had more time to prepare.

CHAPTER 4

"READY?" VORTEX ASKED AS HE removed his cotton pants.

The male jumped, looking like he might have a heart attack, even though shifters were incapable of such medical problems.

"Holy fuck!" the male muttered. "You gave me a… Um! Yes… yes… of course, Overlord." He bowed his head. "I am Pervious, and I am at your service. Um… are you… will you be…" The male licked his lips.

"I will meet with the human and help escort him back with us." He wasn't leaving such an important task up to his subordinates again. This was delicate business.

"As you wish, Overlord." Pervious bowed. "Here is the rest of my team." The male gestured to a group of three others.

They all stood to attention and bowed their heads.

"Overlord," they all said in unison.

"As you were. We need to leave within the next minute." They quickly shifted and jumped from the large balcony one at a time, quickly moving into formation.

It felt good to stretch his wings. To feel the wind on his scales. Vortex allowed Pervious to take the lead, flying in the center of the formation. They flew hard, still keeping watch for anything out of the ordinary. As they reached the outskirts of their territory, they stayed higher, dropping fast when they spotted the farm.

It was land they owned on the border of their territory. An outpost they operated out of. Deliveries were made here. Males heading out on Stag weekends started out from here. There was a landing strip and a large shed that housed a fleet of SUVs. A helicopter was parked on a helipad to the right of the building, which looked nothing like a farmhouse but rather something out of the pages of an upmarket magazine. The house accommodated 20 males comfortably. It worked for them.

They arrived ahead of the human, quickly shifting.

"Hey." A male beamed at them. He wore a Stetson, and a full business suit, sans a tie. He looked very much like a human, even though he wasn't. "Welcome back." The male chuckled. "Let's hope this next human isn't going to wet himself like the first one."

Pervious cleared his throat. "This is our new Overlord."

The male quickly zipped his lips, sucking in a sharp breath. Then he stood a whole lot taller, dropping his chin to his chest. "Overlord. My apologies. I didn't realize it was you. That you were him. That a new Overlord had been appointed."

"Is the human on his way?"

"Yes, sir… Overlord," the male said, removing the cowboy hat and clutching it to his chest. "I'm Typhoon, Overlord Sir, and yes, he is currently en route here as we speak."

"ETA?" Vortex asked.

"Fifteen minutes," Typhoon said.

"Good. I take it that the documents are ready?"

"Yes, Sir Overlord." The male nodded, still clutching the Stetson to his chest.

Vortex bit back a smile. "All of you can call me sir in front of the human. At least until the paperwork is signed."

"Yes, Overlord Sir."

"And then either Overlord *or* Sir will be sufficient," he told Typhoon.

The male swallowed thickly. "My apologies, Overlord."

"You have nothing to apologize for. Now, let's get some clothes on." They all headed into the house, which was set out like a bed-and-breakfast or an upmarket boutique hotel. There were welcome drinks on the table as they entered. They looked like fancy cocktails, but Vortex could scent that they were alcohol-free. The fragrance of flowers hung heavily in the air, since there were several arrangements in various places in the reception, office, and lounge area.

All the paperwork was laid out on the desk to the left of the reception. They made their way down the hall. The last room on the right housed racks of clothing in various sizes. There was everything from casual wear, such as shorts and t-shirts, to formal tuxedos and everything in-between. There were shoes to match and in all sizes. Well, make that all bigger sizes, since dragon shifters were large by human standards. All of them. Some were larger than others.

They quickly changed. All of them chose suits since this was technically a business meeting. The human was expecting to meet a company representative. It would be important to ease the human into the whole dragon thing. It would take tact.

If that meant a couple of males dressed to look like businessmen, so be it!

"I'll handle the human," he growled as the sound of a vehicle pulling up greeted him. "I'll get the documents out of the way and then brief him on the situation."

"Of course, Sir," Typhoon said, putting the hat back on his head.

They made their way to the lobby and walked outside. A female in a black pantsuit slid out of the back of an SUV.

She was of average height, with long dark hair that was left to cascade down her back. The suit said, "I'm all business." The stern set of her features as she gathered her things said the same. Everything else... not so fucking much.

Wait a minute!

A female? He had spoken to the CEO of the company just yesterday, and he had mentioned a male salesperson. He caught the glint of gold as she pulled the strap of her laptop bag over her shoulder. It didn't matter to him either way, as long as she could do the job. They had been clear about their requirements. As long as she fit the brief, he was happy.

The female walked over. Her dark eyes were expressive and as pretty as the rest of her. Her mouth was full and curved into the hint of a smile.

"Hello, I'm Amy Winters," she said as she walked towards him. The other males stayed back.

"Winters," he said, lifting his brows. "That's an interesting last name."

"Tell me about it." Her voice was smoky. "My nickname was the Ice Princess all through high school."

He chuckled, taking her outstretched hand. Her clasp was firm. Her hand warm. Her skin was fucking soft against his palm.

"Why Ice Princess?" he asked as they let go of each other's hands.

"Because I wouldn't put out like a lot of the other girls." She shrugged. "Tony Thomson started calling me that after I broke up with him for getting too handsy." She rolled her eyes. "It stuck. Sorry, this is probably too much information, considering I don't even know your name yet. And considering that you're my client." She laughed. Vortex liked her easy manner.

He also liked how forward she was. Humans could be dull. At least the next few days might not be as big a hardship as he had envisioned.

He smiled. "I'm Vortex."

"Oh! Is that also a nickname? I'm sure there's a story behind that, too."

"Indeed." He winked at her, trying to act human and failing. Why did humans wink? What was the point? "Follow me. Let's get the paperwork out of the way, and then we can continue on the next leg of the journey."

"Are we taking the helicopter or one of the

Gulfstreams? I can't wait to find out what it is that your company does."

"Would you like a refreshment?" Vortex pointed at one of the drinks on the table.

"Don't mind if I do." She grabbed a glass.

"This way." Typhoon gestured to a desk and chair.

As Amy breezed past, he caught a good noseful of her scent. She smelled fresh, like an ocean breeze. Like the sun dancing on the waves. There was also something sweet in her scent, like sweet berries. It was fucking delicious. And then something struck him.

Wait a minute!

Wait just a cotton-picking second.

He stopped walking, cocking his head. *No way. No fucking way!* This was a problem. A huge fucking problem. He needed to get to the bottom of this, and quick.

CHAPTER 5

HOLY FREAKING HELL. MAKE THAT heaven because surely she had died and gone up there. She'd almost fallen onto her ass in amazement when climbing out of the SUV. It seemed that only gorgeous men in tailored Armani suits worked for this company. What kind of business were they in, anyway? Maybe a male modeling agency. Or…? Were these guys sportsmen? Footballers, perhaps? Movie stars? They could be, since she didn't watch much television these days. Not like she used to. It was another thing else missing in her life. Movie nights. What happened to spending a whole weekend binge-watching a series? Things needed to freaking change!

Pulling her head out of her ass, Amy sat down. The leather was soft and luxurious, just like everything else in this place.

Vortex pushed a stack of paperwork her way. "Let's get the formalities out of the way." He put a gold pen on top of the pile.

Out of all the linebackers or male models or rock stars… whatever they were, this guy was the hottest, with his tousled dark hair and bright green eyes. Surely, with a name like Vortex, there had to be more to this. Who was he? These men were larger than life, especially the one who sat next to her. God, he smelled good, too. *Yum.* Woodsy, fresh, all man. She wanted to take a bite. She had to remind herself that he was her client and, therefore, off-limits. *Pity!* It had been a while since she had dated. Work got in the way of any kind of relationship. It was all late nights. Work on weekends. Working like that tended to do a number on a woman's social life.

Amy picked up the pen, looking down at it for a few seconds before putting it on the desk next to the stack. It was heavy. Probably – *ahem* – real gold. It wouldn't surprise her. She really couldn't wait to find out more about all of this.

She caught a glint of the wedding band on her finger as she flipped open the file. She almost rolled her eyes. What kind of company wouldn't do business unless the sales executive was male or a married woman? It was crazy. Surely not actually legal in this day and age.

Amy had to pretend that she was married. *A little white lie!* Nope, it was a huge freaking lie. Huge! It didn't really matter to her as long as she got the business. It was all just a bit weird. From coming out here to the middle of nowhere to the ring on her finger to these larger-than-life male model-types. Were aliens involved? Were these the men in black? She bit back a laugh. The humidity was clearly getting to her.

"The top page is pertains to you," Vortex pointed out. "It's an overview of your basic information given to us by Trivector. Please can you sign the section at the bottom that states the information furnished is true to the best of your knowledge.

What?

Why?

This was weird, too.

"Um… okay."

"Read through the document before you sign it, Miss Winters."

"No problem, I…" Her eyes narrowed. "That's *Mrs.* Winters," she corrected him.

"Strange that you still have the same last name you had in high school." Vortex leaned back in his chair and scrutinized her. "Even though you're married."

Crap!

Crap!

Keep it together, Amy!

"My husband took my last name. I only have sisters and wanted to carry on the family name." Too much information. She needed to keep her mouth shut. She was rambling. Amy didn't enjoy lying to her client. Having said that, she thought it was bull that only a married woman was allowed to deal with this organization. That was plain wrong.

"Interesting," Vortex said. "And your husband didn't mind?"

"Not at all. He has three brothers to carry on his

family name." She shrugged. "If he wanted to marry me, it had to be on those terms."

He was difficult to read. There wasn't a hint of emotion in his expression. "How long have you been married?"

"Three years," she lied. Did he suspect her? If so, what had given her away?

"Do you enjoy married life?"

What did this have to do with anything?

"Yes, I love my man. Jake is just the sweetest."

"No kids yet?" Vortex licked his lower lip, and she had to work not to watch his tongue glide over the perfect plump fold.

"Um… no… not at this stage. We're both career-focused."

"Do you travel a lot in your line of work?"

"Not a huge amount… no." She shook her head. "We have six more branches in all the major centers around the country."

"What does your husband do?"

What was this? Why all the damned questions?

"He's a performer… a singer." It just came out.

"Oh! Anyone I know? Does he go on tour a lot? Perhaps he's on tour now?"

A singer! Holy shit! She needed to learn to lie better. Amy cleared her throat.

"He's more classically trained. I doubt it would be anyone you know. Jake is an opera singer." She had to tell him something. The lie rolled off her tongue before she could stop it.

"Now that's something." Vortex sat further back in

the chair, folding his arms. "I'm intrigued. Is your husband a tenor or a soprano?"

"You know about opera?" *Who the hell knew about opera? Shit!* She knew absolutely nothing.

"I know this and that. I'm no expert. Nothing like Luciano or Andrea Bocelli to fill the soul. I listen from time to time."

She made a sound of agreement. *Fuuuuck!*

"So, is he a tenor or a soprano? I personally prefer a good soprano myself."

"That's what he is." She smiled. "A… um… soprano." She nodded. "He has an amazing voice." Amy held back a wince, praying she sounded believable. "What about you? Are you married?"

"Yes." It was stupid, but she felt instant disappointment. It didn't matter that he was a client and therefore out of bounds or that she was married… at least, according to him. She still felt the stupid emotion. "I'm married to my job. Sad, I know."

"It's not sad. I know exactly what you mean." *Shit!* She was so bad at this whole lying thing. "I mean, I'm not sure how my husband puts up with the hours I keep."

"It sounds like Jake… Your husband's name is Jake, right?"

"Yes." She nodded too many times.

"Well, it sounds like Jake has a pretty busy schedule as well."

"He does."

"You'll need to sign, Mrs. Winters." He gestured to the document in front of her. The one with all of her details. "It's a crime to lie on a legal document."

What the fuck! "I realize that." *Fuck!* Did he know she

was lying? Why was he acting so suspicious? She picked up the heavy gold pen and signed with a flourish.

"You'll be needing this." He opened a drawer, pulling out a piece of paper. "It's a simple questionnaire. Please take your time and fill it in."

She looked over the document. It was basic; most of the answers were yes or no. Then they wanted to know things like special dietary requirements, and—

Wait!

They wanted to know if she was on birth control. It was none of their business. Amy wrote "not applicable" and moved on to the last questions. Nope, she did not get motion sickness. Yes, she was okay with traveling.

She put the document to the side.

"Then the NDA," Vortex said. "I had a copy emailed to your legal department. I'm going to assume you were forwarded the document? If not, you are welcome to take your time and read through the agreement. In short, any information revealed, anything you learn after signing is not to be disclosed to a third party. The NDA is fully binding. There is no time frame or window period. You will take what you learn during your time with us to the grave." He kept his eyes on hers, again not showing any kind of emotion. Cool. Calm. Collected. "Should you decide to contravene the NDA, we will nail you to the wall, Miss Winters."

"Mrs," she corrected. "But you can call me Amy."

The lines around his mouth tightened. "We'll take everything you own, including the clothes off of your back."

"That would make things interesting. I mean, I'd be naked."

"This isn't a joke, Miss… Amy."

"I realize that. I know how NDAs work. I read the document. I found it to be a little overdramatic, but I'm quite happy to sign it. I would never reveal trade secrets. I'd never work in this industry again if I operated in that way. It's unethical, and I'm not that kind of person."

"Fantastic to hear. You can initial all 32 pages and sign where applicable. I believe full signatures are required on page 10 and on the last page."

"Will do."

Her hand hurt by the time she was done. She returned the documents to the file, which she handed to him.

"Shall we get started? I'm going to assume there's one more leg to this journey. I'm eager to find out more about your organization." She smiled at him. "You're not going to make me choose between a red pill and a blue pill? This somehow feels like a red or a blue pill moment."

"A what?" Vortex frowned, looking baffled.

"A red pill or a blue pill. You must have watched *The Matrix*?"

His frown stayed firmly in place.

"The movie where Keanu Reeves is Neo? The white rabbit? The pills?" she tried.

Light entered his eyes. Vortex shook his head. "No. I don't have time for television."

Amy had thought she was bad. This guy had a carrot stuck up his very sexy ass.

"Oh! Pity. That movie was great. The fight scenes were amazing." She tried to stop talking and failed. "At one point, Neo gets asked to choose between two pills and his life changes forever based on the one he ends up picking. Anyway, it's not important. I can't believe you haven't watched it. That's all."

"I haven't." Vortex turned in his chair to the man in the cowboy hat who was lingering in the waiting area. "Give us five minutes, Typhoon."

The big guy nodded and left.

"Typhoon. Another strange name. Really, I feel like I've entered the twilight zone or something." She smiled, trying to come across as playful. She normally got along with her clients. Amy had a knack for reading people, but Vortex was a closed book. She usually knew which tack to take. With him… nothing. It was disconcerting. The fact that she wanted to rip his suit off and ride him like a rodeo cowgirl didn't help matters, either.

CHAPTER 6

NOW THAT THE PAPERWORK WAS out of the way, Vortex could get to the heart of it. He hated bullshit. Could smell it a mile away.

"Let's cut the crap, Miss Winters," he said as soon as Typhoon was out of earshot.

The human sat up straighter in her chair. "Um… I'm not sure what you mean."

He looked down at the gold band on her finger. His annoyance with this female was growing by the second.

"We asked for a male or a married female. We made ourselves very clear on the matter. You're neither."

"I'm married."

"Bullshit! You need to be very straight with me and very fucking quickly, or I'm putting you back in the vehicle you arrived in." He used his thumb to point behind him in the direction of where the parked SUV would be. "You are not married. Jake is made up. A soprano is a high-pitched female voice. You're talking through your ass." Her tight as fuck ass; it also pissed him off that he had even noticed in the first place.

"Jake is not made up!" she bit out. "He sings soprano."

"He's not your husband, and a grown male cannot sing fucking soprano. Soprano is a vocal range for females and young boys. Jake does not exist. Admit it already, so that we can move on."

"Jake does exist. He's my parrot." She half stood from the chair before sitting back down. She pulled in a deep breath. He could tell that she was trying to collect herself. Not because she was worried or afraid, but because she was angry. This female had grit. "I don't get it. Why is it so important that I'm married? I'm the top salesperson on my team. Just because I don't have a set of balls doesn't make me any less capable. I know my stuff when it comes to security systems."

His lip twitched. "Parrot?" He held back a laugh. "Seriously?"

"Look, I don't enjoy lying, so I stuck to the truth as much as possible. I live with a guy. He does sing… not very well, but he tries. I'd say he's soprano since it's high-pitched. Semantics."

"He's also covered in feathers."

"We can't all be perfect."

He cracked a smile, which he quickly schooled. "Long story short, the reason we needed a male, or a mated female, is—"

"Mated?" She raised her brows.

"We're not from around here," he carefully explained.

This was the delicate part. Only, he wasn't sure he wanted to divulge what they were because he wasn't sure she was staying.

"You sound American." Her eyes lifted in thought. "Are we flying out of the US? I didn't pack for cold weather." She lifted a hand, looking sheepish. "That's assuming you let me stay." Her eyes blazed. They were pretty. A very dark brown, like melted chocolate, and then framed by thick lashes. Holy fuck, when this war was over, he needed to get laid. It had been… fuck… two years since he last went on a Stag Run. "I would urge you to allow me to stay, Vortex. It shouldn't matter that I'm not married. I don't need balls to do my job either."

"It matters." He shrugged. "And I would be inclined to disagree; you have a rather large pair of balls. I like that in a female."

"You like your women to have balls?" She lifted her brows. "Now that's kinky." Her eyes danced with mischief for half a second before she schooled her emotions.

"You like your dick with a side of feathers, so I wouldn't judge." *Fuck!* That was seriously unprofessional, and it was headed into a zone that courted danger. He needed to steer the conversation back. "You lied. I get that you were backed into a corner. I don't care. I'm willing to let it slide on a couple of conditions."

Her shoulders sagged with relief. An almost inaudible sigh passed her lush lips.

Lush.

Holy fuck! He really should send her home. If it weren't for the looming threats, he would. As it stood, he didn't have a choice. The lair security needed upgrading asap. It would take days to arrange another salesperson.

"Thank you." She started to remove the ring.

"Stop! I'm not done, *Mrs.* Winters."

She cocked her head, looking confused. "I don't understand."

"There are hardly any females where I come from."

"Are you in the army?" She cocked a brow. "No, the navy, then?"

"Let me finish. It's at least thirty males to every one female. I'm talking about several hundred horny-as-fuck males in their prime who will want nothing more than to get between your thighs."

Her mouth fell open, but she didn't say anything. Good. He had her attention, at least.

"You – and since we have to spend a lot of time together over the next few days – *we* would be harassed relentlessly if they were to find out that you are unmated. It wouldn't matter that you are on our land for important business dealings. These males would be impossible. You have a delectable scent, Miss Winters." *Fuck!* That sounded like he was flirting. He wasn't!

"A delectable scent?" She sniffed her wrist. "I'm not wearing perfume."

"You still smell great and look even better." He put a hand up, palm facing her. "I'm not coming on to you, but hundreds of men would hound you relentlessly if they knew you were available."

"Would I be in danger?" She clutched her chest.

"No." He shook his head. "Nothing would happen against your wishes, but it would be irritating as hell. We're in difficult times. There's a reason we need your services. I need all of my males focused. I need *you* focused. This task needs to happen within the specified timeframe. Our security needs to be upgraded yesterday. You need to stick to your story. You're married. Jake is your opera-singing husband. He is *not* a soprano. Go with tenor instead."

"Got it."

"The ring stays on your finger. Now listen up because this is very important…"

She nodded, her eyes on him.

"Jake – your darling husband – is away on tour."

"Do opera singers go on tour?" She lifted her brows.

"Yes. You haven't seen him for a whole month."

"Wow, poor me. That's a long time." Two frown lines appeared on her forehead. She pulled that lush bottom lip between her teeth. "Why? Why all the song and dance about my husband being away? What does this have to do with anything? I'm married. I have the ring. That should be sufficient."

"I can tell that you haven't had sex in a long time. It might complicate matters, since married couples fuck on the regular. That's a real problem."

"Excuse me!" She cleared her throat. "And how the hell would you know all of that? How is it even your business?"

CHAPTER 7

T HIS WHOLE THING WAS BECOMING more bizarre by the second. This guy could tell just by looking at her that she hadn't had sex in the longest time? Did she look that tightly wound? Like a pathetic individual who didn't have a social life? It would be true, so perhaps he could tell.

Lord no!

"I have an excellent sense of smell," he said by way of explanation, which shocked her.

Smell?

What did a sense of smell have to do with anything? No one could smell whether someone was having a dry spell or not. It simply wasn't possible.

"No way," she pushed out. "You can smell that I haven't had sex in a while?" Did he think that she was a total idiot? This guy was sexist and making up a bunch of shit to get rid of her. The more she thought about it, the more that explanation made sense.

Smell? Hah! No way!

"Yes." He nodded. "Your shower gel is..." He sniffed a few times. "It's cherry with hints of vanilla. You had a chicken salad for lunch." He sniffed again. "No dressing. You also haven't had sex, or even come, for that matter, in a long time."

Come? He could smell all that? Is that what he was insinuating? *Shit!* He was right on the money, though. Her vibrator had died a month or two ago, and she hadn't had a chance to replace the thing. The days had bled one into the other. Had it been that long since she'd orgasmed? Wait just a minute, though. There was no way he could pick that up from smelling her. It was a lucky guess. Had to be.

Amy pulled her gaping mouth closed. It took some doing, but she managed it. There were no words, though. What did she say to that?

"A married female who doesn't smell of sex will be a problem. You're young and attractive. It will make no sense." He kept his gaze on hers. "You've been aroused more than once since we started this meeting. In fact..." He looked down her body, which was growing hotter and hotter by the second with both shame and, yes, arousal. He was talking about coming and sex, and he was freaking gorgeous in that Armani suit. "You're aroused right now." He didn't say it like an accusation. Or in a nasty, weird way. He just said it in that deep, sexy voice of his, making gooseflesh break out on her arms.

Crap!

"I... um... I am not! This is highly inappropriate. There is no way you can tell all of that by just looking at me." How could he tell all of that? It was true, though. She had bought the cherry-scented shower gel. She *did* have the chicken salad for lunch. She'd grabbed a takeout at the airport and was pissed that it didn't have dressing.

"Bottom line, you arouse easily for a mated… married female. Too easily. Excuse the brashness of my words, but, quite frankly, you scent like a female who needs a good fuck. It will cause trouble with my males." He remained impassive.

Amy made this little squeaky noise. Her throat felt small, and her eyes wide. Hearing this man say that she was in need of a good fuck did things to her. Crazy things. Things that made her press her knees together. Things that made her ache inside, especially since he looked so together. So freaking gorgeous and together. It was hard to believe such dirty words had come from a mouth that looked like that. A mouth she wanted to suck on.

Holy crap!

She needed to get it together. It had been a very long time since she had been a schoolgirl so easily affected by a good-looking guy. Why was she acting like one now? Especially since he was being a prick. This was complete bullshit. He was an asshole! And a client. She needed to draw the line, though. This had gone too far.

"This is inappropriate!" she repeated while trying to gather herself.

"I'm *not* being inappropriate." He pushed out a breath through his mouth, sounding almost bored. "I'm stating facts. I'm concerned that your arousal will cause problems with my males. Especially since it isn't something you seem to be able to control. You're supposed to be mated. Mated females don't act this way." He looked her over again, like there was something wrong with her.

Asshole!

"Mated? You really do have a strange way of saying things. Where did you say you were from?" How was this conversation appropriate in any way, shape, or form? By now, her cheeks were burning. Her whole body was on fire, and not in a good way. She was getting angry. Where did he get off talking to her like this? Perhaps where he came from, this kind of conversation was okay.

It wasn't!

"I didn't. We'll get to that soon enough. I'm not convinced you can pull this off."

"The story is that I haven't seen my husband in a month. Of course, I'm edgy. What woman wouldn't be? This isn't an appropriate conversation. It ends right here. Let's move on."

"I'm not convinced that this is going to work, so we can't move on. I'm not convinced that you are the right person for the job. I don't think you're going to be able to pretend to be married."

"Firstly, I'm here to do a job, not to find a lover. I'm a professional. Then secondly, I can pretend to be married just fine. Not everyone will ask me as many questions as you do."

"They will ask."

"Let me guess, they'll all pry into my personal life, and they'll all have a great sense of smell? They'll know I haven't had sex in a long time?" She may as well be straight with this sexy asshole, since it didn't look like she was going to get this account, anyway. Amy almost felt sorry for James. If he was on the verge of a mental breakdown, this would have pushed him over the edge.

Not her!

Forget it!

"Exactly." He nodded. "They'll know everything you just mentioned and more."

She rolled her eyes. "Where's the camera? This has to be a joke."

"It's no joke."

"If this was *The Matrix*, I'd take the blue pill now, please. With all due respect, Vortex, I'm done with this conversation. I'm happy to discuss anything to do with security systems. My personal life and my level of arousal have nothing to do with you or any other employee of this organization. Your poor HR and legal departments must have a field day with all the lawsuits. Is that why I had to sign an NDA? You don't scare me. Are we going to cut the crap, or am I leaving?" She made the same thumb gesture he had made. "I'm going to assume that the SUV is waiting outside, engine revving?"

"No, the motor isn't running at this time, and that's not why you signed the NDA."

She strained to hear an engine or lack thereof, but got nothing.

"Your hearing must be excellent as well," she deadpanned. *Such utter bull.*

"Yes, my hearing *is* excellent, *Mrs.* Winters. Shall we go outside? I'd like you to meet the others. We need to get going. We have a long flight ahead. For the record, your personal life *is* my concern, but only if it affects your ability to do your job and others to do theirs."

"I don't have much of a personal life because I put my job first. I'm going to assume that you've decided to allow me to stay?" *Play it cool, Amy. Play it cool!*

"Yes. Unfortunately, I don't have many options

available to me right now. So, we stick to the story. Can you stick to the story, *Mrs.* Winters?" He kept putting emphasis on the *Mrs.* part. "Can you rein in your enthusiasm for the opposite sex?"

She made a squeaking snorting noise that she hoped conveyed her frustration and extreme irritation. "Yes!" she finally managed to push out.

"I'm sure it will work out, then. Just to be sure, you may not have sexual relations with any of—"

"I'm here to work! You're getting on my last nerve. I refuse to be treated in this way. Just because I'm a single woman doesn't mean I'm looking for a good time. Because I'm really not."

"You're an *attractive* single woman with a scent that could drive even a half-dead male insane."

"Oh." What a braindead thing to say.

"But yes, I like your backbone and grit. You need to be careful. My males can be tenacious at getting what they want."

She leveled him with a dirty look. "Like I'm some sort of item on a menu? I'm not! You really need to talk to your human resources department about sexual harassment and sexism in the workplace." Thing was, the thought of him sexually harassing her didn't seem half bad.

"Sexual harassment?" He quirked a brow. "I don't think so, Mrs. Winters. Stick to your story. Do your job, and we shouldn't have any trouble."

"It's just a few days," she mumbled. "I'm not some sex-starved fiend. I'll cope."

He nodded, not looking like he bought it.

"I'm the right person for the job. You won't regret this. I can keep my sexual urges under control for a few days," she joked.

"Good to know." Vortex was completely serious. *Was this guy for real? Holy macaroni.* He kept his cool, green gaze on her for what felt like the longest time but was actually only four or five seconds. Then he nodded in what looked like agreement. "Let's head outside." Vortex rose to his feet, and she followed suit.

It's a two-mil deal. You've got this!

Amy was half tempted to leave after all of that, but she couldn't. Ray would have her ass. She couldn't believe this jerk. Did he think she was going to jump him? Amy had a little more dignity than that. Then again, he was probably used to women jumping him. *Arrogant prick!*

As they walked, Vortex removed his jacket, hanging it over a chair. She squinted as they walked outside. Her purse, and with it her sunglasses, was with the rest of her things, which were neatly stacked next to the SUV. The sun shone brightly. It was a beautiful late afternoon with not a cloud in the sky.

Vortex undid the buttons on his cuffs. Four of his men stood to the side, talking among themselves, including the guy in the Stetson. One of the men laughed, eyes on her. The other three were all grinning like there was some big joke she wasn't a part of. Another good ole boys' club? Only these guys weren't your typical stuffed suits.

"I hope you don't have a problem with nudity, Mrs. Winters," Vortex said as he opened the buttons on his shirt one by one.

Nudity?

"Um…" Her mind drew a blank. What did nudity have to do with anything? Was he stripping down? It looked like he was. Why? What the hell was going on? Funny how her mouth had gone dry, and words wouldn't form, even though her lips moved.

Vortex slipped the crisp white shirt from his shoulders.

Holy hotness, Batman!

The guy could fill a suit in a way that screamed "tall, dark, and delicious," but he was so much more attractive when he showed skin. Broad shoulders, a smooth chest leading down to a six-pack, and that "V" thing. Holy freaking hell, that vee at his hips was a thing of beauty. All men should have it. She was gaping. All-out gaping.

Wait a minute!

He was unbuttoning his pants… pulling down the zipper… She made this strange noise at the back of her throat as he gripped the material in his big hands.

"Wait!" she finally managed to get out, panting just a little. Who could blame her? First of all, he was gorgeous, and second, what the hell? "What are you doing?"

"Don't freak out."

One of the guys in the group sniggered. Suddenly, she felt a little unsure. She was in the middle of nowhere with a bunch of guys. A two-mil contract? Right then, it had felt too good to be true, and perhaps it *was* too damned good to be true.

"You're okay," Vortex said. That wasn't his name, though. It couldn't be. He'd lied. This couldn't be happening. "Don't freak out. You have nothing to be worry about. You are safe."

Again, that's what they always said before they killed you. Or worse.

He toed off his shoes and pulled his pants down. Just as she suspected, he was naked underneath the fabric. No wonder James had a breakdown. He got to see what a real man packed. *Shiiiiiit!* "Long and thick" had a whole new meaning. He was gorgeous. Even his cock was a thing of utter beauty. Vortex folded the pants. Did serial killers fold their clothing before killing you? They did if they wanted to stay clean. Blood-stained fabric. It was a fact.

What did any of this have to do with security systems? That must have been a ruse to get her there. Serial killers also liked a specific type. That's why he had been so pissed about her not actually being married.

No!

Surely not!

Vortex – or whatever his name was – didn't look like a killer. Her brain felt scrambled. She couldn't think through all the internal noise. It took a few long seconds before it started working again.

"Um… no… I…" Okay, sort of working. She looked up into his eyes, which were glinting.

"Don't scream." His voice was soft and soothing.

Scream? Hah! There wasn't too much point in that, since they were in the middle of nowhere. Who would hear her?

"What are you doing? Put your clothes back on," Amy managed to choke out. "This is inappropriate." She wished she could stop saying that.

"Keep an open mind," Vortex said. "We're not human."

Not human!

Not…!

What?

Something pushed up out of his skin. Something that glinted. Scales! *What the hell?* Yes, scales. They popped up out of his skin… all over. They were mostly a turquoise color, although some leaned more towards blue, while others seemed more green. He grew larger. Limbs stretching, scaly skin fleshing out. His face too. It elongated. His teeth growing longer and sharper. Vortex grew a tail and sprouted wings. Wings that were longer and wider than his whole body. The word "massive" came to mind.

Not human!

Nope. No, he wasn't. A dragon stood before her. It had the same green eyes as the man. They shone with intelligence.

Vortex.

A strange name. A strange way of talking. A superhuman sense of smell and hearing. Not human at all. Her thoughts were jumbled. Racing about a mile a minute.

"A dragon," she murmured, mostly to herself.

"We're dragon shifters, Miss…" one of the guys from the group began to say.

"Mrs. Winters, but you can call me Amy." She couldn't take her eyes off Vortex. His tail thrashed from side to side. He stood up on his massive hind legs, claws digging into the ground, and he roared. Smoke billowed from his nostrils.

The sound was deafening. *Wow!*

"Dragon shifters," she repeated. "I guess it makes more sense now."

"You are safe," the same guy said. At least, it sounded like it was the same one. She still couldn't take her eyes off of Vortex. His scales glinted. He was magnificent. She probably should be afraid. This is what James meant when he said that she would be torn to pieces. James hadn't been that good at reading people. He was a lousy salesperson… a lousy person, full stop. She wished she could have been a fly on the wall when James had witnessed this. A breakdown… She could well imagine. Good thing she was made from sterner stuff.

The dragon came back down onto all fours, and the

whole process happened in reverse. Limbs shortened. Wings and tail retracted to nothing. The massive creature folded in on itself until a man stood before her. He was no less impressive than the creature had been. "We need the security around our lair upgraded as a matter of urgency." His voice was a rich, husky baritone. "Are you able to help with the best possible solution and then later with the installation? When I say later, I mean sooner rather than later."

"Yes. Um… of course."

Vortex took a step towards her and held out his hand. "Welcome aboard, *Mrs. Winters.*"

She took his large hand and shook it. It was weird making a business agreement while one of the parties was naked. Amy had a feeling that this was about to become the norm.

He gave her the ghost of a smile. It lifted the one side of his mouth. If sexy had a specific look, then this was it. It didn't weird her out that he wasn't quite human. In fact, it excited her.

"We need to move out," Vortex said as he released her hand.

The other men began discarding their clothing. Her cheeks instantly felt hotter as she looked away.

This was nuts. All of it! Totally nuts.

"You said you weren't afraid of heights or of flying?" Vortex asked. He'd turned his body away from her, looking towards the vast mountain range in the distance.

Lordy, his ass!

She seriously needed to stop this. Amy had never been this attracted to anyone in her whole life. When romance novels spoke of animal magnetism, this was what they meant. Vortex was her point of contact on this deal, and she was supposed to be married. It was sucky! It was also life.

Get a grip!

What had he just asked her? "Um…" *Flying! Heights!* She shook her head. "No… but—"

"And that's your luggage over there?" he asked, pointing at her things.

She nodded once, feeling bewildered. Who wouldn't, though? *Dragons.* It all made a crazy kind of sense.

"Take the bags, Pervious," Vortex instructed one of the dragons, who gave a low rumble. Pervious was more of a gray color in his dragon form. His scales were iridescent. His eyes had gone from a dark brown like hers to a lighter golden color. He wasn't as big as Vortex. None of them were.

A cracking noise drew her attention. Within seconds, Vortex was gone, and the dragon was back. He flapped his great wings, seeming to rise easily into the air despite his bulky body. Moving quickly and gracefully, he gripped her with his huge talons.

"Hope you have a safe journey." The shifter with the cowboy hat waved; he was grinning broadly.

"I'm not so sure whether—" Amy yelped as her feet left the ground. "I'm not—" She bit back a scream.

Sterner stuff!

Big lady balls!

She could do this!

She could!

Vortex lifted her higher and higher. Then they were flying.

Flying! Crap! Crap! Crap! Craaaaaap!

It was wonderful and terrifying all rolled into one. There was something amazing about that.

CHAPTER 8

The next morning…

AMY GROANED AS THE SHRIEKING noise of her alarm drilled into her brain. She rolled over, patting the side table a few times before encountering her cellphone. It took a few attempts to silence the device. She groaned again, wiping her eyes.

Amy's brain felt foggy. All she wanted to do was to roll over and go back to sleep. It had taken her forever to drift off last night. Then she remembered why. Remembered where she was, and sat up. Sure enough, she was in the apartment. The one in the dragons' lair.

Dragons.

Holy shit!

She fell back again, a smile on her face. Flying had been a pure joy. Once she got over the initial shock, she loved it.

Loved the views that went on forever. Loved the exhilaration of being so high up… in a dragon's talons. *A dragon!* There were lots of them. Just as Vortex had explained, most of them were men.

The dragons' lair.

It was nothing like she had imagined. A lair was supposed to be something dark and dingy. Not this place. This was bright, light, and airy. Opulent but in an understated way. These dragons had taste. They also had money. Lots of it.

Vortex hadn't said much after they arrived. He'd instructed one of the others to show her to this apartment. It was already after hours, so it made sense. She'd been escorted here just as the sun was slipping below the horizon. Even though the refrigerator was full, food had been delivered. Various items, all under gold cloches that were so heavy that she was tempted to believe that they were real gold.

Amy looked out at the vast view. The entire front side of the apartment was glass. It led onto a large balcony. The sun was just peeking over the horizon. The sky was still mostly black, bleeding into dark purples and navy blues, over a vast expanse of ocean. It was breathtaking. So far, everyone had seemed… nice. For dragons. *Holy freaking crap!* She was tempted to pinch herself.

Amy threw back the covers and jumped out of bed. She was a little tired, but nothing a strong cup of coffee or two wouldn't fix. She could not wait to explore the lair. Vortex had mentioned that security needed to be upgraded both here and at various other locations. This was amazing. She couldn't wait to find out more about these shifters. Suddenly, a few days away from home felt too short.

She'd read about non-humans. There were the Sweetwater vampire kings. She knew that human women applied to meet vampire men. At one stage, there had been major marketing surrounding this. Then there were the elusive shifters. As far as anyone was aware, they were wolves. There were rumors of bear shifters. She supposed that it wasn't a far stretch to include dragons.

Dragons!

Holy crap!

Amy walked through the open-plan apartment. It had been built around the view. The kitchen was like everything else in this place, amazing. It was gleaming white granite and stainless steel. All of the equipment was top of the range. This included the coffee machine. It was one of those big commercial-looking ones, the kind that had to have an instruction manual about a mile long. After opening a few cupboards, she found a plunger and a sealed packet of coffee grounds.

"Come to mama," she cooed.

It didn't take long before a steaming cup was in her hand. Amy plonked herself into one of the wingback chairs. She curled her feet under her while watching the sunrise.

"A girl could get used to this."

Once the java hit her system, it was time to get moving. She picked out a navy-blue pantsuit and sensible low heels. Amy did a lot of site surveys. Sometimes taking her to the strangest places, including construction sites. She tended to stick to sensible clothing choices. When it came to presenting a solution, and more importantly to closing, she wore items that were more girly. Items that made her feel subtly sexy. Because why not? She was a woman, after all. Right now, she needed to be sensible. Comfortable pantsuit, white blouse, and comfy cotton underwear in hand, she headed to the bathroom.

Once again, it was pure opulence. The one side was all window with a huge stone bathtub. Then there was the shower with four heads. *Four!* Who needed that many? She could choose from various settings, from drizzle to pulsing to monsoon. And a whole lot in-between.

She spent a bit of time in the shower, enjoying herself far too much. Thankfully, it didn't take her long to get ready. She wasn't big on make-up or fancy hairstyles. She gave her long dark tresses a quick blow-dry and then pulled her hair into a neat, out of the way ponytail. Not very glamorous, but she was here to do a job, not to impress anyone. Her mind wandered to Vortex. She gave a small shake of her head and finished off her makeup with some tinted gloss. Again, nothing OTT.

Amy checked her watch. She had half an hour for a quick breakfast and another cup of coffee. There was enough time to scramble an egg or two. It didn't take her long, and the eggs were on a plate with a bagel and a couple of strawberries on the side. The breakfast of champions. Hopefully, this would see her through to lunch. She hadn't packed any snacks. There probably wouldn't be any time for snacking, anyway. This job was urgent.

There was a knock on the door just as she was about to take her first bite. Amy put down the bagel, looking at her watch. She still had eighteen minutes. Whoever was out there was going to have to wait for her to finish eating first. Being too early was a thing.

"You're early. I wasn't..." The words died on her lips when she saw Vortex standing in the doorway.

Why was she so surprised at his level of hotness when

she'd seen him just yesterday? Not just seen him, but seen him naked and in all of his glory. Also, why did knowing he was half-dragon do weird and wonderful things to her? It had made her attraction problem worse.

He's your client!

"You're early," she blurted a second time. Getting irritated at the fact that he might be able to smell her interest in him. His sense of smell was annoying. "Oh, and apologies for being so forward, but what are you wearing? You mentioned something about an important meeting this morning." And he was going like that?

Screw her life!

His pants were made of soft cotton. They were loose-fitting with an elasticized waist. They looked good on him. Really good. Especially since he wasn't wearing a shirt… or shoes. Just the pants, which were white. A really great contrast against his bronzed skin and all of those muscles. Then, apparently, underwear was too much to ask for as well. Even without looking too hard, she could see the outline of his cock and in all of its wonderful glory.

Screw her life so hard!

"We're a very open and honest species, so forward is good. I like forward," he said, his voice dark and rich.

His words from the day before rang in her ears — *you need a good fucking.* Yep, he was forward, alright. Perhaps a little too forward.

"I mean, I saw you in these pants yesterday, but I thought since today was a workday that you might go back to the suit." She was babbling. "Not that you look bad. You don't. You look great… I don't mean that in… in a weird way." Seriously babbling. "It's just not really work attire." She flapped her hand in his general direction.

"My choice of clothing shouldn't matter."

"I mean, it doesn't. I just… um… never mind." It was hard to think with so much of him on display. She was really beginning to irritate herself. Vortex was a man like any other. No, he wasn't! Okay, he was a shifter like any other, and she needed to pull her head out of her ass.

"I might need to shift to show you certain areas in the lair. It's easier to dress and undress. A suit would be tedious."

Vortex and naked. Two words that should not go together. She'd seen him naked twice yesterday. It shouldn't be a big deal today. By now, she was getting used to it.

"Aren't you going to invite me in? You can finish eating while we talk. Or should I say, you can eat while we talk."

She looked at him quizzically.

"You haven't started eating yet, so *finish eating* wasn't the right term."

"You really do have a great sense of smell." Her cheeks heated. She'd been standing there gawking at him for several minutes and hadn't even invited him in.

He nodded. "We do. It's part of the reason I'm here, so we can just go over a few things." He gave her a quizzical look. "I'm still in the hallway, and your breakfast is getting cold."

She was an idiot. It was that simple. What was it about this guy, aside from the obvious? Tall with a side of dimples and two sides of muscles didn't normally leave her feeling unhinged like this… like he did.

Amy stepped to the side and gestured for him to come inside. "I think I might still have some coffee. I'll pour some for you." She lifted her brows.

"You call that coffee?" Vortex's eyes shone with what

looked like mischief as he looked back at her. "You're using a plunger when there's a perfectly good Barista 1000 standing right over there." He glanced at the gleaming machine.

"I'm sure you need a Ph.D. to operate that thing." She pointed at the coffee machine as he switched it on.

Vortex opened the cupboard below, taking out a filled brown paper bag. "The best coffee is made with freshly ground beans." He measured a scoop or two into a shallow cup that had a handle. "Throw a few beans in here." He put the cup thing into the machine. "Then push this button." There was a whining noise as the beans were ground down. Amy could smell the coffee from where she was standing.

He unhooked the cup. "Tamp down the coffee." He used a nifty device that was attached to the side of the machine. He pushed down on the grounds a couple of times. Then Vortex put the cup back into the machine, twisting until it was secured. He placed two cups under a double silver spout and pushed another button. A few minutes later, two large espressos were ready. "See. Not so hard." He shrugged.

"Like I said, a Ph.D." She laughed. "You'll have to come around early every morning to make me coffee." *Shit!* Did that sound like she was flirting? Amy hoped it hadn't come across that way. She sat back down in front of her food.

Vortex placed one of the cups next to her plate. It smelled delicious. She took a tiny sip, groaning.

"That is good."

"Told you." He took a sip of his own brew.

"Oh! Do you want to share my breakfast? I don't mind. Or I could whip you up a plate in five minutes flat. We might still have time."

"I already ate. Besides, dragons don't eat eggs." He made a face, taking a seat across from her. "At least the self-respecting ones don't."

"Why not?" She frowned.

"There are four different kinds of dragons." He held up a hand. "I don't want to get into all of that right now. There isn't time." He took another sip of his coffee. "To keep it simple, there's Air, Wind, Water, and Fire."

"Interesting." She took a bite of her breakfast. "So, the four elements," she said after swallowing.

"That's right. We're Air, and our females give birth to live young, but that's not the case with Fire dragons. Their young hatch. The females of the species lay an egg and—"

She put a hand in front of her mouth, trying hard not to laugh.

"Oh, my word! That's amazing. I suppose I can fully understand why eggs would be considered…"

"Disgusting! You're essentially eating the unborn young of another species." He grimaced.

"When you put it that way…" She looked down at her plate, seeing her food, the eggs, in a whole new light. "Although most chicken eggs we buy in stores haven't been fertilized, so that's not completely accurate." She pulled her plate back towards her.

"Still…" He gave a shudder. "Don't mind me, though. Eat your food. You're going to need it. Besides, plenty of our males eat eggs nowadays. Some of the males even drink milk. We've changed since mingling more and more with humans."

"I thought that my being here was… unusual. Does your kind mix with humans regularly?" She took another big bite of her food.

"We do… or did. Again, we don't have much time to get into it. There are very few females of our species."

"You mentioned that," she spoke around her food.

"Most of our females are infertile. We found out a few years ago that we are compatible with humans. There have been a large number of matings between our males and human females. Many of these have resulted in offspring."

"So, it's the same as the other non-humans… the vampires, and the shifters, too."

He nodded. "Yes. Up until recently, we mingled extensively with humans. There has been a drive to pair our males with human females. We've had to be discreet, or we would have had more matings with your species by now. As discussed, it's been successful. Only, we're in troubled times, so we've put a hold on our males going into human territory and any new females coming here."

She wondered what he meant by troubled times. Amy had a feeling she was going to find out soon enough.

"I see." She took another bite of her bagel, much smaller this time, keeping her eyes on Vortex.

"Many of our males are single. There is currently very little female interaction. Tensions are running high."

"I'm hoping that this isn't leading to another lecture. I get it, Vortex. You spelled it out for me yesterday. You don't have to repeat yourself to me, and I'm not repeating myself to you. I get it. You all have a fabulous sense of smell, hearing… all your senses are heightened. I need to be very careful. Know that I am here to work." She shrugged. He could go to hell! To prove a point, Amy stuffed the last piece of her bagel into her mouth to show him that she was done talking about it.

Vortex sighed. "I'm not sure you do. Everywhere you

look will be horny-as-fuck males who can scent everything about you. If the royals find out that you are unmated, they will have my head. Possibly my dick too," he muttered the last, his eyes blazing. His jaw tight.

"Royals? As in… a king? A queen?"

"Focus, Amy! If I had sent you back yesterday, delaying this process even further, my superiors would have laid into me, anyway. So, I'm taking a chance on you. Don't fuck this up, *Mrs.* Winters."

Amy managed to hold back an eye-roll, but only just. "For the tenth time, I'm ready. I've done my homework. I understand what's at stake. For the record, my ass is on the line too. I was told that if I don't secure this business, then I'm out. No job. No one in the industry will touch me if that happens. I'll have to start over. The last couple of years of my life will have been for nothing. I've sacrificed a ton to get to where I am. To thrive in a male-dominated industry. I'll do anything it takes to see this through, and that includes lying through my teeth about having an opera-singing husband."

"Good! I'm glad we're on the same page. War is coming, Amy. My people's lives hang in the balance. There is more at stake here than money, power, and prestige."

"War?" she croaked. *Holy shit!*

"Yes! Goblins and the cave dwellers, to name a few. We have enemies who are closing in."

"Goblins? Seriously?" Her eyes widened. "Please tell me you're joking."

"I'm not. Nor are there any red or blue pills, and no, there are no cameras. I'm damn serious. As serious as it gets. If we can see the enemy coming well in advance, then we will be better equipped to stop them."

Goblins!

Cave dwellers? What the…!?

Enemies! War! It was scary shit!

Okay! No sweat! She could still do this. No problem.

"You're right there. We will also look at access control measures." Her company specialized in internal and external security systems designed to protect a company from theft of goods or intellectual property. She specialized in the former. Point being that it didn't matter who the culprit or culprits were. Human, goblin, or other. This would be a job like all the rest. *Goblins, though? Wow!* "I can help you with whatever solution you require." Her voice sounded sturdier and more together than she felt inside. "If anyone so much as breathes close to your lair, you'll know about it."

"Glad to hear it! How was breakfast?" He looked down at her empty plate.

"It was good." Pity she hadn't tasted much of anything. When she looked down at her plate, she noticed that the strawberries were gone. She didn't remember even eating them.

"Let's get going. Meeting starts in half an hour," Vortex said. "We're meeting Thunder, the king. And Storm, who's the prince and Thunder's second-in-command. Then there's Cyclone. I must warn you about Cyclone. He's… he's brash… and rude. He doesn't like people, in general. Hates humans. He's a Dragon Overlord, like me. There are two of us. You could say that we're like Major Generals. Cyclone has been an Overlord for five or six years now. Yeah, he's as salty as they come. Ignore it. Don't take it personally. He's like that with everyone, especially humans."

"Oh! Fun times. I'll manage. I'm sure I can handle

Cyclone. Like I said before, I'm used to surviving in a male-dominated industry. I'm surrounded by assholes and sexist pricks on the daily. I have to play nice and get along. This will be no different."

"Don't flirt or flutter your eyelashes. He hates shit like that."

"I won't!" Vortex really didn't think much of her at all. She needed to be on her best behavior and deliver the goods.

"Don't stare at his dick, either."

Amy put a hand in front of her mouth, having to work to keep from choking on her own saliva or her tongue. "I won't! That's not even a fair comment. Yesterday was a bit of a shock. Today is a new day. I am now officially desensitized to naked men."

"Good to hear, Mrs. Winters." He stood, putting his cock at her eye-level. Right there. Holy crap, but that thin cotton did nothing to hide what was going on…

"My eyes are up here, *Mrs.* Winters." He sounded pissed.

"I wasn't looking at… it… that… there." She looked to the side, flapping her hand at his man zone.

"Right." Vortex didn't sound convinced.

"You were the one who put your junk in my direct view. I didn't put my eyes on it. Besides, that's hard to miss. It's kind of there and in your face." *Shut up, Amy! Stop freaking talking.* "I'm not looking," she added, sounding exasperated. Her eyes were back on his dick, though, so it wasn't true at all. She quickly stood up, cheeks hot. Her whole damned body felt hot.

Vortex's eyes were narrowed. His jaw looked tight. Everything about him looked bristling.

Screw her life!

Argh!

CHAPTER 9

"I N CLOSING…" SHE LOOKED FROM one man to the next, trying hard not to be intimidated by the fact that two of the men were royalty. That one of them was glaring at her like he wanted to kill her and that none of them were human. Hey, she was used to presenting to boards and CEOs of major corporations. She could do this too. Amy cleared her throat. "In closing, I will need to perform a security risk assessment of all the areas in question. I'll start by performing an extensive survey where I will look for blind spots and weak points, ensuring that all of these are eradicated."

"You need to keep one thing at the forefront of your mind, Miss Winters—" the prince began.

"Mrs.," she corrected him.

"Of course," Storm said. He wore a full suit, including a tie. The other two were dressed in the same kind of cotton pants as Vortex. "You'll keep in mind that our enemy is not human. The cave dragons can fly. They can see extremely well in the dark, and the goblins are as comfortable underground as they are on the surface. Their night vision is impeccable as well."

"Yes, I will keep these factors in mind because they do play an important role in my solution. We'll look at systems like CCTV, intruder detection, and possibly even access control. I'll also take a look at your current physical security measures. Perhaps these can be improved on as well."

"Doubtful," Cyclone chimed in for the first time, his voice a deep rasp. His scowl seemed to take up his whole face.

"We need to keep an open mind," the king said. "Mrs. Winters is an expert."

"Expert," Cyclone snorted, sounding disgusted. "What can this female tell me that I don't already know?" He gave her a look of pure hate. "I've been an Overlord for over five years. I was in the guard for nearly ten before that. I've handled goblin unrest and those filthy human hunter scum." His eyes narrowed as he said the word "human" like she was one of those hunters he spoke of. "There is nothing you can tell me that I don't already know."

She kept her eyes on him. Held his gaze, even though she was tempted to flinch away.

"I'm sure that's true, but I would appreciate it if you could humor me."

"There is no time for humoring anyone," Cyclone growled the words, his dark eyes boring into her. "I'm going to excuse myself. One of us needs to be out there.

My Lords." He bowed his head for half a second, then rose to his feet. The guy was a monster. Vortex was tall and powerfully built, but not like this. Cyclone looked like he snacked on steroids for breakfast, lunch, and dinner. He grunted at Vortex as he walked out the door, ignoring her flat. Nothing she wasn't used to.

"Don't mind him." Storm grimaced. "Cyclone is extremely good at what he does. The males all respect him."

"I'm sure he is, and I'm sure they do." Otherwise, he would crush them with one hand. She smiled, leaning back in her chair, hoping she looked more relaxed and at ease than she felt. "I'm not easily intimidated."

"Well," Thunder grinned. "I'm glad you are here, Mrs. Winters. I doubt your colleague would have coped half as well."

Was he referring to James?

"I heard he was terrified when Pervious shifted," the king said.

"Cried like a baby, I am told." Vortex added.

"He didn't!" She tried to bite back a grin of her own. Then quickly changed the subject because it would look unprofessional of her to take such glee at James' tears and terror. It was funny considering how hardcore he always pretended to be. *Asshole!* "Um… my husband sings. If he's feeling nervous during a performance, he pictures his audience naked. Hey," she shrugged, "I didn't even have to picture anything since everyone was naked already." She giggled.

Thunder chuckled.

Storm grinned. "That's true."

Vortex's lip twitched. Aside from that, he remained stoic.

"So, your husband is a singer." Storm looked duly impressed.

"Yes, and opera, of all things. He's a tenor and currently touring around the US. Not that he's famous or anything. They're performing in a small production called *The Magic Flute*. Are you familiar with the performing arts?" she asked Thunder, who shook his head.

She noted that Storm shook his head as well.

Thank god!

"They're performing in tiny theatres around the country. He's been gone for weeks already." She tried to look depressed, pulling in a breath of air.

"You must be proud. I'm sure it can't be easy to be a full-time opera singer." Storm looked duly impressed.

"Oh, no." She laughed. "Jake doesn't perform full time. He's actually an accountant. Thankfully, he can work remotely. Accountant by day and opera singer by night. My Jake is a talented man, and yes, I am extremely proud of him."

Vortex cleared his throat. "Shall we get going? Apologies, Sire." He inclined his head at Thunder. "My Lord." And at Storm. "We should start surveying all the areas. Otherwise, we might go over the allotted five days. I am eager to plug these holes you spoke about earlier," he said to her.

"Of course," Storm said. "Vortex will take excellent care of you, Mrs. Winters. He'll ensure you see everything you need to and that all of your requirements are met. We look forward to seeing you in a couple of days for the presentation."

They all stood.

It was going to be tight. Three days of surveys with only two to put something amazing together. Amy could do it, though.

They said their goodbyes and headed out.

"I'm impressed," Vortex said under his breath. "You *did* some research."

"Yes, I did. It's up here." She touched the side of her head. "I've got this."

"I'm glad." He still didn't look convinced. "Let's get going. I'll show you our current setup. Where would you like to start?"

"Do you have a security room?"

"Security room?" He cocked his head and frowned.

"Do you have a space where someone is viewing CCTV footage?"

"No, we have alarm-activated systems, so no need for constant monitoring."

"We have our first hole in your security. Good to know." She made a note on her iPad. "You'll need to show me what you have in place, as well as all access areas. This should include public areas as well as private ones. For example, my room has a beautiful patio and lovely double doors. That would be considered an access point. I didn't see any cameras or beams in place. There aren't even locks on any of the doors."

"Alright. It's going to be a long day. I hope you brought walking shoes."

She pulled a pair of slip-ons out of her tote. "I always come prepared." She changed into the comfy shoes, putting her heels in the bag, and they started walking.

Fuck!

He could see how the males eyed the human. How a couple of them openly sniffed the air. Bottom line, Amy did not scent like a mated female. Her smell was out of this fucking world. It was downright delicious. Ripe cherries, hints of chocolate… and pussy. There were no two ways about it. This female scented of sticky, salty, musky, tangy pussy. Like arousal and need and yearning. His mouth watered, and his cock kept threatening to harden up. It didn't help that she eyed the fuck out of his dick altogether too often. She seemed to be in a constant state of semi-arousal. Didn't scent of another male. Didn't take care of her basic needs. Vortex wanted to have a word with her about it, but… that would be taking it a step too far. Telling a female that she needed to ease herself… *No! Just fucking no!* He'd power through. The males from yesterday would, hopefully, be spreading the word that she was mated. He'd made sure that Pervious knew about her husband being out of town. Perhaps he needed to have a word with Storm about officially getting the word out there. A thin band of gold on her finger was not going to do the trick. Not when dragons were governed by their snouts and their dicks.

Scent-wise, Amy was not being seen as mated, full-fucking-stop.

Another male scented the air as they drew closer. Amy was inspecting the CCTV cameras outside of one of the common areas.

"Don't even think about it," he warned the male in low tones.

"I can see that the human is working, but—"

"No buts," Vortex said.

"Is she yours," his eyes widened, "Overlord?" The male dipped his head, suddenly realizing who it was that he was speaking to.

Amy continued to make notes on her iPad as she walked around the area.

"No!" Vortex growled, drawing her attention. He waved a hand and tried to smile. It probably looked like more of a grimace. "This female is mated," he said under his breath.

The male sniffed the air a few more times. "I don't scent another male on her. Are you sure?"

This was the kind of bullshit he had been afraid of. So far, this was the only male to have approached them, but there would be more in the coming days. Plenty more. Droves of them. They'd try to talk to her, give her gifts, and ask her out. They'd get in the way.

"She hasn't seen her mate in a few weeks. Trust me; this human is as mated as they come."

The male didn't look too convinced as his gaze tracked where the human was walking. He made a low noise deep in his throat. The dragon version of a whine.

"If you say so, Overlord."

"I do say so."

The male nodded and walked away. His gaze was still on Amy, and he still didn't look convinced. Vortex would speak to Storm. The male could send out an email or something. Many of the unmated males hadn't been into town in months. When he said that tensions were running high, he was underestimating what too much testosterone could do to a male. Her scent was like throwing gasoline on an open fire.

"Everything okay?" Amy asked, a smile curving her full lips.

"All good. Did you get what you needed?"

"Yes. I'm ready to see more." She made a face. "I get the feeling that we haven't explored even half of it."

"You'd be right. From here, I want to show you—"

Her stomach rumbled loudly. Amy grabbed her belly with one hand. "Sorry!" She widened her eyes. "I had hoped that the bagel would see me through to lunch. I should have brought a snack along. I'm one of those people who eats breakfast and then a snack. Lunch and then a snack, followed by dinner with dessert and sometimes another snack."

"You're lucky." Vortex didn't mean to do it, but he gave her the once-over. "You're tiny. Not all humans have good metabolisms."

"Tiny?" She snort-laughed. "No one in the history of my life has ever called me tiny. I think I like it. No. Make that, I *definitely* like it." She chuckled. "I'm not tiny. There's a bit of junk in my trunk, but I'm okay with that. I'm certainly not going to eat lettuce."

Junk in her trunk. By junk, she meant ass with a side of tits. *Holy fuck!* "You must work out then?"

"God no!" She laughed some more. "I don't have the time." She shook her head. "The only exercise I get is when I carry out assessments like these. That's it!"

"As I said, you're lucky."

"What about you?" Her eyes tracked him from head to toe. Her scent wrapped itself around him. *Fuuuck!* "You must work out a whole lot." Her gaze was on his abs and then his pecs before locking back with his eyes.

"Most of my workouts take place out there in my dragon form. We're lucky; dragons are naturally muscular and strong."

"I see that. I mean, not just on you, but all the men here." She looked around them. "Cyclone is like a beast, even in human form."

"You should see his dragon." He whistled low. There wasn't anyone strong enough, other than the king, perhaps, who could take on that particular male and come out of it still breathing. "You handled him well, by the way. He can be intimidating."

"Thanks. You weren't exaggerating when you said that he's not too fond of humans. If looks could kill…" She raised her brows. "I got the distinct impression that he would have taken me out if you guys hadn't been there."

Vortex laughed. "Nah… I think in this instance, he's more bark than bite. He would never harm an innocent female."

"Maybe I'm not that innocent." Her voice had turned slightly husky, and not for the first time that day, he got the distinct impression that she was flirting with him. She seemed to realize it as well because she sucked in a little breath, her eyes flaring. "Um… why does he hate humans so much, anyway?" She quickly brought the conversation back on track. He'd let it slide… this time.

"There are rumors that he had his heart broken by a human female."

"Wow! She really must have done a number on him."

"Rumors say that she did. He was always a moody fuck. Not as bad as he is now, but still. Apparently, he became quite pleasant when he was dating her. You could even have a conversation with him about things other than hunters, war, death, and fighting techniques. Then she broke his heart. Broke him, and he's now twice as bad as he ever was."

"Makes me almost feel sorry for him. Not that I know what that feels like. I've never been in love, and so…"

"Not out here, Mrs. Winters."

She made a face. "Oops, I forgot." Her stomach grumbled, much louder this time. Amy's cheeks turned a bright red. "I'm sorry. That must have been deafening for you."

His mouth twitched. "Let's go and find some food."

"I'm sorry." She widened her eyes, looking as cute as fuck. Vortex found that he liked the human. Liked spending time with her. Good thing that he had plenty of willpower.

CHAPTER 10

HER CHEEKS HEATED.

Her whole body warmed and then grew hot.

It was like a pool of molten lava spreading from the core in her belly, right through her veins.

Amy was getting used to the nudity. She really was. Butts, abs, and cocks weren't that big of a deal. They really weren't. Not after several days of looking at them. It was *him!* Vortex!

Crap! She'd hoped this dumb attraction, infatuation, whatever the hell it was, would be over by now. It really wasn't. It was probably worse. Turned out that Vortex was a really great guy. A little "anal." A little too serious, perhaps, but he was really, really nice anyway. His serious ways made him even more attractive to her. What if he let himself go a little, just a smidge? She had a feeling that would be something to behold.

Right then, she was trying so hard not to stare at him. All those muscles. His ass. Everything. All of it. Especially his eyes, which could dance with mischief from time to time.

Vortex cleared his throat, and she realized that she was staring at him. At least her gaze was fixed above his shoulders this time.

"Sorry." She smiled. "I was thinking of options for security measures in a location such as this."

A lie!

Dammit!

She really needed to focus. As much as she relished the thought of picking up this business… The commission on a two-million-dollar deal was nothing to snort at. Perhaps she could start her own business with the money. Or travel. But it wasn't the money or the prestige a contract like this would bring to her; it was helping these people. The dragons seemed… nice, for lack of a better word. She'd seen a few women and children. A family, just this morning. It was horrible to think that they might be in danger.

"Here, Mrs. Winters." One of the others offered his hand. "The ground is rocky and uneven."

That it was. She took the guy's hand, trying hard to remember his name. There were several of them. All guards, there to protect her if the need arose. Several more dragons circled overhead. They were at the wide opening of a cave that was perched on the side of a huge mountain. The wind ruffled her hair.

"Thank you." She began walking, taking careful steps, trying to get closer to the entrance, where a broken CCTV camera was hanging from wires from the rocks above the entrance. There was broken glass on the rocky ground beneath it.

When she looked up at Vortex, he was scowling, his eyes fixed on where her hand was locked with the other guy's. Was this a problem? Surely not? The poor guard wasn't coming onto her. He was just being helpful. That was all.

Since word of her being married – or mated – had gotten around, the men were mostly leaving her alone. One or two shifters had tried to ask her out, but Vortex had growled at them. She noticed that they sniffed at her. It was all very strange, but still made sense.

"The goblins keep breaking our cameras in the more remote areas, such as the caves," Vortex said.

"They've at least left the solar panels alone," she said, looking up at the wide panels mounted to the side of the sheer cliff. That must have been fun to install. "I would suggest putting a cage around the camera and reinforcing—"

"They'd pull it off. They're strong. Bigger than Cyclone when he's in his human form."

"Wow… that *is* big. What I was going to suggest is reinforcing the cage with silver. I'm hoping that goblins are the same as the rest of the non-human species. Are you guys also affected by silver? I know the other shifters and the vampires are."

His eyes lit up. "That's a fantastic idea. We would never have thought of using the metal. Sure, we infuse bars for keeping species in, but why not do the same to keep them out? That's good thinking, Mrs. Winters." She noted that he always called her that when they were in public. "And yes, to answer your question, we are affected as well."

"So, you would need to utilize the services of an outside

company to install and then service the equipment? That makes it a little bit trickier." The dragons planned to limit any outsiders on dragon soil. Firstly, the fewer humans who knew about them, the better, and then secondly, the dragons were under threat; they didn't want to put anyone's life in danger. They'd built this entire lair, so installing the security systems themselves was more than doable, but not if the devices or equipment were silver.

"Not necessarily." Vortex scratched his chin, the stubble catching. "There are many of us, particularly the guards, who have undergone treatment to make us more resistant to our silver allergy."

"It's an allergy?" She took another step on the rocky terrain and nearly fell on her ass. Vortex reached out and grabbed her arm.

"You okay?" He kept his grip firm, taking a step towards her, his eyes filled with concern.

"All good." She smiled. "I'm trying not to look down, is all."

"Afraid of heights?" He frowned.

"Nope. Tell me more about the allergy sensitivity thing, please." She quickly changed the subject, noting that his jaw had tightened.

"Many of our people have had desensitizing training. We're not as allergic as we once were. Some of the males haven't been for desensitizing, while others have gone through the process more than once."

"I don't know how you did it, Overlord," Gust remarked, dipping his head as Vortex looked his way. "The Overlord did the desensitizing training three times. It makes you as sick as a dog. There were running bets on who could hold down their puke for longer. We'd sleep for a whole day after doses were upped. Draft lost all of his hair and half his teeth. It wasn't uncommon to lose one or two teeth or a couple of nails."

"That's terrible," she said, making a face.

"They grew back… eventually. It sucked going through the desensitizing just once. I'm not sure I could do it a second time, let alone a third."

"You would be fine," Vortex said. "It gets easier each time. It's important that our children are born more resistant, which will only happen if *we* are more resistant."

"So, babies born since the desensitizing have been naturally more resistant?" she asked. This was fascinating.

Vortex nodded. "It looks like it might be the case. Our silver affliction is a major weakness. Any improvement is a step in the right direction. We've made strides."

"Does that mean you'll be able to install and service the equipment if it's housed in silver cages?" she asked.

"Yes, there are several males who went through two rounds of desensitizing. They should cope well enough. We'll work on being better prepared. We can't have those bastard goblins breaking our cameras. We need to have eyes on them."

"Agreed," she said. "I'll include silver-plated cages—"

"Pure silver will work best."

"Silver is a relatively soft metal. I'll look into silver alloys that might work better. We want the structure to be as strong as possible. Let me do some research."

"Sounds good." He licked his lips. "There are another four caves in our territory. Do you need to see them all?"

"Yes. I'd also like to see inside. You said that the goblins might use the cave systems to travel underground. That they might emerge from any one of the five caves?"

"That's right." He frowned hard, looking concerned.

"I'd like to take a look inside. We have infrared CCTV cameras, and we could install motion detector beams into passages as they lead to the outside. It might be easier to hide sensors. Also," she looked out over the valley below, "we might want to look at putting eyes up out there. Again, we'd be in a better position to hide self-contained units in strategic places within wooded areas. You could track goblin movements after they leave the cave system."

"I like it."

"I might suggest that for a phase two of the rollout. It might put pressure on the budget now. There is a lot to cover here, especially considering you guys don't even have locks on your doors."

"Our budget isn't capped at two million dollars, Mrs. Winters. We figured that would be our minimum spend."

"I see." *Holy crap!* "Wow! This is bigger than I thought. This rollout might need to take place over several phases. We would—"

"No! It needs to happen within the next month."

She took a step back and tripped over a stupid rock. Vortex grabbed hold of her. She grabbed him right back because… she was falling. Her hands grasped his biceps. Glorious biceps! Hard, thick, and solid. She wasn't just referring to his biceps, but to all of him. Every last bit of him.

Vortex kept a hold on her upper arms. She noted that his nostrils flared a few times. Was he sniffing her?

Their eyes were locked. Her lungs felt tight. *Shit!* Amy let him go.

"You need to be more careful," he bit out, looking irritated.

She ignored his outburst. "I'm not sure that's possible. I'm beginning to think that five days isn't long enough. We can only start mobilizing once I've given you figures and received the go-ahead. Silver cages for every camera. Jesus, Vortex, that's big money. We'll need to have everything custom made. I estimate we'll need in excess of a thousand cameras, and that's for the lair alone. We don't keep stock of—"

"Start mobilizing then, Mrs. Winters."

"You haven't signed off on anything. You don't even know what it's going to cost."

"Right now, we don't care."

"But…" She opened and closed her mouth a few times. "We might rip you off."

"You won't."

"You've never dealt with Trivector before; how would you know?"

"I've dealt with you. I trust you, Amy. You won't rip us off."

This was probably hands-down, the best compliment anyone had ever given her. Especially given the circumstances under which they had met. Then again, he had told her that she was a shitty liar. That was also an awesome compliment. This was better, though.

"I won't." She shook her head. "I'll make sure you get a fair price… a discount even, since you're ordering in such big numbers. I will need you to sign for the stock."

"No problem. Let's go inside." He pushed out a heavy breath. "Damn!" He sighed again. "I didn't think to bring a flashlight."

"Oh… no problem. I have one." She pulled the sleek black flashlight from her bag.

Vortex smiled for half a second, and holy dimples alive, she felt things go nuts inside her. She almost dropped the damned light because… color her freaking gobsmacked.

He was gorgeous when he smiled. *Wow!* It left as quickly as it appeared, though, leaving her wanting. She was tempted to tell him a stupid joke just to see his eyes light up like that again. Just to see that smile and those dimples.

"I'm shocked at how much stuff you have in that thing." He glanced at her tote. "Not just bullshit, either, but handy items."

"I've been at this job for long enough." She shrugged, still reeling from all that dimply goodness. "I have to say," she switched it on, "if I had known how rough the terrain was going to be, I would have packed hiking gear. These little slip-ons don't exactly cut it." She looked down at her pumps. She almost freaking tripped again. Loose rocks and uneven ground were not her thing.

"I've got you." Vortex picked her up.

Picked.

Her.

Up.

It took a few seconds for her startled brain to realize that she was cradled against his broad chest. She had to stop herself from nestling into his arms. Into his neck. He had the best smell. It was weird. She'd read that different people had different scents. That attraction could be based on smell as well. If that were true, holy freaking moly, she was in over her head. She wanted to bottle him.

"Um. Thanks," she squeaked.

Dark enveloped them. Even the light from the flashlight was swallowed by the darkness. Amy closed her eyes for a few seconds as Vortex walked deeper into the cave. She could hear that the others were following. When he set her down on her feet, she was a little wobbly. Who could blame a girl?

CHAPTER 11

That evening…

THE DOOR OPENED. AZURE LOOKED disappointed when she saw him.

"Where is she?" She put a hand on her distended belly. "It's good to see you." She quickly smiled, looking the picture of health and happiness. Vortex felt a pang. *Pang?* Was that the right term? He felt *something* seeing Azure ripe with child. The fleeting emotion was gone before he could put words to it.

"That's a lovely way to greet a friend." Vortex feigned annoyance as he walked into the house. "What am I, chopped liver? I would swear you invited me just so that you could meet her."

"I did." Azure laughed.

"Nice!" Vortex pretended to walk back to the door. "In that case…"

"Are you sure you want to leave? I cooked your favorite," she added.

"Elk roast?" he asked, eyes wide, walking back into the room.

"Yep." She bobbed her brows. "With buttery potatoes and a red wine *jus*."

"You're speaking my language." He rubbed his stomach.

"Don't believe a word she says." Ice walked up to him, handing him a cold beer. "Elk with potatoes happens to be Azure's favorite, especially now that she's with whelp. Slathers her elk with mustard, of all things." He wrinkled his nose.

"I take it that's a pregnancy craving thing?" Vortex said, taking a sip of the beer. He didn't know much about such things.

"Yes." Azure nodded, looking sheepish. "I also crave soda, especially the bad kind. The more sugar and caffeine, the better. I'm trying to refrain since it's not good for the little one." She gave her belly another rub.

"Only a few weeks to go," he said, still unable to believe that Ice was going to be a father. Up until a few months ago, Ice was steadfastly single. Although Vortex had never seen the male this happy. Both of them, for that matter. They made a great couple. That feeling in his chest was back. It couldn't be indigestion; he hadn't eaten anything yet.

"Then we'll be parents." Azure shook her head, looking bewildered. "I still can't believe it."

"You're going to make such a great mom." Ice kissed the top of her head, snaking an arm around her and pulling her against him.

"You're going to be an even better dad." She gazed up at her mate adoringly.

"Okay… that's enough, you two. You have a guest."

"That's why we invited your human friend." Azure narrowed her eyes. "So that when we get all googly-eyed, you have someone else to talk to. Why didn't you bring her along? I should have invited her myself."

Vortex shrugged and shook his head. "She's my work colleague." Thing was, he enjoyed her company too much. He thought it was better that they didn't spend more time together outside of work, too. "It felt wrong to invite her along." He gave a shake of his head.

Azure scrunched up her nose. "I know she's a work colleague; what of it?" She put her hands on her hips. "I heard that the human is mated, so what difference does it make? Why would it feel wrong?"

Fuck! He'd almost stuck his foot in it.

"Um… what I meant was that this is a huge project. Amy is burning the candle at both ends. She might even need an extra day or two to finalize the quote, which will put us behind on our project timeline. I would've invited her, but she has to work again this evening."

"You're a slave driver," Azure said. "Surely she could have stopped to eat?"

"Those goblin fucks could attack at any moment. One or two days might mean that we are too late."

"Aren't we blowing this out of proportion?" She frowned heavily. Her hand was clutching her belly.

"No!" He shook his head. "I wish that were true. More and more bands of goblins are being spotted in our territory. Either the goblins themselves or, more often than not, signs of them."

"Yep, it's true, sweetheart. I've seen them on several occasions," Ice chimed in.

"They're breaking our surveillance equipment. They're up to no fucking good. They're spending more and more time on our lands, coming ever closer to our lair. They're watching our comings and goings. They're up to something."

"The goblins still work for us in the mines, though. How can we be preparing for war against them and still have them as allies? It makes no sense," Azure asked, sounding animated. Her eyes were filled with fear. Her hand continued to clutch her belly protectively.

Ice rubbed the side of her arm. "They're pretending to still be our allies while preparing for war. They did it once before, all those years ago."

"In the great uprising," Azure said. Her eyes had a faraway look.

"That's right! Plotting and scheming. They're not happy working for half the gold. They feel it should all go to them since they mine it. They feel that we do not deserve any of it."

"That's nonsense." Azure's eyes blazed. "We have the human connections. We have the market. There's no point in mining a commodity without a buyer. What? Do the goblins plan on going into human territory themselves?"

"Who knows?" Vortex shrugged.

"That would work well for them." Ice laughed. "Goblins in among the humans. It would be chaos and would not end well for the goblins."

"All we know is that there's something afoot. They're planning another uprising. All the signs are there," he said.

"Exactly! We believe that's exactly what they're doing.

The goblins claim that there are vigilante groups who wish us harm. They say that the bulk of the goblin community has nothing to do with these factions. That they are innocent of wrongdoing. And we can't prove otherwise," Ice added. The male was well informed.

"So, we have to keep working alongside them." Azure shook her head. "Surely more can be done? It just seems crazy to wait."

"We're not waiting," Vortex said. "We're preparing. I'm taking Mrs. Winters to the mines tomorrow to conduct assessments there as well."

Azure made this weird sound. "Okay, firstly, why are you calling the human 'Mrs. Winters'? You're not Christian Grey. Then secondly, you're taking her to the mines… where the goblins are? Hordes of them? Is that wise?"

"What my dear sweet mate is trying to say is, are you fucking crazy?"

"Who's Christian Grey? And no, I'm not crazy. It's a necessity. Mrs. Winters understands the risks and is fully prepared to do what it takes to deliver the best possible security solution. The mines are the most important place for strategic surveillance. I need our expert front and center."

"Thanks, Christian." Azure looked at him pointedly.

"Who the hell is Christian?"

"Didn't you watch any of the *Fifty Shades* movies?"

"No. I don't watch television. I don't even own one." He pushed out a heavy breath. "What does a movie have to do with anything?" Why was everyone suddenly quoting movie lines?

"You keep calling the human by her full title instead of by her actual name. Why is that? It's a strange thing to do.

It reminded me of Christian Grey from the movie. He does it to distance himself from the female lead because he's attracted to her. Incidentally, their relationship starts in the workplace."

"I told you… the human is mated. The problem is that she hasn't seen her mate in a while. He's an opera singer and is on tour." It sounded crazy. Fucking nuts. Jake the soprano-singing parrot. He smiled. Couldn't help it. He managed to reel it back in and cleared his throat. "Bottom line, she doesn't scent like she is mated, so I do it to remind the males." Now that was a plausible explanation.

"And you're taking her to the mines tomorrow?"

"Yes, it's important that all of the areas are covered. I have a meeting with Shrakka."

"Fuck me!" Ice widened his eyes.

"With the goblin king?" Azure's eyes went wide.

"Yes. It's too dangerous to send royalty in. I'm going instead. We're going to discuss the vigilante groups, among other things."

"It's too dangerous for royalty, but you and the human will be quite safe? Is that what you are saying? That doesn't sound right." Ice took a big swig of his beer.

"We don't believe that they are ready to show their hand just yet. Shrakka and the rest of the goblins will be on their best behavior, biding their time. The human will be at my side at all times. We are taking a full guard."

"Excuse me a sec." Azure slid out from under Ice's arm and went to the kitchen.

"Why bother talking to Shrakka or with putting up cameras anywhere near the goblins in the first place? They'll smash them. There's not much point."

"That's exactly what we're banking on. It'll be tough to

both work the mines and attack any of the lairs. When they suddenly stop working or smash the cameras, we'll know they're coming."

"I agree that they won't have the numbers if workers remain at the mines." Ice nodded. "They could trick you, though. They might fake a tunnel collapse or something like that." Ice didn't sound convinced. "They're a cunning bunch."

"Any kind of loss in signal will be interpreted as a potential threat. We need to get eyes on the mines. All the tunnels, all the exits and entrances; all areas. The mine will be our first warning. We'll have time to access and mobilize from there. Otherwise, we have to wait until they're almost on our doorstep. That might be too late."

"It sounds like you've given this some thought."

"I have." Vortex took a sip of his beer. "It's all I think about." His mind strayed to a certain human from time to time as well, but he wasn't about to admit that to anyone.

"Here." Azure handed him a package. He looked down. It felt warm to the touch and smelled delicious. "It's food for the human. I cooked extra. Go and take this to her."

He frowned. "I already organized for food to be delivered from the kitchens. It should arrive within the next half hour."

"No." Azure shook her head. "Home-cooked is better. I even packed some key lime pie for her."

"There's pie?" His voice was animated.

"Yes, there's pie." Azure laughed. "Now, take this to her. We'll wait for you to get back. Dinner will hold."

It couldn't hurt. He'd check in on Amy. Leave her some dinner and be back here in 10 or 15 minutes.

"That's thoughtful of you," he said. Azure was a sweet female.

"If she feels like a break, she can come back with you and eat with us."

"Sure thing." He had no intention of inviting Amy. The less time he spent with her outside of work, the better. Vortex took another sip of his beer, putting the bottle on the table. "I'll be back soon."

He left the apartment and walked down the hallway. Ice and Azure were in one of the family homes. It had three bedrooms. Whereas Amy was in a single-bedroom apartment on the other side of the lair. It took him a couple of minutes at a brisk walk to make it over there. He'd decided not to cancel the dinner she had ordered for herself. Perhaps she didn't eat elk. Humans had a strange taste in food. Also, she had a fantastic appetite. His mouth twitched with the start of a laugh just thinking about how often her stomach rumbled. The little female had to eat every two or three hours.

Vortex knocked on her door. It took a good minute before it opened. Amy took a step back, her eyes widening as they landed on him.

"Oh, hi." She smiled. He noted that she was holding her iPad. "This is unexpected."

Clearly! Judging from her attire, she hadn't been expecting anyone. She wore a tight red tank top and a pair of sleeping shorts. The shorts exposed her lush thighs. And from the way her ripe little tits molded themselves against the top, he'd say that she wasn't wearing a bra.

"I can tell." His voice was gruff.

"Oh…" She looked down. "Shit! Yeah… um… I'm working. I thought you were the guy who brings me my food." She turned, walking back into her apartment, her eyes on the iPad. Her ass was fucking amazing. It had substance. Good for holding onto during— *Not going there!* "Did you want to go over some notes? Is there something you needed to add?" She turned back towards him, her iPad in her hands, ready.

Fuck! Some of her hair had slipped out of the loose bun on her head; it framed her face. She pulled a plump lip between her teeth. Her tits made him want to fucking drool.

He walked inside, closing the door with a bang. "Do you always look like that when the male from the restaurant brings your delivery?" He could see her nipples. There was no doubt about it. She wasn't wearing those human coverings. His balls had tightened. His cock wasn't far behind. He put the container of food on the table, turning back to her.

Her eyes were narrowed in thought. "Ahhh… no, I wore my peach tank and white sleeping shorts yesterday. Is it a problem?"

Peach! Holy fuck! That male would've gotten an eyeful. "Yes. You're not wearing a bra," he growled. "You let males into this apartment while practically naked."

"What?" Her eyes narrowed. "I'm *inside* my own private space, and I'm far from naked." She gestured around them. "I like to get comfortable when I'm compiling—"

"I'm not trying to be rude here, but I can practically see your breasts." He pointed at her chest, and her nipples pointed right back. "That's not appropriate, Amy."

"Not appropriate? What are you talking about? All of you let your dicks hang free on the regular. I saw a lady shifter on the balcony yesterday; she was completely naked for a good couple of minutes before she found herself one of those dresses. No one cared at all. No one even looked."

"You're human!" Anger and frustration churned inside him. He wasn't sure why.

"What does that have to do with anything?" She threw her hands in the air.

"Humans are highly attractive to our kind. You're driving my males insane with your scent. If you start walking around like that—"

"I don't plan on leaving my apartment dressed like this, and I'm not driving anyone insane. A few guys asked me out yesterday, but since word has gotten around that I'm married, it's been fine. What the hell, Vortex?! You're acting like, like… You're acting like a jealous boyfriend." She took a step towards him. "Why? What is this? Why are you so angry?"

Jealous?

Was he jealous?

"Not a fuck!" he pushed out. "We have a working relationship. My job is to keep you safe. I told you how you scent." He took a step towards her, his nostrils flaring.

"You said that I smell like I need a good fuck." Her eyes were blazing.

"Yes, dammit! Why haven't you done something about that?" he growled, getting more irritated by the second.

"What the hell should I do about it?" she half-shouted. "I can't help the way I smell."

"You can take care of it! You're driving me fucking insane." He ran a hand through his hair. "Your nipples are hard. You're aroused right now. I'm pretty sure your pussy is wet. Driving me fucking crazy," he mumbled again.

Amy looked down. She gasped when she saw the erection tenting his pants. The soft sound she made went straight to his balls, causing them to tighten even more.

"This is such a mess." He put a hand over his cock. "I'm sorry. This is… It's a problem," he muttered, anger still churning in his gut. Except it wasn't aimed at her. It was aimed at himself.

By now, they were almost standing chest to chest. She had to crane her neck to look into his eyes.

"You're attracted to me." Realization lit her eyes. "Oh, my god." She covered her mouth with her hand. "I never thought… I… This is great." She giggled. "It explains your shitty behavior."

"Of course, I'm attracted to you. A male would have to be deaf, dumb, and fucking blind not to be. I mean, look at you. It's just… it's…" He inhaled her scent, taking it deep into his snout. "It's hard to be around you."

"I can see that." She was grinning. Looking down at his cock, which strained behind his hand.

"This isn't funny."

"I disagree. This feels like another red or blue pill moment. Which will it be?"

"Why does everyone keep quoting movie lines?" he groaned.

She frowned. "Who else quoted a movie line? And you really have to watch *The Matrix*. It's a great film." Then she licked her lips. He tracked the movement of the pink tip of her tongue. Even that was erotic. He was so fucking dead and buried. "What are we going to do about this?" she asked; her eyes glinted with mischief.

"There is nothing that…" That wasn't entirely true. "I can make you come a couple of times." He shrugged. If she wasn't going to ease herself, he could help her out. It would make life easier for all of them. No one ever needed to know. If he kept it to brief touching and only one hand, there would be no after scents.

"I don't… fool around with clients…" she whispered.

"Not normally. Then again, I've never been this attracted to a client before."

"I never mix business with pleasure."

"Does that mean you're going to turn around and walk out of that door?" she asked, looking disappointed. "That would probably be for the best."

"No."

"Thank god." She clasped her chest. "I'm going to make an exception, even if you can be an ass from time to time." She put her hands flat on his chest. "Kiss me."

"No kissing."

"Why not? Humans like to kiss. I like to kiss."

He wanted to kiss her. Wanted to kiss her altogether too much. "Kissing complicates things. This will be about taking care of business. Nothing more and nothing less. I'll make you come, and then your scent should be more bearable." He shouldn't do this. He should ask her to carry out the deed herself. Vortex couldn't bring himself to do it. He wanted to watch her come undone.

"I'm not sure I can get into the mood without making out."

He cupped her breasts. They reminded him of ripe peaches. The smaller, tastier kind. Her nipples were hard underneath his thumbs.

She groaned. "I might just take that back." Her eyes fluttered closed. "You're good with your hands."

"I'm going to make you come twice," he whispered into the shell of her ear, hearing how her heart kicked up a gear of two.

"Twice." Her voice was husky. "Arrogant much?"

He chuckled. Twice was shitty by shifter standards. Not being able to use his cock or his mouth was shitty, too, but it would have to do. "Stating facts, Amy. That's all."

"Okay, then," she moaned softly. "Have at it."

He rubbed on her nipples a few more times before running a hand down her back and squeezing her perfect ass. "All you have to do is tell me to stop, and I will." Her eyes were already hazy with lust. Her breathing was elevated. "You can change your mind at any time." This was a bad idea. Maybe she would be the voice of reason.

"There'll be no stopping." Amy pushed herself against him. He could feel her plump little breasts against his chest.

He needed to lay down the… rules. For lack of a better word.

"Tomorrow is business as usual. This won't get in the way of doing our jobs?"

"Hell no!" She rubbed herself on his cock, and he had to bite back a groan. *Holy shit!* "I haven't had a relationship in a long time," she went on. "I know how to compartmentalize. You're right. I do need this, and then it's back to work."

"Good to hear." Vortex pulled down her shorts, which dropped at her feet. Then he pushed a knee between her thighs and clasped a hand over her mound, all the while keeping his eyes on her. Her slip of a thong was soaking fucking wet. He bit back another groan. He rubbed her through the underwear a couple of times, watching her eyes flare with lust.

They lit up, and her mouth dropped open. Amy moaned, her head falling back. She rocked against his hand.

"Oh god! Oh, Vortex." He knew she'd be needy as fuck. That she was aching. This was something else, though. She was so highly strung. As she'd said, she needed this. Who was he kidding? He needed this, too. He was going to enjoy watching her come apart… seeing her sated. At least he'd be able to think more clearly around her for the rest of her stay.

He slipped one finger under the lace and zoned in on her swollen clit. His finger slipped and slid over the tight nub.

"Yes," a choked-out plea. His dick throbbed. It all-out fucking throbbed. His balls hurt they were so tight. He had a feeling that if he picked her up and slammed inside of her, she wouldn't resist. Vortex was shocked at how much he wanted to do just that. To feel her tight, wet heat… *Fuck!*

She hissed through her teeth as she buried her face in his neck. Her breath was hot against his skin. It didn't take more than a few soft rubs, and she was gripping his biceps and groaning hard.

"Oh shit! Ohhhhh…" So tightly wound. He'd hardly touched her.

"You poor baby," he growled. His voice had dropped about a hundred octaves.

She took sharp little gasps of air. When Amy lifted her head, her face was pinched. He kept his finger firmly on her clit… rub… rub… rub.

Amy's back bowed as her body began to jerk against him. She bit down on her lower lip, her eyes wide.

"Holy shit!" she gasped.

His cock actually twitched inside his pants. Everything in him told him to put her on her knees and to take her… hard and fast. To make her come again with his cock buried to the hilt.

She mewled and gave a shudder as the last of her orgasm moved through her. Then she sagged against him.

"I'm so embarrassed," she whispered against his chest. "I don't think I lasted ten seconds."

Using both arms, he held onto her while she tried to catch her breath. "There's nothing wrong with being a receptive female."

"It's…" she was panting, "it's been too long… too…" she swallowed thickly, "long."

Vortex pulled some of her thick, glossy hair behind her ear. Her mouth was so inviting. He wanted to devour her lips. Devour her. Instead, he leaned in and sucked on her earlobe, nipping at the soft flesh. She moaned.

"You're so fucking sexy," he whispered. His voice sounded choked. Her grip on his arms tightened as he shoved her panties to the side. Amy made a gasping noise as his finger breached her pussy.

Tight as fuck. He knew she would be.

Her walls clamped down around his finger. She was so fucking wet. So perfect. Vortex moved in and out of her a couple of times, loving the wet, sucking sound it made inside her. He ground his teeth together, wishing he could replace his finger with his cock. Warm. Wet. Tight. She groaned deeply. And so fucking sensitive.

Her back bowed, and she groaned again. Her head rolled back. "Oh god! Oh, my holy fuck…" She gripped him by the wrist, her nails digging into his bicep. "Jesus… more… more… don't you dare stop," she groaned.

He inserted a second finger. Her pussy was so tight around him. "Amazing," he murmured.

"Fuuuck. Oh wow! Yes! More!" Her eyes were wide. Her breath came in sharp pants. One hand now clawed at his back while the other tried to drag his hand closer. Her hips rocked. Amy was riding his hand. Her ripe breasts bounced a little under the tank, which he wanted to rip off. Her panties were red… fire-engine fucking red. Like her tank.

Lacy. Sexy as fuck, like the rest of her. He could see a thin strip of fur and glistening pink lips he wanted to suck on.

Vortex groaned. His cock wept from sheer frustration. He pushed a little deeper and moved faster, urging her on. His willpower dropping by the second.

"I need to come again… make me come again… Oh god, yes… just like that… Oh fuck… Please, Vortex… please…" She was so fucking vocal. "There… right there…" Her eyes were wide. "You found it… the spot… there… Jesus! Holy fucking shit!"

He'd never been so damned turned on in all his life. About to come from just watching her. And this was just two fingers. How would she react to his cock? He needed to get out of there. Finish this and leave before he did something stupid like fuck her. She was just that spectacular.

Keeping his fingers deep inside her, he slid his thumb over her swollen clit while finger-fucking her hard and deep. Her pussy went from snug to impossibly tight.

Her mouth fell open as she sucked in a ragged breath, then her eyes widened up a whole lot before she all-out growled. The growl slowly turned into a high-pitched groan. He kept working her, slowly easing off the pressure as she came down. Amy slumped against his chest, burying her face against him. He anchored an arm around her to hold her up. She was breathing hard. Still moaning softly.

"I'm sorry… I don't know what that was. Actually, I'm not sorry! That was insane. So good!"

"That was perfect." He pulled her panties back into place.

She rubbed a hand over his length. Vortex groaned, moving away from her touch.

"What about you?" She was frowning. "Don't you have to—?"

"What about me? It was you who needed that. It needed to happen, and now it has." He tried to give her a smile. His was pulled too tight. He'd never been so desperate for a female.

Her brow furrowed. "What does that mean? *I* needed that? I think *we* is a more appropriate term. *You* also look like you could do with—" Her eyes were on his hard-as-nails cock.

"No! I'm fine." If she so much as touched him, he'd shoot off. If he got even a drop of his seed on her, it would be tough to mask the scent. Make that impossible. Vortex didn't want rumors and speculation. He didn't want others thinking she was mated and yet still fair game, like so many humans were. Firstly, yes, he was jealous of others making moves on her, and secondly, and more importantly, he didn't want this female being seen in that light. Amy was feisty as anything, but she was also sweet.

"I've eased you, Amy. You should feel better now. Your scent won't be quite as pronounced."

"I must say, I prefer it when action is a two-way street." She picked up her sleeping shorts, pulling them up. "You know, give and take? Mutually beneficial and all that."

"Unlike you, I will take care of my own needs. We agreed that I would make you come twice. Then we would go back to business as usual. That was the deal."

Her eyes flared with anger for a second, and her jaw tightened. "Still… I don't see why we can't renegotiate. I give a fantastic hand job."

This female was too much. He liked her. His balls had to be blue under the fabric of his pants. It wouldn't take much. A couple of tugs. Her hands would be soft and— It couldn't happen, though. Vortex walked over to the washbasin, pumped a whole lot of hand wash into his palm, and began to lather his hands, turning the faucet to warm.

"I'm sure that's true, but I'm going to have to decline." He rinsed his hands. Wiping them on a washcloth. Then he squirted some sanitizer into his hands and rubbed them together. "To mask the scent," he told her.

"So you're just leaving?" She looked baffled.

"Yes. I said that this was a means to an end and that I was going to make you come twice. I didn't say I would fuck you. We can't fuck. You know that, right?"

"Yes, I know that." She snort-laughed. He didn't quite believe her nonchalance. "I thought this would be a two-way street, though. You're acting like you did me a favor. I don't like favors." She shook her head. "I prefer for things to be even. Now I feel like I owe you something.

"I did us both a favor. You don't owe me a thing." He pushed a breath through his nostrils. "That's not entirely true. I'll take a kickass security solution."

"You mean I should do my job? Well, you don't have to worry about that. Thanks for taking care of things. I'm so much more relaxed now." Her cheeks were flushed. "Unless there was something else you needed, I'd better get back to work." She glanced at her desk.

He couldn't read her. Was she angry? Upset? She held his gaze, looking completely calm. Nope, she was fine. They could move on.

"I brought you food." He pointed at the package on the table. "A home-cooked meal, compliments of a friend of mine."

"Thanks, but I already ordered from the kitchen."

"It's better than the restaurant food. It's elk roast. You should eat it. She's an excellent cook."

"You're on a date and fucking around with me?" Her eyes blazed.

"No. I would never do such a thing. Azure is mated to a good friend of mine. They are expecting their first child. She asked me to give you that." Why was he telling her all this? "It's business as usual tomorrow." He lifted his brows.

"Sure thing, boss." She pretended to salute him.

"Don't call me that," he grumbled.

"Sure thing, Overlord." She winked.

"Business as usual, Mrs. Winters." He used a stern voice, his mouth threatening to curl into a smile even though he was tightly wound.

"I need to work, Vortex." She gestured for him to leave. *Fuck!* Why was he still there? Ice and Azure were waiting for him.

CHAPTER 12

The next day…

AMY WAS MORTIFIED.

Completely and utterly humiliated. If she could leave, she would. If she could send someone else in her place so that she never had to look at Vortex again, she would. What was that? Who did that?

He'd somehow left her feeling dirty and used. At the same time, he'd taken no pleasure from her, so her feelings of being used made no sense.

A means to an end?

Taking care of business?

What the hell did that even mean?

I said I would make you come twice. I never said I would fuck you. Again, all so condescending, like she'd been gagging for his cock to fill her or something. She made this groaning, squeaking noise and covered her face. Amy *had* been gagging for sex with Vortex. As to his cock filling her? *Yes, please!*

She'd wanted him so badly. If not sex, then to touch him, to see him come. There was something vulnerable in that, something special that he had denied her.

Vortex had admitted to being attracted to her after acting jealous but couldn't stand the idea of her touching him back, though. What was wrong with him? Was it her? Why did she care? She was there to do a job. That was it! Thankfully, she'd managed to hold it together and pretend like it didn't matter to her, when it did. Otherwise, she would have been doubly humiliated. Why had she even let him touch her in the first place? He was a client, dammit. Mixing business and pleasure was dangerous.

Why was she so upset? Was she developing feelings for him? *Nah!* That couldn't be it. They hardly knew each other. Yet… if she really dug deep and was honest with herself…

And there he was. She *did* care. She cared altogether too much. Amy liked Vortex. She really freaking liked him. It wasn't just a simple attraction. There was more there.

Argh!

She wanted to run. She wanted to hide. Instead, she pulled her shoulders back and adjusted the straps of her backpack so that it fit a little snugger against her body.

Nothing had changed.

She could do this.

Amy was going to put last night right out of her head as if it had never happened. As if two of the best orgasms of her whole entire life had never freaking happened. Thing was, she had orgasmed before. She wasn't like other women who complained about never getting to Pleasure Town. She'd been there, and with more than one partner, but never like that. It was especially noteworthy, considering he had used his hand to get her there. Just two or three fingers at most.

Nope!

She was pushing it out of her mind. Pushing *him* out of her mind. He was a jerk. A gigantic asshole. There was no way she could be attracted to a shitty prickmiester. Not happening! No way!

Vortex slid out of his cotton pants, leaning over as he pulled them down his legs, stepping out of them.

Arghh!

Screw her life all the way to hell!

All she could see were broad shoulders and tightly ripped abs. Oh, and then there were his thick thighs and a cock that could make grown women weep. She wasn't even going to mention all the acres of bronzed skin or his mesmerizing green gaze, which was fixed on her.

She narrowed her own eyes in what she hoped was a no-nonsense business look. Then she glanced down at her iPad, making sure that it was fully charged and ready for a full day's work at the mines. Her heart stuttered. She was going to see the goblins. The enemy, by all accounts. Only, the dragons and the goblins were still working together in a grudging truce. It was weird. It might be dangerous. She glanced over at Vortex, who was speaking to one of the others. She wasn't worried. As big of an anal-retentive jerk as he was, she knew Vortex would keep her safe.

She was going to focus on getting the job done. On putting together figures and a stellar presentation. The presentation would be a formality, considering she'd already put in an order for a ton of equipment. Vortex had signed off on the order yesterday without even seeing the bottom line. It was insane. He trusted her. He was also a big jerk. What was wrong with him? He trusted her. He was kind and protective of her, but then he went and did what he did last night. Made her feel cheap. She couldn't get a handle on him, which was hugely disconcerting. Amy couldn't read him.

"Morning." Vortex had snuck up on her. He was right there. *Crapola!*

"Morning," she mumbled back, eyes still on her device. She didn't want to look at all of his sexiness up close. Not today. Not after what had happened last night.

Mortified!

"You look prepared. I see they delivered your gear this morning."

She looked down at her steel-toed boots and nodded. "The coveralls are in my backpack, along with the hard hat." Amy finally forced herself to look up and wished she hadn't.

Holy hotness personified.

She disliked him even more for being this freaking gorgeous. It wasn't fair. It wasn't right.

"Are you sure you're comfortable going to—?"

"Yes. The sooner we go, the better." She walked away from him. Putting some distance between them was the right thing to do. "Pervious… would you mind giving me a—?"

"I will take the human." There was a biting edge to Vortex's voice.

Really?

Was this still jealousy? Even though there was nothing between them. Less than nothing.

"The safety of the human is my responsibility," he added when Pervious quirked a brow.

"Of course, Overlord."

It wouldn't help to argue, so she set her jaw instead. She tried to ignore him as he shifted. Tried not to see all of those bright scales bursting out. He was even pretty in his dragon form. How was that possible? From his sleek back and wings to his even greener eyes. The others looked dull in comparison. She had a feeling that men were ruined for her after this. That they'd all pale in every way, even though he was a huge asshat jerk.

He'd been upfront with her. Amy knew this. Logically she knew it, but she was still hurt. She needed to try to move past this. No more fooling around with her client.

He made this rumbling noise as he lifted her into the sky. She tried not to enjoy herself as the wind whipped about her face.

Deep down inside, there was this nagging little voice that told her that Vortex wasn't a jerk, or an asshat, or an asshole. That there must be a good reason — aside from the obvious — why he had left things the way he had. The obvious being that he was her client. That she was there on business. That everyone thought she was married. That they couldn't be together. That there was no future for them. Those were the obvious facts, and more than likely, why he'd pulled away so abruptly. It wasn't Vortex's fault that she had feelings for a guy she hardly knew. Feelings for her client.

This was driving her mad! Insane! No more. Back to her original plan, she'd focus on the work. She'd have as little to do with Vortex as humanly possible. Amy would be cordial. She had this.

Amy turned her focus outward and tried to calm her mind. The terrain grew more arid. Grass and trees gave way to rocky ground. They started their descent. They seemed to be making their way towards large rocky outcrops. Areas with big, stacked boulders and sand. Lots of gravel and dirt. *Were those…?* Yes, there were people down there. One of the people grew in size, and… a dragon took to the sky. More dragons appeared from over a tall, barren mountain that seemed to be made from sand.

As they drew closer, she sucked in a breath. Goblins. Vortex had briefed her. He'd told her that their skin would be green-tinged, and it was. They were huge. Bigger than the shifters when in human form. Much smaller than the dragons. They wore clothing made from sackcloth. The brown hessian-type material was worn in short, skirt-style garments around their waists. They had leather wraps around their wrists and biceps, with thick gold hoops in their ears. Some had one earring. Some had several. Their facial features were… scary. Everything was more pronounced. Big ears and thick lips. As they looked up, several of them grinned, exposing big, sharp teeth.

Orcs. They looked so much like the orcs in *Lord of The Rings.* Perhaps marginally better than orcs. Although, "better" was the wrong choice of word. They looked slightly less terrifying than orcs. Their eyes were large and black as night. They seemed to look right through her. Every eye was focused on her. She felt a shiver run up her spine. It felt like she was being sized up for dinner.

How many of these creatures were below the earth mining the gold? At least they weren't going too deep into the mines, just the upper tunnels. Still, how many would be down there with them? She twisted around in Vortex's talons. A huge formation took up the rear. There were at least twenty dragons. Suddenly it didn't feel like that many. Amy licked her lips. She could do this. Vortex would keep her safe.

He gave a soft rumble. It sounded like it was meant for her. Like it was meant to be soothing. Funnily enough, it did soothe her.

They landed. Her eyes were still trained on the goblins, who openly sniffed the air. Vortex roared. It was deafening and a threat. There was no missing that part. Smoke wafted all around her.

The goblins moved off, their gazes snapping away momentarily. Some of them glanced back as they walked.

Vortex roared again. The goblins picked up the pace. She couldn't look away from the strange creatures. Only when a hand closed around her hip and squeezed, snapping her out of her daze.

"You okay?" Vortex asked.

"Um… yes… They're pretty frightening. How many of them did you say there were?"

"We're not sure. They live in the caves. I've never seen a female. There are rumors that the males and females look the same."

"That's strange."

"It is." He pulled a pair of pants on. Many of the men didn't follow suit. They stood guard, naked, ready to shift at the drop of a hat. "Let's go inside."

Inside?

Were they going underground already? Vortex had mentioned meeting with the king in the mine offices. She looked to where the goblins had disappeared underground.

"This way." Vortex went in the opposite direction. Her mouth fell open as she turned. Those weren't big piles of boulders or rocky outcrops. They were clever disguises. Anyone flying overhead would miss these large buildings.

Up close, she could see that everything was state-of-the-art. Just like the lair, only streamlined and functional instead of opulent and comfortable.

"I'm not sure what I was expecting, but this isn't it."

"Pervious, Lightning, and Vapor, you are with me. Gust and Squall, man the door. The rest of you, be vigilant."

Pervious, Vapor, and Lightning fell in behind with the other two. The others answered, "Yes, Overlord." Those in dragon form gave a rumble. The dragons overhead did too, the sound carrying.

"Are you sure you feel happy to proceed?" Vortex asked her. "I can send you the layout of the mines… at least for the areas we are comfortable traversing." He had explained their aversion to confined spaces. It was the whole reason they'd needed the goblins in the first place.

"I'm fine." She nodded once; her voice sounded better than she felt. It was preferable to see an area in person. It was hard to distinguish blind spots on a map. Storm had explained how this was the most crucial part of her assessment and why that was. The first indication that war was coming would start here. It all made sense. She'd steel her nerves and do the assessment. Amy would do it to ensure the safety of the dragons. Not just the Air lair but the others as well. Especially now that she had seen for herself how terrifying the goblins were.

"I have a meeting with the goblin king. I had planned on leaving you with the—"

She looked toward the entrance of the cave. A group of goblins had gathered and were staring… at her. Just standing there staring.

"I'd rather stay with you. Is that okay? I'm sure you don't want me tagging along. It's just… they make me nervous." She glanced at the group.

Vortex's jaw tightened, and his eyes narrowed.

"I… I don't want to be left out here."

"Humans have a heightened sense of self-preservation, especially the females of the species. You're right to trust your gut. If you feel uncomfortable at any point, we'll leave. Just say the word."

"I will." She nodded. "And thank you." She appreciated the fact that he was taking her seriously.

They arrived at the entrance to one of the buildings. Vortex put his thumb on a scanner at the door, then keyed in a code. The door opened. He gestured for her to go inside.

"I'm impressed. This is much better security than you have at the lair."

"We have more need for it here," he stated. "And you will help us upgrade our security at the lair."

"I most certainly will." Their conversation was stilted, but at least it was cordial.

She noted that each of the others placed their thumbs on the pad as well. A beep sounded each time. There were CCTV cameras mounted throughout the building.

An older dragon shifter sat behind a desk. He rose to his feet when they walked in. His hair was salt-and-pepper, and he had the start of crow's feet around his eyes. His physique was not quite as built as the others, but he could still put most human men to shame.

"Overlord." He bowed. "Human," he said to her, bowing his head again.

"Amy," she corrected.

"Of course." He bowed again.

"Is Shrakka ready to see me?" Vortex asked; the sharpness of his voice made it clear that he wasn't going to take no for an answer.

The shifter's eyes clouded. "No." He shook his head. "Shrakka did not come. Dommak is here in his place."

"Dommak?" Vortex frowned. "There had better be a very good explanation for this."

"I am sure there will be," the elderly shifter said. "Dommak is expecting you." He gestured to a wide hallway. "He is waiting in the boardroom."

"Let's go," Vortex told Amy, putting a hand to her back as they walked.

The three shifters followed silently behind them. They walked for a time down the bright hallway. The wall on the left was made of glass and looked into a large warehouse. It was full of equipment, including dump trucks and other earth-moving machinery she didn't recognize. There were a handful of goblins in the warehouse as well. One seemed to be fixing an engine. They all stopped what they were doing and stared. Two of them started talking and laughing.

Vortex growled low, and they stopped instantly. She snapped her gaze back to the hallway ahead of them. Vortex touched his hand to her back for a second. Just a quick brush of the fingers, and she felt calmer.

To the right of them were rows of offices. They all had glass panels. Most of the rooms were empty. There were shifters behind the desks in a number of them. They all briefly glanced up and then got back to whatever it was that they were doing.

At the end of the hallway was a beautiful stainless-steel staircase. It gleamed in the morning light. The whole back section of the building was glass and steel. It was quite something.

"The conference room is at the top of these stairs," Vortex told her as their feet clunked on the steps.

Amy was ashamed to admit that she was a little out of breath when they reached the next floor. One stretch of hallway and one flight of stairs. She made a mental note to work on her fitness. She could see why they would put the boardroom and conference areas up here; the views were amazing. There was still beauty in the arid landscape and rocks. A scattering of scrub bushes dotted the terrain here and there.

"Ready?" Vortex asked. "You can stay out here with Pervious if it would make you feel more comfortable."

She realized that she had stopped walking. That she was staring over the view, her heart racing in her chest. Amy was wringing her hands together; her palms felt distinctly sweaty.

For the first time, she looked into the boardroom. A goblin sat at the head of the table. He wore suit pants and a crisp, white button-down shirt with the top two buttons undone. No tie. He had many gold hoops in each ear. He looked calm and collected. His hands rested on the table in front of him. He dipped his head, his dark eyes on Vortex.

Maybe it would be better if she met a goblin up close and personal before going underground with multitudes of them.

"I'll go with you."

"We won't be long," he told the others.

The door to the boardroom slid open as they approached. The goblin rose to his feet.

"Dommak," Vortex said. "This is a surprise."

"It is good to see you, Vortex." The goblin held out his hand, and they clasped at the wrist for a second or two before letting go. Then he turned to Amy, and Vortex growled.

It was more of a vibration of the chest. A noise so low she could hardly hear it. It was all the more terrifying as a result.

"I was going to introduce myself, but I won't look at the human if that would make you happier."

This was ridiculous. He seemed well-spoken. She noticed that he wasn't wearing shoes. His feet were huge, and his toes were grotesque. Just like everything else about these goblins. Having said that, he seemed polite enough. Seemed indifferent to her.

"I'm Amy," she said.

"Dommak." The goblin held out his hand, and she took it.

His shake was firm. His skin was callused, like he worked the mines himself. He let her go almost as soon as they touched.

"I was expecting Shrakka," Vortex said.

"The goblin king sends apologies. There was an urgent matter that needed attention. I came as second-in-command. I'm a Horde Captain, which is a similar rank to an Overlord. I trust that is in order?"

Vortex's eyes darkened slightly; other than that, there was no change in his demeanor. Amy could sense that he was displeased, even though he concealed it well.

"It should have been conveyed sooner."

"The urgent matter was unexpected. Up until not so long ago, King Shrakka was going to be here. My sincerest apologies. I would be happy to reschedule for another day? Perhaps one of the Air royals would be free at some point in the near future?"

"I'm here now, so let's move on, Dommak." Vortex pulled a chair out for her and then took a seat next to her.

Amy unclipped her backpack, placing it on the floor beside her before sitting in the comfortable leather chair.

"Can I offer you some refreshments?" Dommak

gestured to a table that was laden with various food items, including pastries, fruits, and little sandwiches. There were sodas and waters in an ice bucket, as well as jugs of various kinds of juice.

"I already ate," Vortex said, leaning back in the chair.

Amy took her cues from him, even though the cold water looked refreshing and the pastries looked lovely and buttery. "No, thanks."

"Let me know if you change your mind." Dommak poured himself a cup of steaming coffee, adding cream and several spoonfuls of sugar. He stirred noisily. "The latest figures are in the file in front of you. I emailed them to Thunder yesterday."

"King Thunder," Vortex corrected.

"Of course. My apologies. Slip of the tongue." Dommak's voice was deep and thick. He placed four pastries on a side plate, putting the items on the table in front of him before sitting.

"I'm not here to discuss figures. If you're making quota, great. If not, there had better be a good explanation and a plan to rectify."

Dommak nodded once. He took a large bite of one of the pastries; a glob of custard leaked out the side and landed on the table with a splat. Dommak didn't seem to notice. Perhaps he didn't care because he continued eating, finishing the pastry in two bites and as many chews. He swallowed, smacking his lips.

"They're delicious. I would recomm—"

"Let's cut the crap." Vortex sat up taller in his seat. "The human is here to conduct an assessment of the buildings and the upper areas within mines."

"The buildings will not be a problem, but the mines…"

Dommak shook his head, looking solemn. "I cannot guarantee the human's safety if you venture underground."

"That's bull," Vortex growled. "You just said that you're a Horde Captain. You are in charge. You keep telling us that you have nothing to do with these so-called vigilante groups. It's time to prove it, Dommak. If you have nothing to hide, then you will allow us a full and safe admission into the mines with the human."

Dommak shook his head.

"No?" Vortex said, his voice chilling. "Are you declining? What do you have to hide?"

"Nothing. You are welcome to go into those mines, but I cannot and will not guarantee the safety of the human. Our goblin males have taken a great interest in humans since you started bringing them onto our territory."

"Our?"

"A slip of the tongue, I assure you, Overlord," Dommak said, taking a noisy slurp from the coffee cup, sucking down most of the contents in one go. He licked his lips. "We're a base species. If we see it and we like it, we take it. It's survival of the strongest. Humans are weak. Both males and females alike."

"What about you?" Amy asked. The question just slipped out. "You… are… different."

Dommak laughed, putting a whole pastry into his open mouth. He continued to laugh around the food. Again chewing just twice before swallowing.

"I like you, human. I can see why you would be considered interesting." He ran his tongue along his teeth, cleaning them of crumbs and bits of food. Even his tongue was a ridiculous size and green-tinged.

That was it. The others had leered at her. Not Dommak.

He also hadn't done that sniffing thing all the others had done to her.

"You said that if goblins want something, they take it. That your species is interested in humans… attracted to them?"

Dommak nodded. "Yes." He frowned.

"Not you, though?" *Why not?* She was onto something. She just didn't know what that something was.

Dommak grinned. "You are not my type. Weak and pathetic."

Vortex shifted in his chair. She could feel the irritation and impatience rolling off of him.

"I take it that you like your women strong? Are goblin women very strong?"

"Oh, yes." Dommak's black eyes glinted. "I'm not one for weakness. I like my males strong and fierce as well. The more fight, the better."

"Can we get back to the more pressing matters at hand? I have nothing against your sexual preferences, Dommak, but—" Vortex began.

She squeezed Vortex's thigh, which shut him up with a sharp intake of breath.

"Holy macaroni," she whispered. "You're not a male. You're… you're a woman, aren't you?"

"No offense, Dommak," Vortex said. "Amy is not trying to be rude; she is interested in goblin society, that's all."

"Clever human who asks the right questions. I like you. Stronger than you look. Perhaps there is some merit to the hype surrounding your kind." Dommak nodded. "Yes, I am a female."

CHAPTER 13

EVERYTHING WENT SILENT FOR A few long beats.

"What?" Vortex finally pushed out, sounding confused.

Amy glanced his way, and sure enough, his green eyes were clouded, and his was brow furrowed. She couldn't believe that after all these years of working with the goblins, the dragons had never figured this out.

"That can't be," he added.

"The human is right," Dommak said.

"My name is Amy."

"Feisty little thing. You would have done well as a goblin," Dommak added, popping another pastry into his… her mouth.

"You look like a male. You sound like a male." Vortex wasn't convinced.

"Females are the stronger of the genders. We are the

brains and the brawn. We are the leaders. We may look like males, but I can assure you that we are strong." She beat a fist to her chest. "We are female."

"What about Shrakka? Surely—?"

Dommak laughed; it was hearty and deep. Amy saw an Adam's apple on her throat. Dommak didn't seem to have breasts, either.

"Shrakka is also a female. Every position of leadership is filled by a female."

"King Shrakka is actually a queen?" Vortex sounded gobsmacked.

"As I said, all leadership positions are filled by females. We are the more superior of our species, but what does it matter? The vigilantes are all male. They heard about small, soft females. Females who are easy to dominate. Females with an open hole."

"Open hole?" Amy cleared her throat, suddenly feeling queasy.

"We are built like males in all aspects. It is only when we choose to breed that we retract our cocks and allow ourselves to be penetrated. Otherwise, it is the females who fuck. The males are there to please us." Dommak shrugged. "There have been mutterings of anger and disgruntlement. Some of our males have left. They don't want to be ruled. They are supposedly tired of being dominated. They wish to do the dominating."

"They want humans," Vortex said.

"Yes."

"Those vigilante groups are definitely working on their own?" Vortex muttered.

"One hundred percent." Dommak's voice dropped a few octaves, sounding so manly it was astonishing.

"So, it's not Shrakka who wants to start a war with the dragons?" Vortex asked. He didn't look like he believed Dommak.

"The king… or king, however you want to see her, is strongly opposed to this uprising. She's fucking livid. Her favorite male left to join the vigilantes. A group of our strongest warriors has gone after them. Shrakka put the word out this morning that deserters will be put to death. We are done entertaining our males."

"Fuck!" Vortex whispered under his breath. "There really are vigilantes," he said, almost to himself.

"The majority of our kind are comfortable with our agreement with the dragons. We're wealthy. We have built golden cities beneath the earth. We have all we could want. All we could possibly need."

Not the males, though.

"Right now, the deserters are few." Dommak's eyes narrowed, her stubbled jaw tightened. "But keep parading human females around these mines… take her underground for them to sample, and we will have a mutiny on our hands. There will be an uprising the likes of which you have never seen before. Forget gold; there is something more valuable to those idiot goblin males than gold."

"Understood," Vortex said. "You should have brought this to our attention sooner. Perhaps you could offer some positions of power to your males? Give them more… more say."

Dommak laughed. "Because you are doing the same for your females. Because there is such equality among the dragons?"

"We are working on being more progressive," Vortex said.

Dommak looked over at Amy. "I suppose that is true. This female is in charge of your security. I must say, I prefer dealing with a female. This has been a fruitful meeting."

"Why didn't you say something sooner? Why not be open with us?" Vortex asked.

"You never asked. You dragons always assume. Our species are like the dirt beneath your feet and just as expendable."

"You have been well rewarded for your services." Amy noted that he didn't outright refute the claim.

"We are like the yoked ox who plows the earth. A means to an end. Skin, sinew, and bone. Perhaps now you will see us as more."

"More?" Vortex asked. "You're goblins. There is no more."

"Males!" Dommak snorted, looking in Amy's direction. "They are as thick as two planks."

"I understand you just fine. So, there is more to goblins than meets the eye. But if you're saying that we would be eager to get to know you more, to delve more into the goblin psyche and culture, then no, thanks. That's not fucking happening. Our species are like night and day. We don't need to get into bed together."

"I like defiance in a male. You are strong." Dommak licked her lips, suddenly looking a touch more feminine in that instant.

"Not happening." Vortex managed a smile. It lasted all of three seconds and was gone. "We should work together to stop these groups."

"That is unnecessary. They are but a fraction of our numbers. We will be hunting down—"

"Going into our territories?" Vortex's voice was clipped.

"Yes. Shrakka has already asked your king for special permission this very day. We need to put a stop to this behavior. We need to get these males back into line before others get ideas. As I said before, stop parading delicious morsels." She locked eyes with Amy for a moment. "If we need your help, we will ask for it."

"We won't tolerate goblins in our territories. Trespassers will be dealt with swiftly and without mercy. We will be implementing further security measures here and inside the mines themselves."

"We have no problem with that. But we should be allowed to hunt down our own, however. To make examples of them. That's all we ask."

"I'm sure our royals will be in touch with answers." Vortex stood.

So did Amy. "It was nice meeting you," she said as she put an arm through one of the straps of her pack.

"Go home, female," Dommak said. It sounded like there might be a hint of anger in her voice.

"Be respectful, Dommak," Vortex warned.

"I am worried about the human. That is all. We will be in touch." She nodded once.

Vortex followed Amy out. No one said anything while they made their way down the stairs. They started down the hallway. "Can you b—?"

"Not here," Vortex said. "There are ears," he added. They walked down the stairs and started down the next hallway.

"It's just—" The incident happened in a split second. So quickly, her stomach lurched. One second, she was walking down the hallway, and the next, she was being yanked away. Her neck actually cracked from the whiplash.

There was a loud bang and the sound of a lock automatically engaging.

The room was small. The light dim. It looked like a supply closet. The creature inside with her took up half the space and had to crane his neck slightly. It was a goblin, up close and personal. He leered at her, his black eyes glinting. He sniffed noisily, inhaling deeply.

He moaned, "Human." He sniffed some more. "Mmmmmmm…" he rumbled. "Human cunt."

CHAPTER 14

*H*OW THE FUCK HAD THAT *just happened?*

A goblin fucker had Amy.

It was so unexpected. So left-field. Who would ever have expected that one of those green bastards would make a move on Amy in the mine offices?

Out in the open? *Perhaps.*

Underground? *Definitely.*

Right here and right now while walking between four dragon males in their prime within a contained area? *No way!*

Perhaps, as Dommak had implied, he was a little arrogant for thinking this wouldn't happen. Okay, a lot fucking arrogant. And if he got Amy hurt or killed, he would never forgive himself.

Vortex threw himself at the door. There was no handle. It didn't open automatically, didn't so much as budge. It was made of steel. Reinforced fucking steel. He threw himself at it again, denting the surface, but that was it.

Then he spotted the keypad. As an Overlord, he should have access to all areas. He quickly keyed in his password, but the device went red and made a hard-sounding beep.

Access denied!

Someone screamed behind the steel door. It was loud and piercing and distinctly feminine. *Amy!* His hackles went up. All of them, and all at once. His teeth sharpened in an instant.

"Fuck!" he snarled, gripping the edge of the door and pushing with all his might. The steel creaked and started to buckle, but the frame was holding.

There was another scream from behind the door. It was still high-pitched, but different. *Wrong! What the fuck?* He lost it. Saw red.

Vortex roared, feeling the cotton pants tear from his body as he shifted. It happened so quickly that a shock of pain raced through him. When bones lengthened, tendons pulled. Scales pushed through skin, and wings ripped outward. He ignored the piercing agony of shifting too quickly. It was fleeting. Smoke billowed from his nostrils as he heaved the door clean off the wall, throwing it down the hallway.

His eyes clouded and shut against his will. He sneezed. Fighting burning eyes and skin. Vortex shifted back as he moved into the small space. The sting in his eyes and on his skin redoubled as his scales retracted. The goblin was writhing on the ground.

What?

This was unexpected. The first scream had been Amy, but the screaming taking place right now was all coming from the goblin.

Huddled in a little ball. He was screaming, clawing at his face. Rubbing at it.

Amy sneezed too. She was using her torn-up jacket to shield her face and held something in her hand, which she pointed at the goblin even though the male was down.

"Pepper spray." She coughed and spluttered. "I won't leave home without it."

At this point, he could barely fucking see. His eyes were streaming. His face burned, and he wasn't even covered in that shit. He couldn't imagine what the goblin must be feeling. *Good!* Motherfucker deserved it!

He walked further into the small space, his face be damned. He kicked the male several times. There was satisfaction when he heard a rib or two cracking. Bastard deserved that too. He'd heard Amy scream. She'd been terrified.

"Lightning, make sure he gets put in a cage," Vortex choked out. Even his throat was burning. "And that he stays there. That he fucking rots." His vision was blurred. "What is this shit?" he asked Amy, leading her out into the hall.

"Pepper spray." He could hear that she was struggling as well. "It's made from capsaicin, which comes from chilis. It's oil-based, it sticks, and it burns like a bitch."

"That would explain why my eyes feel like they're on fire."

"Don't rub! It makes it worse."

Dumb fuck goblin was rubbing that shit all over his face.

"I figured," he said.

"We need water. A restroom," Amy added. "We have to flush our eyes." She coughed a few times.

"Follow me." It was Pervious. He looked like he was leading Amy. Vortex's eyes and nose were streaming. The burn wasn't as intense anymore after leaving the closet.

Half a minute later, they were in the nearest restroom, splashing water on their faces. It didn't take long before he felt better. Vortex wasn't sure whether it was because they had moved away from the spray zone or whether the water was helping. In his case, it was probably related to his fast healing ability.

He put his hand on Amy's back, feeling her pack still secured there. He gently took it off her, handing it to Pervious.

"You okay?" he asked.

"Yeah," she replied. "I pulled my shirt over my face after I nailed him." Her voice hardened up.

Amy was some female. "You got him right in the eyes." He'd seen the way the male was clawing at his face. "He's going to be in a world of pain for a while. The silver cage won't help matters."

She snorted. "Good! Nasty creep! His eyes were wide open. He wasn't expecting it."

"Thought you were some helpless human."

"Yep." She nodded, splashing some more water on her face.

"He was wrong," Vortex said.

"So wrong." Amy turned the faucet off.

"Better?"

"Much."

"Can we go?" Her voice softened. "Back, I mean? Home… to the lair?" Her face was a little red. Her eyes were bloodshot. Her hair was half in the ponytail and half out. *Fucking beautiful.* "You said I could say the word, and I'm saying it: word. There!" There was a tightness to her face. A pinched look of fear.

Fuck! He hated it.

"We're leaving right now." He said to Pervious. He tried not to snarl and failed. Vortex picked her up and carried her.

"I can walk," she whispered.

"I know." He kept her in his arms where she was safe. It didn't take long before they were at the exit.

The male at the reception was panicking. "I heard the commotion. I've called for—"

Vortex didn't wait to hear the rest of it. Lightning would deal with it.

"Let's go," he told his team as they marched outside.

He set Amy on her feet so that he could shift. Then he was picking her up, and they were flying as fast as they could with a human in tow, making it back to the lair in record time.

Again, Vortex put Amy on her feet and shifted. He picked her up.

"I really can walk." Her protest was weak.

Pervious handed him Amy's backpack, which he pulled over one shoulder. He nodded once and then started walking.

"You've been through an ordeal."

Amy put a hand on his shoulder and buried her head in his chest for a few moments, probably because her eyes hurt. She was handling this well, but it had to have been rough on her.

Just as he stepped into the lair, a male approached at a jog. "We heard there was trouble at the mines." Vortex kept walking, forcing the male to follow. "The king wants a debriefing, both on the incident and on your meeting with Dommak."

"Not now!" he growled. "I need to get Mrs. Winters to her apartment."

The male jogged to keep up. "Of course! Can I bring anything? A healer? A human doctor?"

Vortex stopped, pulling back slightly so that he could get a look at Amy.

"I'm fine," she said. Her eyes were still quite bloodshot, but otherwise, she did look okay.

"He didn't hurt you?" Vortex asked.

"No. I sprayed him before he…" She swallowed thickly. "Then you were there."

Vortex picked up his pace again. "Mrs. Winters needs rest. I will speak with Thunder later."

Thankfully, the male stopped following them. They got some strange looks as he walked down the hallway. Some of the males sniffed and wrinkled their noses. Yep, that shit was potent. Pepper spray. He didn't put her down until they were inside her apartment.

"What can I get you?" he asked as he stepped back so that he could assess her. "What do you need?"

"What I really need is a shower. My skin is still burning a little. Also, my clothes are… They're… " She looked down at her torn jacket. He noticed for the first time that her blouse was open, too. Most of the buttons were missing. Thankfully, she was wearing a top underneath, or her bra would have been exposed. "I n-need to change." Her lips trembled once. That was it.

His blood fucking boiled in his veins. For a moment, he was tempted to go back and finish that goblin bastard.

"I'll wait here. Can I get you anything in the meantime? I could help you wash. Just ask, and it's yours. Anything."

Amy pulled a plump lip between her teeth. "No. Look, I know you're busy. You don't have to—"

"I do have to. I want to." He reached out to her and pushed some hair behind her ear. "You were so brave. You took him down on your own."

Her lip trembled, and so she sucked it inside her mouth.

"I'm not all that brave. I was terrified."

"You think that brave people don't get scared?" He wanted to step in closer. To take her into his arms. He wanted to erase everything that had happened. "They do. It's just that brave people don't submit to that fear. They use it to fuel them… to fight. You fought back. You won. You're a fucking warrior."

"It was pepper spray. I'm hardly—"

"Don't put yourself down. You were in a terrifying situation and kept a clear head. You handled it. I'm in awe of you right now, Amy." He couldn't help it. He cupped her cheek in his hand. "I'm sorry that happened to you. I let my guard down for a second, and—"

"Don't blame yourself." She shook her head, and he took his hand away. "It wasn't your fault."

He ground his teeth together. "Actually, it was. You're *my* responsibility, and I messed up. I'm sorry! If he had… If you had been… Fuck!" He pulled her into his arms. "You scared the living shit out of me. You could have been hurt."

She chuckled. "And yet you kept a clear head and handled it. Thank you for saving me."

"You saved yourself. That was all you."

Amy tensed up. "Vortex…"

"Yes?"

She tensed up a whole lot more, turning to ice in his arms.

"Um… you're naked and hugging me. If you're not careful, you're going to get your scent all over me. That would be bad, wouldn't it?" She cleared her throat. "You should probably go now. I'm safe. I'm fine."

Vortex deserved that. He pulled away, letting her go. He hadn't been able to tell if she was upset with him last night. Her outward appearance pointed to the contrary, but in this moment, he realized that she was upset about it.

"About last night… I'm sorry. I acted like a jerk. I *am* attracted to you. Your scent drives me insane. Still does, if I'm being honest with myself. All I wanted was… I wanted more. I wanted to taste you. Wanted to bury myself so deep inside you and hear you moan my name. I can't do any of those things. It's not possible." He shrugged. "It's as simple as that."

"We could fool around. I mean, we *could've* fooled around. It's a two-way street." She gestured between them. "You… made me feel. I guess I felt cheap. We didn't have sex. You didn't let me so much as touch you, and yet you left me feeling awful. Worse than I've ever felt before, and I've done the walk of shame once or twice in my life." She licked her lips. "I was in a serious relationship a couple of years ago and found some text messages on his phone. He'd been cheating on me. Believe it or not, I felt worse after you left last night than I did the day I found those texts. I don't know how that is, only that it's true."

"Fuck!" He pushed his fingers into the corners of his eyes.

"The reason I felt worse is that I know you're not like that. I expected it from Rob – my ex. It still came as a shock, but… I knew deep down that he was an asshole. You're not that guy. You acted like a jerk, but you're… better than that. I was hurt and disappointed."

It tore at him to hear her say that. "I'm so sorry. I mean that. You have to know that I wanted you to touch me. I still want you to touch me… Fuck! We can't, though. If I get so much as a drop of my seed on you, they'll know." He pointed at the door. "They'll scent it on you. A male's seed is designed to do two things. The obvious is to impregnate a female. And the other is to mark her. To leave a scent on her. One that others can smell. If a female has sex with the same person regularly, it changes her scent in such a way that it tells others that she is off-limits. The other way around is also true. I can't mark you in any way. We can't use condoms because they are pungent too. The scent of rubber lingers. I don't want a mated female getting a reputation. I don't want *you* getting a reputation. I would be nailed to the wall too, but I could care less about that. I ran like my ass was on fire because I almost gave in to my desires. I was this close," he held up two fingers a millimeter apart, "to putting you on your knees and taking you. I won't do that to you. I have too much respect for you. I'm also not in a space where I can have a relationship. It just isn't in the cards for me right now."

What he didn't tell her was that he could easily fall for a female like her. If there was a picture of a definition of his perfect female, it would be one of her. He could see in her eyes that she could fall for him, too. It was dangerous. A road they needed to avoid. If he brought her here, she would be in danger. Today had proven that all the more to him.

"I should have explained things better. I never meant to hurt you. I certainly never meant to make you feel cheap. I should never have touched you in the first place, but I couldn't help myself. It wasn't just for you, either." He cupped her sweet face in his hands. "It was for me, too. To see your eyes hazy with pleasure. To hear the noises you made. To see you sated… Fuck, I'd do it again. I should never have done it, but I would do it again in a heartbeat."

Her breathing hitched, and her heart rate sped up. Vortex swiped his thumb, skimming the underside of her lip before letting go.

"I know that now. I understand. For the record, I'm glad you touched me." She got this naughty little smile. "It was nice."

Nice.

Fucking nice?

He wished he could show her that he could do a lot better than "nice." It wasn't to be, though.

"I'd better go. I need to shower." She gestured in the direction of the bathroom with her thumb.

"One last thing," he said. "I just… have to do this one little thing," he closed the distance between them, his eyes were on her mouth; her eyes were wide, "and then we go back to being business associates." He leaned in, his mouth a breath away from hers.

"I'm not sure that's possible."

He brushed his lips against hers. "Friends, then?"

"Um… I'm pretty sure that ship has sailed." She slid her hand around his neck, her eyes on his. Vortex kissed her, soft and sweet, going easy. Tasting, savoring. Altogether too soon, he pulled away. "Nope." She licked her lips, her lashes still fused together because her eyes were tightly shut. "Definitely not friends." She opened her gorgeous dark orbs. "It sucks that you're such a good kisser. I'd kind of hoped you'd be terrible."

He chuckled.

"You have a great laugh. You should use it more often."

"Maybe I will." It wouldn't be a hard thing to do while she was here. Amy had a way of making him feel… of making him *feel*.

Her stomach grumbled loudly. Their eyes locked. Amy cracked up laughing.

"It's nowhere near lunchtime," Vortex said.

"What can I say? Everything makes me hungry. Being happy, being sad, stress… almost getting mauled by a creepy goblin is now number one on my list."

"You shower. I'll order some food. Anything in particular that you want?"

"That elk you left last night was delicious. Oh, I get massively hungry when I'm pissed off, so I ate it all."

He chuckled again. "Elk it is."

"And pizza. Do dragons eat pizza?" She gave him the cutest frown. She walked backward, taking one slow step after the other.

"Who doesn't eat pizza?"

"That's true." She was grinning by the time she reached the bathroom. "You really don't have to stay. I know you have things to do. Kings to meet. Goblins to beat up."

She knew him well already.

Vortex shook his head. "I'm staying right here. We're going to eat elk pizza—"

Her eyes lit up. "Elk pizza is a thing?"

He nodded. "It's definitely a thing. We're going to eat pizza, and we can watch a movie. I was thinking *The Matrix?* Although, I know you've already seen it, so we can watch something else instead."

Her mouth dropped open. "You want to watch *The Matrix* with me? And no, I do not want to watch something else. *The Matrix* is a classic."

"I do. I wouldn't want to miss out on a classic."

"You're going to love the part about the blue pill and the red pill." She was smiling broadly.

"I have a feeling I will, too."

She gasped. "Wait, no! What about work? I'm super behind on—"

"You're taking the rest of the day off."

"But—"

"No arguing. I can stay for a couple of hours, but then I have to go. Tomorrow we'll pick up where we left off. I'll bring plans and schematics for the mines, workshops, and office areas. You can inform your superiors that you'll be staying an extra day."

"Do you think what we learned today will change things?"

"No, it doesn't change anything. We'd be stupid to trust them. We proceed as normal."

"Didn't you believe Dommak? Do you think she was lying about her gender?"

"Not necessarily. That part might be true. I'm not sure what to believe and what not to believe. Ultimately, it doesn't matter. They are not to be trusted. That's where it ends." He ran a hand through his hair. "No more talk of goblins. Forget about them, about work, about all of that. Go shower." He pointed at the bathroom door. "I'll have everything ready for when you're done."

"Popcorn." Her eyes went wide and bright. "We'll need some."

He found himself smiling again, broadly. It felt good. "I'm on it."

CHAPTER 15

Later that day…

S TORM LEANED BACK IN HIS chair. "This changes everything."

"With all due respect, how do you figure?" Vortex asked.

"We now know that it *is* vigilante groups and not all of the goblins who are involved in an uprising this time." Storm rolled his shoulders a few times. "I don't even think it can be called an uprising. It's a couple of irritated goblin males, sick of being under female rule." He sniggered.

"You're under female rule," Thunder deadpanned.

"Like fuck I am."

"You are totally under female rule. If your mate asks you to jump, you don't even ask how high; you just do it."

Storm shook his head, looking shocked. "That's bull. I wouldn't—"

"Relax, little brother." Thunder held up a hand, smiling. "I'm also ruled by my female. It's how it is. Our females are mostly subtle about the fact that they have us by the balls. It's not so with the goblins. There is nothing subtle there." Thunder laughed. "I can't believe that Shrakka is a female. You said that the females have cocks?"

"That's what Dommak said. They have cocks, and they like to use them on the males." He shivered.

"Poor fucks." Storm shrugged. "Unless you like that kind of thing. Personally, I think I might revolt against that as well."

Thunder shrugged. "I have to say that I agree with Storm. I think this changes things. Makes them less urgent."

"Sire, we can't take the word of a goblin… a Horde Captain. They could be lying to get us off our guard and to catch us with our pants down."

"You say that the female from the security company figured this out? That after prompting Dommak, the goblin revealed the male-female thing and the real reason behind the groups we have been seeing?"

"That is correct, but… he… she… whatever the case is, might have been lying. Perhaps it was Dommak's intention to reveal all of this to get us to relax our guard."

"I'm not saying for one second that we relax, just that we can stress a little less about it," Storm said. "We still go ahead with all of our plans. We increase security. Where are we with that?"

"The female had an ordeal today. I insisted that she

take the day off. The presentation will take place a day later. I rescheduled with your PA already. I will sit with Amy tomorrow and go over the plans and schematics for the mines."

"I don't think she should go back," Thunder said. "It's too risky."

"Agreed." Vortex heaved an internal sigh of relief.

"I will set up a meeting with the goblin king… queen." Storm made a face, trying to suppress a smile. "I need to try to get used to that."

"I'm not sure that would be safe, my Lord."

"I will be well guarded. I want to talk more about these matters. I want to be sure that they have the situation contained. I want to see how we can work together to stop these vigilante males. They're after our females. They want the humans, and they have to be stopped. We are technically still in an alliance with the goblins. The salesperson from Trivector taught us something today. Why didn't we ask the goblins about the vigilante groups? Why didn't we try to find out more? How is it that we didn't know that all the positions of power are held by females? We assumed, and we were wrong. We need to do better."

What the hell did he say to that? It all made sense. He still worried that this thing would blow up in their faces. It churned in his gut and made bile rise up his throat.

"I'll assemble the team when you are ready to meet with them."

Storm nodded once. "I am told that you rescued the human today."

"Amy did an excellent job of taking care of herself."

"You're too modest." Storm smiled. "We stay our

course." He went on before Vortex could say anything else. "The cave dragons have been quiet. Too quiet, perhaps? No, we can't let our guard down just yet. I look forward to hearing what the human has to say. You were saying that her team is already mobilizing?"

"Yes, my Lord. They've started the production of CCTV cameras and motion detectors. Tomorrow they begin the manufacture of silver alloy cages for cameras at the caves and possibly certain areas at the mines as well."

"Good. I look forward to hearing all about it," Thunder said.

Vortex couldn't help but think that despite what they said to the contrary, Storm and Thunder were no longer as worried about the goblins. It was a mistake!

"We must call a meeting with the royals of the other tribes," he heard Thunder say.

"This is important information." Storm sounded like he was smiling. *Fuck!* There was nothing to smile about. Not a damned thing. Vortex didn't trust those green bastards. Male, female, they were all the same. Dangerous. Cunning. Tough as nails.

CHAPTER 16

The next day…

AMY TAPPED THE MAP WITH the back of her pen. "This setup is going to require a lot more cameras than I ever imagined."

She'd just finished calculating the length of the mine tunnels they needed coverage for. There were a ton of shafts.

"They will need to be able to switch between normal and infrared. Do you think we'll need silver alloy cages for the mines as well?" she asked Vortex, who was sitting next to her. Close enough that his thigh brushed hers every now and then. They sat closer than they had on the sofa yesterday. He'd sat on one side and she on the other. The pizza and popcorn rested between them so that they could share. Her lips had still tingled from that kiss.

That kiss.

That earth-shattering kiss. It hadn't lasted long, but it had awakened things inside her she hadn't known existed… and it wasn't sexual this time… Okay, that was not entirely true. Her body had reacted. How could it not? Vortex was six and a half feet of raw power. Make that raw, naked power.

It wasn't her attraction that shook her. It was what happened inside her chest. Vortex was right; they needed to keep their distance. This couldn't go further, or she'd get hurt. Not just hurt like she'd felt the other night, but the bad knock-your-socks-off kind of hurt. The kind that left a person curled up in bed for days. The kind she had never felt before.

Her eldest sister, Jennifer, had an ex who had broken off their engagement. It had happened years ago, but Amy could remember Jen's face. The look in her eyes. It was sad and hollow. It took a long time before she smiled the same way again. Too long. Jen was married with two kids now, but it had taken her sister two years before she even started dating again. Amy didn't want to go through that. To feel like a piece of her heart was missing. And a guy like Vortex could easily do that to her. Possibly even to the point where she might never recover.

"Amy?" Vortex touched her arm. "You zoned out there for a second."

She was looking at her iPad, thinking about things she shouldn't be thinking about.

"Sorry! As I said, that's a crap ton of cameras. I need to work on the final figures. It should bring the overall price per unit down. Should we start manufacturing the infrared units as well?"

"Yes. Storm and Thunder advised me that we will continue as normal. That we won't let our guard down based on the new information. I don't trust the goblins." His jaw tightened.

"You're right. I wouldn't trust them either." She felt a shiver run through her just thinking about her run-in with that goblin. The way he'd looked at her. The way he'd sniffed her. How he'd wanted to see her naked. How he'd wanted to see her "down there." He'd used the C-word. Those goblins were disgusting creepazoids.

On top of all that, he kept telling her that he wasn't going to hurt her. *Yeah right!* He'd been so busying pawing her that she'd been able to get her pepper spray out of the nifty side pocket on her backpack easily.

"Should we manufacture extra cages as well? I'm talking specifically for the caves."

"No, I think let's leave the cages for the mine areas." Vortex shook his head, his eyes on the site map. "If cameras are destroyed, we'll know that something is going down."

"You want to leave them unprotected on purpose?"

"Yep, that's the plan." He nodded.

"It will be important to have someone heading up security. I'm specifically talking about the monitoring of the information coming in from all areas. It's going to be key to the success of the security at this lair. You'll need a designated area with several individuals. I'll work out exactly how many staff will be required. It'll be a dedicated team of surveillance experts who will be the eyes and ears of this lair twenty-four-seven." She paused, opening her iPad. "On top of that, there will have to be a dedicated team who will need to carry out maintenance on all equipment on a regular basis. I would put the same person in charge of both duties. I would be happy to train this individual. Anyway," she smiled, "I'm getting ahead of myself. I'll bring all this up during the presentation."

"Then you'll be here for the installation?"

"Absolutely. I will personally inspect every nut and bolt wherever I can. I'll make sure that all areas are fully covered. There may be a need to add in extra measures later. Sometimes holes are found post-installation. I doubt there will be many, but you never know." She swallowed thickly. "I won't be able to assist at the mines." Her voice changed as fear crept in.

"I'll be involved during the installation as well. You can train me on what to look for, and I'll be hands-on at the mines to ensure that the same standards are met. I don't want you going near there again." His voice deepened, and his eyes seemed to darken.

"Perfect. Then it will be a matter of training the team who are going to work maintenance and security, with a focus on the manager of that department."

He leaned back in his seat, clasping his fingers behind his neck. "It looks like you have everything well under control. I'm liking what I'm hearing."

She groaned. "Not really. I have so much work to do to try to come up with a final figure for the presentation. I can say that it's going to be higher than the original budget. Quite a bit higher."

"That's not a problem. Again, I know I can trust you."

Amy nodded. "I'm waiting for figures on some of the equipment. We don't normally sell in such volumes, and the cages in silver alloy have never been done before. I should have them in time to present on Thursday. In the meantime, I have a mountain of work to keep me busy."

"I'm sure you will have final figures, and if not, we'll work around it."

That wasn't entirely true. Amy had been sent figures; only they were far too high per-unit price. Trivector wanted to charge inflated prices for the items already being manufactured. It was wrong. Amy had asked Ray to review it. There was no way she was presenting those kinds of figures. Her company was wanting to take advantage of the dragons. Well, not on her watch.

"No, I'm sure I'll get them in time." She forced a smile.

Vortex sat up straight. He breathed out through his nose, his eyes on her. "Are you doing okay? After yesterday?"

She nodded. "I'm fine. It was a bit of a shock." She couldn't help but shiver again. "They're scary creatures. I would hate it if a whole… What is it that you call a group of them?"

"A horde," Vortex said.

"I would hate it if a whole horde descended on this place. Hundreds of them. I've watched too many movies. I immediately picture the orcs in the final battle scene… I can see I've lost you. I'm talking about *The Lord of the Rings*. I read the books twice, as well. JRR Tolkien; have you heard of him?"

Vortex chuckled. "No."

"His stuff is epic. All the books, starting with *The Hobbit* and the movies as well. There are three movies, and they're long, so we wouldn't have time to watch them." She looked at her watch. "In fact, if I don't hustle, there isn't going to be a presentation." She needed to email Ray again. There had been radio silence since she'd last spoken to him, and he'd promised to do something about the prices.

"I should probably get going as well. I have a couple of things I need to do. And then I'm having dinner with my mom."

So freaking sweet.

Vortex was a good guy. A keeper.

"I have dinner with her once a week, especially since my dad died." His eyes clouded for a moment.

"Oh, no! I'm so sorry. I had it in my head that you guys lived forever."

Vortex smiled. "We're mortal, just like everyone else. Non-humans do live longer, especially the vampires. I think it comes from drinking blood."

"Argh!" She wrinkled her nose.

Vortex grinned. "I've killed a deer or two. Ripped their throats out and then eaten them raw, heart practically still beating."

"In your dragon form?" She felt her eyes widen.

He nodded. "Not all that different from a vampire."

"It's totally different. Killing something and eating it is pretty darned normal. Sucking on someone's neck for food… um… no." She shook her head.

He laughed. She loved the sound. He was sexy when he was all brooding, but absolutely gorgeous when he smiled and laughed. It did things to her insides.

"What are you doing later? I know you'll work for the better part of the evening, but after that?"

Her heart beat a little faster, which was shitty, considering he could hear it and would know that she was affected by such a simple question. Part of her was hoping he was going to suggest hanging out... as friends... Well, not friends, but not more, either. The other part of her, the logical side, knew she had to work until late and that they shouldn't hang out. That they couldn't be friends. There was just too much there. Too much of a connection. Too much of an attraction. She considered lying and saying that she had nothing planned but stuck to her guns in the end.

"You're right; I have to work until late. In fact, I'm staying between these four walls until this presentation is squared away. I'll be communicating back and forth with the office during working hours, so I can do the number-crunching. Exciting, isn't it?" Before he could say anything, she went on. "I'll probably call home and chat to Jake." She bobbed her eyebrows.

"Your bird."

"My parrot, yes. My sister is looking after him for me. According to her texts, he hasn't been his usual vocal self, so I want to Facetime him. I think he misses me."

"He *is* your husband, after all." Vortex smiled, taking her breath away. *Take my breath away...* It was such a clichéd thing to say, but she had come to realize that the saying was true. Every now and then, when she looked at him, her lungs seized up. The air seemed to thin.

She giggled. "That he is."

"How long have you had Jake?"

"Since I left home. Years... six, maybe seven. He's my buddy."

"I wouldn't mind meeting him some time. The infamous Jake opera-singing parrot."

"Actually, he squawks, really loudly. Especially when the sun comes up."

"Jake thinks he's a rooster, then?"

Lordy, but those dimples were out in full force, and so were the butterflies. The ones that lived in her stomach. The ones she never knew she had.

Amy laughed. "I never thought of it that way, but now that you mention it." She nodded a couple of times. "He swears too. Likes to scream 'fuck' at the top of his lungs. I knocked my toes really hard about two or three years ago."

Vortex's shoulders were shaking with laughter he was trying to hold in. "I can guess the rest."

"Yep. He sounds just like I did that day. I can even hear the pain laced into the word, which he shouts full force. I broke my toe and my parrot on the same day."

"That's not broken; that's awesome. Jake sounds like a character." Vortex stood, putting his dick at eye level. "I'd better get going."

Amy jumped to her feet as well, almost knocking over her chair. "Let me see you out."

"I won't see you until the presentation. Let me give you my number in case you need anything."

Amy handed him her phone, which she unlocked.

He looked at her from under his lashes. "You have a picture of your parrot as a screensaver?"

"Yes. What's wrong with that? What do you have on your phone, then?"

His face went pale.

"What? Show me."

"I should be going."

"Show me!" She cocked her head. "I showed you mine, and now you have to show me yours."

"You don't want to see." He handed her his phone, anyway. "One of the guys changed it to that, and…"

Her eyes went wide. It was a voluptuous blonde bombshell in the tiniest bikini. Her boobs were each about the size of her head and barely covered.

"Very pretty," she said.

"…I just haven't changed it. Should've done it by now."

"I don't blame you. She's… Wow! A lot of woman." Amy didn't have the biggest boobs. It wasn't something that had bugged her… until now.

"Nah! Not my type at all."

"What are you saying? A woman like that is everyone's type. Heck, she might even be my type, and I don't swing that way." She smiled, hoping it looked breezy.

"Not my type. I prefer dark hair and chocolate eyes. For me, if breasts are more than a handful, it's a waste." His eyes seemed to drift down to her breasts for a second. Was he talking about her? "I really have to go. Call me if you need help with anything. Or if… You have my number."

"I do." She nodded, watching him leave. He had such an amazing back. And his ass in those pants… Also, he was nice. So freaking lovely. Why, oh why, were things so complicated? He might just be the perfect man. Pity he couldn't be *her* perfect man. Now wouldn't that be something?

CHAPTER 17

Three days later…

"WE WISH TO GO AHEAD," Thunder said as she finished her presentation.

"But," she frowned, "you don't have the final figures yet." Her office was still giving her the runaround. Their CEO, Mr. Taylor, had been answering her emails in one-liners. In short, they weren't budging on the elevated pricing. They wanted the dragons to pay more per unit price than the smaller companies they did business with. It was daylight robbery, and she wasn't having it.

"Get us the best deal possible, and we'll sign," Vortex told her.

Only they wouldn't be getting the best deal freaking possible. She was going to tear down Ray's door and raise hell at Trivector when she arrived back in the morning.

This was unacceptable. Amy would have no part in them taking advantage like this.

"Of course." She nodded once.

"And the installation will take place in three weeks?" Vortex asked.

"Yes. It will be tight, but I'm sure it's doable, considering we already got the go-ahead on certain items."

"You did a great job," Thunder said. "I can see a lot of work went into your presentation. You certainly tailormade the solution to our needs. All I ask is that once you AirDrop the presentation to Vortex's device," he pointed at the laptop in question, "that you delete the document as well as all the finer details pertaining to our lair. Figures and general area descriptions are fine, but you have pictures, diagrams, and schematics of classified information that cannot be leaked."

"I will be sure to destroy all of it, including my notes. As long as you have the presentation." She glanced at Vortex. "Please keep everything. I'll need it for the installation."

"No problem," Vortex said.

"Perfect." Thunder nodded.

They really did trust her. It felt good. It also felt like a whole lot of pressure. It was all good, though. She could take it.

"Get us the final agreement so that I can sign and get the formalities over with." Storm was smiling. "Thank you for all of your efforts. We'll see you in a couple of weeks."

"Are you all packed and ready to go?" Thunder asked.

"Yes, my things are out there in the waiting area." Vortex had told her that he was taking her right after this meeting.

"I'm sure you're happy to be heading home?" Thunder remarked.

Amy was excited to see Jake and her family, but otherwise, not really. She'd miss this place. She had to force herself not to glance in Vortex's direction. It was stupid. They hardly knew each other, but she felt like she'd miss Vortex. That she'd miss this place.

"For sure." She nodded.

"Your mate will be happy to see you," Thunder continued.

"He's still on tour, isn't he?" Vortex frowned.

"Yes, he is, but he'll be back the week after next." She smiled. It sucked to have to lie.

"Um…" Vortex was frowning. "I thought you said that they were on tour for three months. It hasn't been that long yet." He widened his eyes, looking relaxed.

That didn't sound right. Three months seemed like a long time. A married couple wouldn't stay apart for that long if they could help it. Was Vortex trying to tell her something?

She was on the spot. Had to talk quickly or it would look suspicious.

"Um… he'll be home for a couple of days before going back on tour," she lied through her teeth. "I won't see him again for another six or seven weeks." She hoped her calculations were correct. "I can't wait to spend some quality time with him, even though it'll just be for three days."

"I could not imagine being away from my mate for so long," Thunder said, leaning back.

"Me neither," Storm added.

Vortex's eyes were dark; his whole demeanor suddenly

seemed tense. Was she doing a bad job? He'd told her that she was a bad liar. Wasn't she believable? *Crap!*

"We're taking a trip. We're going camping… more like glamping since we have all the gear and all the bells and whistles. We're going to the Rocky Mountain National Park. It'll be just the two of us."

"That sounds like a good way to make up for lost time." Storm rose to his feet. He did up his suit jacket button. "I know I don't have to remind you about the NDA you signed before coming here."

Phew!

They bought it.

It was all fine. All good!

"You don't." She stood as well, gathering her things together before looking at Storm and then Thunder. "I understand the threat to your people, not just from the cave dragons and the goblins, but from the humans as well. I mean, look at what we're doing to the planet… at how we're killing each other off. Your secret is safe with me, and not just because I signed an NDA."

"You can't tell your husband either."

"I would never." She shook her head. "He's not all that interested in my work, so I doubt he'll ask very much." She put some files into her bag.

"In that case, it was nice doing business with you. Vortex will be in touch." Storm glanced at Vortex, who nodded.

"We'll see you soon, Mrs. Winters," Thunder said. "Safe travels, and enjoy your camping holiday."

"Oh, I will." She slung her laptop bag over her shoulder.

Vortex glanced at the clock on the wall. His jaw was set.

"We'd better head out. My team is waiting to escort you." He locked eyes with her.

Shit!

There was something wrong.

Vortex tossed her backpack over his shoulder and picked up her wheelie bag with one hand. Apparently, he was so strong that carrying it was easier for him than pulling it along. He held the door open, waiting for her to go through.

"Thanks. Bye." She waved at the PA, who waved back.

"We'll see you in a couple of weeks." The woman said with a smile.

They headed down the hallway but hadn't gotten very far when Vortex pulled her to the side. He put down her things, looking up and down the hallway. He was frowning heavily.

"Is everything okay?" she whispered.

"No. I was trying to signal you." He ran a hand through his hair, sighing. "Your husband is coming back from tour for a couple of days, about a week before you're due back here for the installation."

She shrugged. "Yes. I thought it would be a nice touch. A married couple wouldn't be separated for so long. It isn't natural."

"How will you explain the fact that you don't scent like you've been with your husband?" He raised his brows. "Because we will be able to scent it."

"Shit!" she said under her breath. "You're right. I guess I didn't think it through. Ummmm...." She scratched her chin. "I'll say that it was canceled, that he couldn't come home after all. I'll make something up."

"*We're going glamping in the Rocky Mountains,*" Vortex pretended to be her. "It's going to be tough to come up with a plausible excuse as to why you didn't go." He sounded angry. "I knew this was a bad idea." He roughed up his hair again. "It needs to be you who handles the installation. The fewer humans who know about us, the better. You will need to scent of a weekend away with your mate in the Rocky Mountains when you come back here."

"How the hell am I going to get that right?"

"There really is only one way." Vortex's eyes blazed. Why was he so angry?

"You're going to have to spell it out for me. I'm not following you."

"You're going to have to have sex, Amy."

"How? What do you mean?" she whisper-shouted.

"I think you know how the deed is done," Vortex countered

"Who with, though?" For a second, her heart actually beat a whole lot faster. Maybe he was offering. Maybe this wasn't so bad. They could figure this out.

"It doesn't matter, Amy. You're a beautiful female. You said you've had hook-ups before. You mentioned the walk of shame, so I'm assuming that you have. Make a plan," he growled the last.

It hurt hearing him say it.

One-night stands were not her thing. Amy wasn't a college student anymore. She'd grown up. She'd reached a point where she wanted more. "You want me to take some random stranger home and screw his brains out the weekend before I come back here so that it will smell like I've been with my husband in the Rocky Mountains?" she deadpanned. Surely, she was misunderstanding him because that wasn't what he was saying. It couldn't be.

"There is no other choice." His jaw was tight. "I should have planned for this better. It's my fault. We should've had a game plan." He squeezed his eyes shut for a second or two and shook his head. "I'm sorry, I messed up." This sounded more like the Vortex she knew.

"What if Jake is sick? Too sick to... you know."

"The male would have to be in a hospital not to fuck his mate after being away from her for so long. That's not going to fly." Vortex shook his head.

"Okay, yes, we'll say he was admitted to the hospital. I'll think of something. I'm not picking up some stranger in a seedy bar. No way!"

"And you're leaving your sick husband to do an installation? You'll be here for several weeks. Nope, doesn't sound plausible." He made a low, groaning noise. "We're in a corner here. You need to come back scenting of a male, any male. I can't see a way out of this. I'm sorry, Amy."

This stung. It hurt a whole damned lot. For half a second there, she'd thought that Vortex actually cared about her. He didn't! She was wrong! He was telling her to sleep with some random stranger so that her lie would remain credible. If he cared even a tiny bit about her, he would not be asking this of her. Pain slowly turned to anger.

"Sure, no problem. There's this hole-in-the-wall bar down the road from me. It's called Bottoms Up. It's the place to go if you like greasy burgers, cold beer, 80's music on a jukebox... It's also the best pick-up joint in town." She breathed in deeply. "I'll go there on Friday night, the weekend before the installation. I'm guaranteed to score." She had no intention of going. Amy would find another way.

She kept her eyes locked on his, and Vortex didn't so much as flinch.

"Okay, then. It's that, or you have to send someone else."

Bastard!

"I've worked too hard to hand this over. I said I would do what it took to make this work, and I meant it. You've been telling me for days that I need a good fuck, and I guess I do. I'll go to Bottoms Up, then. No problem!" She put on fake bravado, looking him in the eyes.

Nothing!

Not a damned thing!

She'd been so wrong about Vortex. He didn't say anything, just picked up her bags, and they continued to walk to the balcony.

"You've got my number. I mean, if there's a problem with the contract," he spelled it out. It would be all business going forward.

"I have your details, including your email address." She'd do her best not to have to talk to him.

"I won't be part of the group that takes you back today." He opened the door that led to the balcony area. A group of shifters were standing waiting. Pervious waved at her.

She waved back. "So, this is goodbye, then."

"Yes, we'll be in touch." Vortex turned and walked away. Just like that.

Asshole!

Good thing she didn't waste any more time on him. Good thing it hadn't gone further. He didn't deserve her. Heck, a guy like him didn't deserve her pinky finger.

CHAPTER 18

Her step faltered as she walked into the room. "What are you doing here?"

"Do you like it?" James gestured around him. "My new office." He winked at her. "I still have to hang up all of my sales awards." He looked up at the bare wall behind him. "Good thing it's spacious in here."

"I don't understand." She frowned. This made no sense. "Where's Ray?"

Why in the hell was James Oliver sitting behind the Sales Director's desk? Why was he looking so damned smug? Where was Ray?

"You're looking at your new boss, Ames. We're going to make magic together, you and me. Pure magic." He leaned back in his chair, a smirk on his face.

"You're the new Sales Director?"

"Don't look so shocked, little lady. Yes, I got promoted when Ray stepped down this week. He decided to take an early retirement."

What?

This made no sense. Ray wouldn't just leave.

"Ray loves his job. He would never take an early retirement. He was a workaholic who lived for the close." She sank down into a nearby chair.

"It doesn't have to make sense." James shrugged. "It is how it is. Ray has retired."

There was something going on here! Something that reeked of bullshit.

James leaned forward in his chair, his eyes wide. "I cannot believe," he looked around them, like he might be worried that the walls had ears, "you were willing to do business with those creatures." He made a face. "Fucking hell! Scaly reptiles." He shivered, making a sound of revulsion. "Disgusting animals."

"They were fine." This wasn't a conversation she wanted to have. "They're dragon shifters."

"Dangerous as hell."

"Yeah, I guess." She nodded. "But also quite civilized."

"I wasn't sure—"

"Back to Ray… What's going on?"

"Nothing! Well done on securing the business. Monsters or not, it's still good money for Trivector. Money the company needs. The contract is worth over three mil. I'm super proud of my top little sales gal." He winked at her. "Not just a pretty face, Ames. You mentioned in your email that there might be further opportunities for equally large contracts… also with those creatures." He made another face, looking disgusted for a few seconds.

There were three more lairs that would require a similar setup.

"Only if we sharpen up our pencils on this deal. The per-unit prices Mr. Taylor is suggesting are ludicrous for such large orders. You're wanting to charge them more per unit than we would for a small enterprise ordering small quantities. I discussed this with Ray. It seemed like he agreed with me." She'd been sure he had been on board. Now he had retired. She smelled a rat.

"Why are you making such a big deal about this, Ames? It isn't. Mr. Taylor has the final say."

"My name is Amy, not Ames. Let's get that straight right off the bat." He was going to work on her last nerve. "Stop with the nicknames."

"I'm your boss. I can call you whatever the hell I want. Ames is better than sugar lips or sweet tits, both of which I happen to like for you." He winked.

Prick!

"There is such a thing as sexual harassment in the workplace."

"There is such a thing as keeping your head down and doing your fucking job, *Ames*."

"That's what I'm trying to do. I need to get my client the best possible deal, and that isn't the case at the moment." Her voice had risen a few octaves. It couldn't be helped. He was getting on her sugar tits.

Screw her life!

"You will take the prices that Mr. Taylor put forward. You will finalize the quotation and get the contract signed off. It will happen by the close of business today, or we are going to have to delay the installation."

Her mind went straight back to the goblins.

"No. Scale Top Mines need the installation to happen on time." She shook her head. She and Vortex may not see eye to eye. She'd started to develop feelings for him. Stupid her. He didn't reciprocate. Not his fault! Still, it hurt. Her wayward emotions aside, the dragons were good people. They didn't deserve to be screwed over.

"If they want the installation to happen on time, they need to sign today." James smiled at her.

"It's over-inflated, and you know it."

"They have to accept. They signed for the equipment already. They're not complaining. I don't see the problem, little lady."

"*I'm* complaining, James. It's not good business practice to over-inflate prices just because we can. It's downright unethical. We're overcharging them. I won't stand by and watch that happen." She folded her arms.

"I'm trying to help you here, Ames." James got this fake sappy look and puppy dog eyes. "Ray also wouldn't budge. He was insistent, just like you, and look where that got him."

She gasped. Of course… And there it was. She would need to play ball or leave. The writing was on the wall.

"Are you saying that Ray was fired over this?"

"Not at all." He shook his head. "Ray chose to retire early." James gave her an evil smile. He winked. "You'll be fired though, unless you accept the pricing structure for those… things."

"I won't." She shook her head.

"Ames, Ames, Ames… Trivector needs you. I need

you. You'd be walking away from a huge payday on this account. I'd planned on giving you a nice raise, too." He winked at her. "Possibly an assistant manager position in the near future. Don't throw away what could be a lucrative career. Think it through."

Amy wondered what she would have to do to get the position. Wondered what position James would want to see her in. *Jerk!* She wasn't sure she could work for someone like him. In fact, she knew she couldn't. It wouldn't be long before he took his short pencil dick out and told her to suck on it again. Then she'd have to laugh at him and get fired, anyway.

Little lady!

Ames!

She'd have to look at that smirk on his face every day. Have him leer at her in much the same way as the goblins had.

Nope! Nope and nope!

She couldn't do it.

"You'll have my resignation on your desk within the hour." She stood.

"Don't be like that, babe."

Babe?

Holy fuck!

No! Just no!

Holding back an eye-roll, she walked out of the office. Both James and her CEO could go to hell. Trivector could go to hell. The one positive in all this was that she wouldn't have to deal with Vortex anymore. She'd already updated her resumé; she'd get it out there. Amy was great at her job. She'd find something else in no time.

CHAPTER 19

The next day…

"COME TO MAMA." LISA CAREFULLY slid the cocktail a little way across the table so that it was closer to her mouth. The orange contents were almost at the rim. Without lifting the glass, she leaned in and took a sip, groaning loudly. "This is perfect. Pretty much the same as *Smith & Wesson* makes it."

"I asked the barman for the recipe. I had a hard time getting it. I had to tell him all about you. How you couldn't drink for a year. How you recently stopped breastfeeding."

"You didn't!" Lisa giggled.

"Of course I did. Then I told him how you hate to leave your baby and that there were two options. One, you bring a three-month-old into *Smith & Wesson* to get your fix; or two, he gives me the recipe so that we could stay here instead."

Lisa laughed. "You are evil. I would never have taken little Christopher into a cocktail bar. I'm not that kind of mother."

"The barman doesn't know that." They both laughed.

"What's in it anyways?" Lisa took another big sip and groaned again.

"Everyone knows it's gin, simple syrup, and champagne. *Smith & Wesson* make theirs with blood orange gin. That's the secret ingredient. I brought everything along, only…" Amy wrinkled her nose, "I couldn't afford actual champagne, so I used sparkling wine instead. I'm sorry. I guess we can't call it a French 75 on account of it being sparkling wine and not the real deal."

"I'm really sorry you lost your job."

"I resigned." She shrugged. "It was time to move on. I would have preferred to have had something else lined up first."

"You're so good at what you do. Any organization would be lucky to have you on board."

"I sent my resumé to all the major security companies. I've also sent it to several agencies. I have an interview lined up for Tuesday."

"That's great!" Lisa smiled, taking another sip of her drink. "You could go into bartending. Sparkling wine or not, this is amaaaaazzzzzing!" She sang the last word.

Jake squawked behind them, flapping his wings.

"Easy, boy." Amy grabbed another piece of apple and gave it to her parrot. "We don't want to wake up the baby." They normally would have met at Lisa's place, but she was having her rugs cleaned.

"You always land on your feet." Lisa took another sip, closing her eyes, a look of bliss on her face.

"I have money saved. I'll be fine." Amy took a big glug of her drink. It was delicious.

"You can always move in with Peter and me. Jake would have to stay outside in the shed though." She widened her eyes. "Sorry!"

"Jake and I will be just fine. Thanks for the offer, though."

The doorbell sounded.

"Expecting someone?" Lisa asked.

"Nope, not at all."

It chimed again.

"I'll be right back."

"Howdy, Ma'am." A tall, middle-aged man touched the peak of his cap.

"Oh… hi. Can I help you?"

He held out a clipboard. There was a large cellophane-wrapped basket on the floor at his feet. "I have a delivery for a Mrs. Amy Winters."

"Miss," she corrected him. "I am she."

"Of course." He smiled broadly. "Please, will you sign here, Miss Winters?" He showed her an open space next to her name.

Amy signed.

"It's…" the delivery guy checked his watch, "it's just past three." He wrote the time down next to her scribble of a signature. "You enjoy the rest of your Saturday now." He touched his cap again. Then he picked up the large wicker basket and put it in her arms. The cellophane crinkled.

"You, too." She smiled, using her foot to close the door since her arms were full.

"Wow!" Lisa exclaimed as she walked back inside.

Jake squawked.

She put the basket down and grabbed a cracker for Jake. "Shhhhhhh, boy."

Jake squawked again just before tucking into his treat.

"What is that?" Amy's sister asked, taking another sip of her cocktail before sliding off her chair to take a closer look.

"I don't know. A delivery for me." It was covered in too many layers to properly see what was inside.

"Do you think Trivector is trying to get you back?"

"They can try," Amy said as she pulled on the ribbon to untie the package. The basket was huge. Inside the wicker structure were about a ton of different candies and snacks. "What in the world…?"

Lisa laughed. "Someone knows you well." She picked up a packet of parrot treats. "There are even various snacks in here for Jake. What is this?" Her sister made a face. "Deer jerky. Deer, as in Bambi? I'm not too sure about this. What in the world?" Lisa looked at her strangely, pointing out another item. "Is this what I think it is?"

Amy giggled, biting down on her lip. It couldn't be. It had to be.

"It's pepper spray."

"Yeah, but a three-pack of the stuff? Who would send you this?"

"It's the last client I took on board at Trivector."

"Pepper spray, though?" Lisa made a face. "It's weird!"

"There was an incident. One of their workers got a bit handsy with me."

"Nooooo!" Lisa's eyes went wide. "Why didn't you tell me about this?"

"It was a non-event. He got out of line, and I sprayed him in the face. I'm fine. Nothing happened."

"That's not a non-event, Amy. You had to pepper spray some guy. That's serious!" Lisa's eyes were narrowed with concern.

"I'm fine! It's all good. This is a lovely gesture." This had to have been sent by Vortex. There were all kinds of candy and snacks. As well as numerous items for Jake, including a seedlog and a mirror with his name etched in the corner.

Lisa picked it up. "It's customized for your parrot. There's a card as well." She handed it to Amy.

Her name was handwritten on the front. Amy opened it and pulled out the card. It was covered in pictures of mini donuts covered in sprinkles. She opened it.

Dear Amy,

I'm sorry!

Best,
Vortex
P.S. Take care of yourself!

"I'm sorry?" Lisa said from over her shoulder. "What does he have to be sorry for?"

"Nosy much!" Amy closed the card, holding it to her chest so that Lisa couldn't read it, which was crazy since she already had.

"Who's Vortex? What a strange name."

"My contact at Scale Top Mines. No one." She stuffed the card back into the envelope.

"No one?" Lisa lifted her brows. "I don't think so, girl. Spill! Who is he really? He knows your affinity for snacks. He knows you have a parrot named Jake. He bought you pepper spray. Take care of yourself?" She looked at Amy through narrowed eyes.

"He's my client. That's all."

"What is he sorry for?" Lisa asked again.

"For what happened… I guess."

"You said it was a non-event. It either was a big deal, or it wasn't; can't be both. Nope… I know you. Who is this Vortex guy? Have you met someone? Is that what this is?" Her voice got all weird, and she got this little smile.

"No… yes… sort of. No! Definitely not." She shook her head hard. "He's my client. We almost had a thing. He's focused on his career, and…" She sighed. "He's too hot and then cold for my liking. He's not looking for anything serious."

"I knew it." Lisa smiled, sliding back into her chair and taking a sip of her cocktail. "So, you *are* looking for a serious relationship, then? Since when? The last serious relationship you had was years ago. I can't even remember his name."

Amy shrugged. "You're my younger sister, and you're married with a kid. I guess I've started to hear my biological clock ticking. I've realized that work isn't everything."

"You're serious about this guy." Lisa was grinning from ear to ear.

"I am not! I hardly know him. I just finished telling you that it's not like that between us. He was standoffish when we first met. Then he had his hands all over me. Then he couldn't run away fast enough. Then he's sweet but in a friend-zone kind of way. We watched *The Matrix* together. Then it's all business, hardcore business. And now he sends me this." Amy touched the side of the basket. She skipped the part where he told her to sleep with someone else.

Lisa laughed. "Yep, that's what I thought."

Amy frowned hard, going back to sit across from Lisa and sipping her drink.

"He's running scared because he really likes you. It sounds like he's trying extra hard to push you away because he actually wants to pull you closer."

"That doesn't make any sense." Amy sipped again. "What are we, in kindergarten?"

"It makes perfect sense. Guys can be very immature when it comes to relationships. So, kindergarten would be about right. Remember how Sean was? I eventually had to give him an ultimatum. Look at us now. I can tell you right now that if I hadn't put my foot down, we'd still be living together." She rolled her eyes. "Men!"

"Nah! We hardly know each other. I'm not giving him an ultimatum."

Lisa laughed. "No, that would be crazy. Spend time with him, though. It'll be even easier now that he isn't your client. You have nothing to lose. It's clear as the nose on your face that you like this guy. He would not have sent you that huge basket if he didn't like you a little as well, or at least want to get into your panties." She bobbed her brows.

"I won't see him again." Amy was shocked at how disappointed she sounded.

"Bullshit. Organize something. You have his number, don't you?"

Amy picked up her phone, looking at it. Her mouth dropped open. There was a message from Vortex.

Did you like my gift?

"What is it?" Lisa asked.

"Nothing. You're right. I'll think about it." Vortex lived… she wasn't actually sure where their territory was located, only that it was far. He wasn't her client anymore, and so there was no reason to see him anymore. Also, he might have apologized, but he'd been a jerk to her for a second time.

"You're not going to call him, are you?"

"Probably not." Amy took another sip of her cocktail, surprised at how much the thought of never seeing him again hurt.

CHAPTER 20

Two days later…

Vortex finished typing the email and pushed send.

He'd fucked up where the human was concerned. Kept fucking up at every turn. His mother had raised him better. His father would roll in his grave if he knew how Vortex had treated a female. Not just any female, one he liked and respected.

What was wrong with him?

Vortex had done the right thing by keeping Amy at arm's length, but he could have handled it better. He scrubbed a hand over his face. He'd told her to go out, to find someone, anyone, and to fuck them just to keep the Air dragons' business.

Was he insane?

Had to be because no one in their right mind would do such a thing. He was ashamed of himself. Amy was clearly angry with him, and rightly so. Perhaps she wouldn't want to handle their account anymore, and he wouldn't be able to blame her.

Vortex sighed, pulling his phone from his pocket. He checked his messages for the hundredth time. There they were, the two messages he had sent her. Both of them had been read, but there was no response.

> Did you like my gift?

> I'm sorry! I acted like a complete jerk. Forgive me, please.

Nada. Nothing. Zip in return. He couldn't blame Amy. He wouldn't respond either if the tables had been turned.

His feelings for her scared him. There! He'd said it – to himself… inside his own head – but he'd admitted to feeling more for Amy than he should. It had been tough to stay away for the two days she'd worked on the proposal. He'd forced himself. Then they'd been ill-prepared for the meeting. His fault. Then he'd told her to fuck a random stranger. He groaned, letting his head drop into his hands. He'd expected her to be shocked and upset. Deep down, he'd hoped she'd ask him to step in. Instead, she'd held her head up high and had wholeheartedly agreed. He'd been able to see the hurt and anger in her eyes, but he had ignored it. Vortex had hurt her.

Fuck my life!

Knowing she was leaving made him feel cut up. He hadn't been able to stick around to watch it happen. He was too afraid of what he might do. What he might say. He sighed, head still in his hands.

"What got your G-string in a knot?" a gruff voice boomed.

Vortex sat up in his chair. "Nothing. It's all good." He turned.

"Shut the fuck up, then. All your sighing and groaning is making it hard for me to concentrate." Cyclone kept typing on his laptop, using two fingers. "I hate these fucking reports enough without you making it worse for me. Un-fucking-bearable even."

"Sorry," he mumbled. Vortex had been so lost in his own thoughts he hadn't even noticed the male arriving. They shared office space. He gathered his things and stood, heading for the door.

"Call her!" the male growled.

"What was that?" He wasn't sure he'd heard correctly. Surely, he'd been mistaken.

"Call her! Stop being a pussy, pick up the phone," Cyclone looked at the device in Vortex's hand, "and call her. It doesn't take a genius to know that you're crying over some female. Pull your finger out of your ass and fix it." He turned back to his computer and carried on slow-typing.

Vortex didn't respond. He grunted something that sounded like thanks and left. As much as he hated to admit it, the male was right. He'd sent two texts and an email. He needed to suck it up and call her. To speak to her. He pulled up her cellphone number and then thought better of it, choosing her business number instead.

"Trivector Security, how may I direct your call?" a droning female voice asked.

He asked to speak to Amy Winters.

"Who might I say is calling?" the female asked.

"Mr. Vortex from Scale Top Mines."

"Please hold just a second." Vortex walked further down the hallway. This section of the lair was quiet; he should have the privacy he needed. A whole minute ticked by.

Fuck!

She wasn't going to take his call. It was another full minute before a male answered.

"Good morning, Mr. Vortex. It seems you beat me to it. I'm Ronald Taylor. I'm the Chief Executive Officer here at Trivector. It's wonderful having you on board."

"I'm sure there's been a mistake. I asked to speak to Amy Winters," Vortex said.

"No mistake." The male chuckled. He sounded older. "As I said, you beat me to this call. Amy resigned on Friday; she is no longer with Trivector. I had planned on calling you a little later today to inform you of the situation."

What?

No!

Surely not! Had he scared her into resigning from her job? It was quite possible.

"Why did Amy resign?" he asked.

"I'm afraid that's information I am unable to disclose, Mr. Vortex. I just wanted to let you know that you will be well taken care of moving forward. Our Sales Director will be handling your account. I will stay firmly in the loop to ensure that all of your needs are met. You will receive your contract by the close of business today. Apologies for the delay. None of us expected a resignation from Miss Winters. We are doing our best to get up to date with all of Scale Top's particulars."

Fuck! Shame flooded him. He'd done this. He'd forced Amy's hand.

"That's fine," he mumbled.

"We will need a signature within 24 hours to avoid delays." The male sounded like he was grinning.

"Sure thing." Vortex disconnected the call.

Something felt wrong about this. Amy was not a quitter. She just wasn't. She may have hated the way he treated her. Nope, she had definitely hated the way he treated her, but she would not have left her job because of him. She was hardheaded and strong. A fighter. He dialed her number. When she didn't answer, he tried again.

"You're not getting the message, are you?" she said.

It was great to hear her voice. So much so that he smiled, probably for the first time since she had left. And it felt fucking good. Now he just stood there with a mouth full of teeth and a stupid grin on his face.

"Vortex… are you still there?" Amy asked. "If you're going to stalk me, you might want to do some heavy breathing or something. I have your number saved, so I know it's you."

"Sorry! Fuck!" He scratched the back of his head. "I know you know it's me. I was just shocked for a second that you answered."

"You called me twice in a row. That's the universal sign for something being up. Is something up?"

"Did you get my gift?"

"Yes, thank you." He was going to have to work for this, but Vortex was okay with that.

"Did you like it?" He heard the vulnerability in his voice.

"The basket was great, yeah. You know I like snacks, love my parrot. Surprisingly, the jerky was good. And I needed a replacement pepper spray. What's not to like? For me, though, actions speak louder than words… or gift baskets."

"Noted." He shifted the phone to his other ear. "I'm really sorry."

"You already said that you were sorry." He could hear that she wasn't accepting it. She was still mad at him, which was fair enough. "Or you wrote it, which is the same thing."

"I'm a jerk," he added.

"Yes, you are. You already said that, too."

He smiled again. She was fucking awesome. "I should never have treated you that way. I'm an idiot."

"Again, no arguments from me."

His smile grew, but he forced himself to stop. Vortex didn't want her thinking that he didn't mean all of this, because he did. Wholeheartedly.

"I *didn't* want you to leave. I *didn't* want you to come back for the installation, either."

She made a noise of frustration. "There you go again. You're the most irritating man I have ever met. Which is it? Because it can't be both."

"It's complicated."

"Not really, Vortex. You either want to spend time with me and see me again, or you don't."

"It's not as simple as that. I've worked hard to get to where I am today, and if I don't stay one hundred percent focused, I could lose everything. Speaking of which, I heard you resigned. I just got off the phone with your CEO."

"Is that why you're calling me?" Her voice had hardened up. "Because if this is actually a business call, you—"

"I wanted to talk… to make things right, so I called you at the office since I couldn't reach you by other means. My main reason for calling has nothing to do with business. Why did you resign, though?" If it was because of him, he was talking her out of it.

"It's better this way. We don't have to see each other again. You'll get the security solution I designed for you. We can—"

"No!" His voice was rough. "The idea of not seeing you again doesn't sit well with me." His chest tightened. His whole body seemed to tighten.

"Well, that's too bad, Vortex. I don't deserve to be treated like shit. You made me feel cheap for a second time. Once was one too many. Twice, though... that's unacceptable."

"I like you, Amy. I like you altogether too much. I know it's a terrible excuse. I just... I pushed you away both those times because if I hadn't pushed, I would have grabbed hold of you and... Going down that road would have resulted in you in my bed... under me... calling my name... loudly and often."

She pushed out a tiny puff of air. "Holy shit, but you're arrogant." He couldn't be sure, but it sounded like she might be smiling... just a little.

"It's a fact, Amy. All fact. It wouldn't lead anywhere. It couldn't. I get the feeling that you're looking for more, but I'm not ready. Even if I were, I can't take a mate now. Not with war on the horizon. I wouldn't be permitted, and even if I fought that, I wouldn't want that for you, Amy. Living at our lair would be too dangerous."

"Living together? A mate? What the hell, Vortex? We've only shared one kiss. Look, it was freaking great, but you're talking about marriage?"

Marriage? No! He was talking about mating her, which was a deeper bond. How did he explain how shifters worked? How quickly they bonded. How quickly he suspected he would fall for a female like Amy.

"All I'm saying is that we would start something we would never be able to finish."

"Never?" She pushed out the word. "Did you just say never? Because never is a long time?"

"It *is* a long time."

She giggled. "I never thought I would be saying this to a guy, but given that you're so serious, I suppose it makes sense. You're overthinking this. How's about having a bit of fun and letting tomorrow take care of itself?"

"Okay." What the fuck was he doing? Why was he smiling so hard?

"Seriously?"

"Yes." He would probably live to regret this. When Amy walked away, or when he was forced to break her heart, they'd both be crushed. Or maybe just him. Cyclone was right; he was a pussy. Yet this felt right for now.

She laughed. "I should tell you to go to hell."

"Who's overthinking things now?"

She huffed out a breath, definitely smiling. "Okay, but don't make me live to regret this."

"I can't promise anything."

It took a little while for her to answer. "I know."

He sighed. *Thank fuck!* "Are you going to tell me what happened at Trivector? You didn't resign, did you?"

"How do you know that?"

"I know you. For a second there, I thought it was me, and then I realized that you'd sooner have kicked my ass than quit. You're not a quitter. What happened?"

"They're a bunch of dicks," she blurted. Then she told him the whole story.

"They essentially fired you because you wouldn't fudge the numbers, is that right?" Vortex had to force himself to ease his hold on the phone. If he wasn't careful, he was going to crush the thing.

"Yep."

"I'm going to insist that they hire you back."

"Don't." She heaved a sigh. "Like I said, they're a bunch of dicks. I don't want to work there anymore."

"There's more."

"Yes." She breathed out the word. "The Sales Director also resigned for the same reasons, and they hired James Oliver in his place."

"The male who pissed himself?" Vortex frowned.

"James pissed himself?" Amy laughed so loudly he had to hold the phone away from his ear. She howled with laughter, making him smile. "Oh, my gosh!" she finally muttered, still sniggering. "It figures. I'm not sure why I'm surprised. The biggest bullies are normally the biggest crybabies. That's the thing; I can't work for someone like that. He's a pig."

Vortex clenched his jaw. "A pig, how?"

"He tries his luck in piggy ways. That's all."

"Tries his luck how?" Vortex growled.

"He might have whipped his dick out the other day. The disgusting prick wanted me to give him a blowjob for—"

Vortex growled, his lip pulling away from his teeth, which had sharpened up. He knew he'd popped a few scales as well.

"Yeah, I told him what he could do with his offer. He's a disgusting human being, and I can't report to him. As long as James is Sales Director, forget about it."

"Leave it to me," Vortex finally managed to push out.

"What are you going to do?"

"I'm going to offer Trivector a red pill or a blue pill."

Amy laughed, and he felt instantly slightly less murderous.

"I love it when you talk dirty."

That put a smile on his face. "I'll see you soon, Amy."

"Soon." It sounded like she was licking her lips, which may or may not have caused his balls to pull tight and his dick to harden. "Soon as in…?" Her voice had gone all husky.

His dick twitched. This was so wrong and yet so fucking right.

"Really soon." Vortex ended the call because he had plans to put in place, and it couldn't wait.

CHAPTER 21

The next afternoon…

THE ONLY REASON SHE WAS in this building, on the top floor, was because of Vortex. She knew it like she knew her own name. Mr. Taylor had asked her to come over for a meeting. Make that begged her, since she had declined initially. She was here purely for Vortex. He'd told her that he would fix things, and perhaps he had. Amy had her doubts, but, as Mr. Taylor had requested, she'd take the time to hear him out. That was all he'd asked her to do.

It would be easier to find a new job if she was still at Trivector. That's how these things worked, and so… here she was.

The door to Mr. Taylor's office opened before she reached it. The Trivector CEO was smiling too broadly. There was sweat glistening on his brow. He looked… nervous.

"I'm so glad I could convince you to come by today, Amy." He stepped to the side. "Please… come inside."

She faltered when she saw Ray sitting in one of the high-backed leather chairs. Her ex-boss smiled and winked at her.

What was going on?

"It's good to see you, Ray," she said. "I was sad to hear that you had resigned."

"It was a misunderstanding," Ray said.

"Please take a seat, Amy," Mr. Taylor said, stepping behind his desk. "What can I offer you to drink? There are the usuals – tea, coffee, water… all of that. Or I can offer you a whiskey. Or shall I pop some champagne, since we're celebrating?"

"Celebrating what exactly, Mr. Taylor?" she asked as she sat down, noting that Ray had a tumbler with a few fingers of golden liquid inside it.

"You can call me Ronald. Or Ron," the CEO remarked as he pulled the foil off a bottle.

Ron? Really?

"We're celebrating the new contract. All your hard work." He pushed the cork, which popped off with a loud bang. A trickle of liquid spilled over the top. The cork landed on the far side of the office.

"I no longer work at Trivector. I resigned, remember?" She frowned.

Mr. Taylor held out a flute full of bubbly liquid to her. Amy took the glass; she was frowning. Not sure where this was going.

"We want you back, Amy. What happened last week was a mistake."

"Which parts? Over-inflating the prices for Scale Top

or pushing me into a corner to the point where I was forced to resign?"

Mr. Taylor winced, turning away as she finished talking. "All of the above." He poured himself a good few fingers of whiskey, drinking half in one go. Then he took a seat. "I regret allowing the two of you to walk out of the door." He looked from Ray to her and back. "I'm grateful that Raymond has agreed to return to Trivector, and I'm hoping you will do the same. I will make it worth your while, of course. You'll keep the Scale Top business. Furthermore, I'm making you Regional Manager. You'll get a sizable increase and your own office. You deserve it."

This had to be Vortex's doing. She'd never seen Ronald Taylor beg and grovel like this before. Because, make no mistake, the man was practically on his knees. His shoulders were slumped. He looked utterly defeated.

"I would like you back as well, Amy. You are the best salesperson we have… hands down." Raymond smiled at her, looking sincere. Funnily enough, she believed him.

"What about James?" she asked Ronny Boy. *Hah!*

He looked down at his glass and then back up at her before taking another big gulp, almost finishing the whiskey.

"Um… James's position wasn't official. It was a knee-jerk reaction on my part. One I regret. He understands that he's not getting the Sales Director position. That it was temporary. James will report to you going forward," he told Amy.

"No. That's one of my conditions for coming back. The less I have to see of James, the better. I want the Scale Top pricing adjusted to the amounts I recommended."

Ronny's jaw tightened. "It's already done. Scale Top

signed an hour ago. That's why we're celebrating. They've specifically asked for you, Amy. Congratulations, you've made a lot of money out of this deal."

"Money I deserve to make." He was making it sound like she'd lucked out. "It's a deal I closed when James couldn't."

"Absolutely!" Ron groveled some more. That look of desperation was back on his face. "You did a fantastic job, hence the promotion. I can see you taking a corner office one day."

The thought left her cold. And yet, it was everything she'd ever wanted, wasn't it?

Ron's gaze dropped to his lap for a second. He chewed on his lip. Then he lifted his eyes, forcing a smile.

"Also, you don't have to worry about James for the next few weeks. He won't be coming in."

"Why not?"

"He was attacked in the parking lot this morning after arriving at work early."

"Oh!"

"It's the most bizarre thing. The assailant took his wallet but not his cellphone or Breitling watch."

"Oh? That *is* strange." She glanced over at Ray, who took a sip of his whiskey.

"That's not the most bizarre thing about it all. The weirdest part is how they left him. I mean, aside from beaten… badly beaten. What man crushes another man's balls?" Ray got up and poured himself more scotch, taking another huge gulp. He wiped his hand across his mouth. His eyes looked wild. "They broke several ribs. Fractured his skull. His right arm was broken. His left leg and both balls. Crushed them." Ray clenched his fist.

"The surgeon is confident that everything will still function, but poor James is in a world of pain. He'll be in the hospital for a week… maybe even two, and then he'll have to work from home for a while. The surgeon reckons that it will be a month or more before he's back on his feet. We'll have to give him admin duties, which means we'll be short a salesperson and overstaffed in the admin department." Ron sighed heavily.

"Not necessarily," Amy said. "I think that Kerry, who's currently working in admin, would make an excellent salesperson. James can work in admin, and I'll train Kerry to be a sales executive. I think she has the knack for it. I've heard her on the phone with clients. She upsold the Henry Lane account."

"Upselling an account and bringing in brand new business are two different things." Ron wrinkled his nose. "She doesn't seem… I don't know; she just doesn't seem like quite the right fit."

More like she didn't have a dick to swing around. *Argh!* These assholes would never change.

"I strongly disagree, Ron." She looked him in the eyes. "Kerry has instincts I like, and as the new Regional Manager, I'm going to offer her the job. Unless you're changing your mind about offering me the position?"

His eyes widened. "No, no! You have the job. You run with it however you see fit. I know Ray will stand by your side."

"Absolutely!" Ray said. "I also like Kerry for a sales position." He rubbed his chin.

"Let's toast to new beginnings and to the Scale Top business. May this be the first of several contracts." Ron lifted his glass.

"Before we toast," Amy said. "You mentioned that there was something more bizarre about the attack on James than them leaving his watch and cellphone. What was it?"

Ron pushed out a shuddery breath and shook his head. "Whoever did that awful thing also wrapped James' body up in purple cellophane and tied a ribbon around him. Can you believe that?"

Amy choked out a laugh, quickly covering her mouth with her hand.

"I mean, shit! That's terrible. What kind of freak would do something like that?"

CHAPTER 22

That evening…

FOR A SECOND THERE, SHE almost couldn't quite believe her eyes. Then she tossed out a laugh. Vortex had assured her that she would be seeing him soon, but she hadn't expected it to be quite this soon. Although, after what happened with James…

"You freak!" she laughed harder. "I mean purple cellophane and a ribbon tied in a bow?"

"You told me that actions spoke louder than words." He shrugged his broad shoulders. "That you preferred them to actual gifts."

"I do."

"Well, then?"

"It still makes you a freak, *and* you're a stalker, just by the way." She narrowed her eyes. "I don't believe I ever gave you my address."

Vortex leaned against the doorjamb. *Sexy freak!* He was wearing a tight gray shirt. It clung to every muscle group. *Holy hotness, Batman!* Maybe she was the freak for eyeballing him like this.

"You signed that form with your basic information that day I first met you." He gave her a lopsided grin. "I might have stolen your address off of that."

"Like I said, you're a bit of a stalker. Good thing I'm hungry," she looked down at the box of pizza balancing in his hand, "so I'm willing to overlook that kind of behavior."

Pity she was hungrier for him than the pizza in his hand.

Amy needed to play it cool. This was technically their first date. Vortex was running a little scared; she needed to take it easy on the poor guy.

"Fuuuuuuuuuuuck!" Jake shouted from the living room, ending on an agonized sounding shriek. The one Jake had been making ever since she broke her toe on the coffee table.

She covered her face with her hand, peering at Vortex between her fingers.

"Is that the infamous Jake?" Vortex laughed.

She nodded.

"I like him already." He was still smiling broadly. *Those dimples, though!* "It's pepperoni." He held up the box. "But we could go out to eat." He looked back over his shoulder.

"Nope. My place is good." She chewed on her lip for a second. "Do you want to come in?" *Crap!* She'd left him standing there… again.

"That would be nice." His green gaze was locked with hers, and suddenly the air felt charged.

His eyes moved down the length of her body as she stepped back.

"Holy fuck!" Vortex groaned. "You look amazing."

To think she'd been slightly embarrassed when she realized it was him. It wasn't like she could change. Now she was glad she hadn't. "Um… these are my old shorts. This t-shirt has a hole in it."

"The shorts are short as fuck. You have great legs, by the way. And the shirt is white and threadbare, and you aren't wearing a bra. Fuck, female!" he growled. The sound shooting straight to her nether regions. "Did you know I was coming? Because I think you couldn't look sexier if you tried."

That was one point for dragon shifters. They were easy to please. His eyes were filled with lust, making him all the sexier. Jeans looked so good on him, too. The way they molded his thighs just right. It all emboldened her. Amy swallowed thickly.

"I have this fantasy…" She licked her lips, and his eyes seemed to track the movement of her tongue.

"What kind of fantasy?" His voice seemed deeper.

"Of being taken hard and fast against a door by a big, bad dragon shifter." She wasn't sure where that had come from, but once she said the words, they became true. Then again, she *had* fantasized about him. In her head, they'd had sex loads of different ways. Normally in ways that involved him showing her how strong he was.

"Really now?" He lifted his brows.

Finding courage inside her she never knew she possessed, she grabbed the hem of her shirt and pulled the garment over her head.

The look on his face was almost comical. His mouth slackened. His eyes both brightened and darkened.

"You'd better come in before you give my neighbors an eyeful," she said, pulling her shoulders back. Amy's breasts were one of her best features. Not too big and not too small.

"Fuuuuck!" Vortex purred, his voice deep. He half slammed the door behind him, tossing the pizza box onto a side table, then gripping her hips and putting her back against the wood. His jaw was tight. His eyes locked with hers. His hands tightened on her hips.

"I… shit… I want this. So fucking much, but—"

"Let's not overthink things. Let's… have fun! Let's just enjoy each other. Don't think about tomorrow. Or war. Or anything else."

His eyes clouded, and he looked down, his eyes unseeing.

She tilted his chin up. "Stop that! Sex. Fun. You and me. No tomorrows. Hell, no todays; just us and right now."

"That's all good and well. It sounds fucking amazing; only I can't promise you—"

She put her finger over his lips to shush him. "Has anyone ever told you that you talk too much?"

His Adam's apple worked.

"Do you want me?" she asked.

"Hell, yeah." He nodded once.

"I want you, Vortex. So we're doing this. Right here and right now!"

His low growl sent shivers up and down her spine. He cupped her chin and kissed her like there might be a tomorrow. It was full of tenderness and hope. It stole her breath. Started to steal more than just that when he slid a hand between them, cupping her sex through her shorts. He rubbed her through the material a few times, eliciting a moan from her.

Then he tugged them down her thighs until they pooled at her feet. Vortex made a sound of irritation when he put his hand back on her. Obviously feeling her lace panties. A low rumble left him as he shoved the fabric aside and slipped his fingers between her folds, zoning in on her clit.

Holy crap!

Amy cried out, but he swallowed the sound as his fingers softly circled her bundle of nerves. *Oh! Shit! Fuuuuck!* She arched her back, breathing heavily through her nose.

More!

More!

She'd forgotten how good he was with his hands. How the hell had she forgotten? Using the same two fingers, he pushed into her.

"So damned wet," he mumbled against her lips. He crooked his fingers a little, zoning in on her g-spot. It was clear that he knew exactly where it was because he hit it right off the bat this time.

Her eyes widened, and she gave a sharp intake of breath as he rubbed on her using firm, easy strokes. Amy had hoped she'd last longer this time.

She was wrong. So wrong!

Wrong!

Wrong!

Wrong!

Her breathing became ragged as her belly tightened. Her skin tightened. Everything tightened.

Just as she was about to come, he moved back to her clit. Using one finger, he made lazy circles around the swollen nub. Round and round and round. Her back arched, her eyes closed, her head rolled back against the door. Amy bit down on her lower lip, holding it between her teeth, and moaned loudly. It was pure bliss, and pure torture all rolled into one.

Vortex took back her mouth. Amy kissed him right back, sucking on his tongue and nipping at his lips. She groaned against his mouth as he pushed three fingers into her.

Three!

"Oh God," she moaned. "Oooohhh... yes." She rolled her hips, unable to do anything else but give in to the sensations.

His thumb found her clit while his fingers kept pumping... pumping. They hit the right spot over and over. The coiling sensation became a tight pull as everything seemed to stop for a split second. She was sure that her heart missed a beat. That everything in her paused... just before the rush of her orgasm hit. She moaned. The sound raw and untethered. His hand continued to pump, the pad of his thumb dragging across her sensitive nub.

He eventually slowed his movements, softened his touch, until he finally stopped. Her head fell back against the door. She clasped his biceps. Her legs were shaking.

"You're good at that."

Vortex chuckled. "You should see what I can do with my cock."

Arrogant man... shifter. He was a shifter. Her shifter. Not hers, but maybe someday. It was important that she not overthink this either. They were having fun and enjoying each other's company. *No tomorrow!*

Amy struggled to catch her breath. His thumb found her clit again and gently rubbed her there. Amy arched her back and moaned. Her eyes went wide. That's all it took to get her blood hot all over again. That and looking into his eyes. They had turned a bright green. Brighter than anything she'd seen before and filled with so much lust… for her.

"You said up against a door."

She gripped the bottom of his shirt. It looked good on Vortex, but she liked naked better.

"That's exactly what I said," Amy replied as she pulled his shirt over his head, letting it drop to the floor.

"The bed would be better." He nuzzled her neck.

"We can try out my bed later."

His eyes found hers. "I can't stay… I'm sorry." His gaze softened.

"We're having fun. It's all good. I know you have responsibilities…"

He kissed her, talking against her lips. "We're not thinking about that now."

"Nope. You were about to make my dreams come true."

Vortex chuckled, nipping at her earlobe. "You put 'not applicable' on your form."

"What form?" Her brain felt slow.

"You put 'not applicable'," he repeated. "On your form next to the question referring to birth control."

She sniggered. "You really are a stalker."

"I need to know, since we're about to fuck. I want to come inside you."

Amy swallowed thickly. Why did that do strange things to her insides? He was so forward about such things. Amy liked that about him.

"I can't scent an ovulation, but… I would rather be sure. Mistakes happen. Not often, but they happen. I'm not ready to be a father."

Amy felt a pang, but she shoved it aside. "I'm on birth control."

"You can't get anything from me." He had this desperate look that he pulled off better than almost anyone she knew would ever be able to. So darned freaking cute. "I brought condoms, but… I want…"

"…to come inside me. I can't get anything from you, and you can't get anything from me."

He made that same rumbling growl she'd come to recognize as lust. Vortex was hugely turned on. She couldn't wait to feel him deep inside her.

"What do you say, then?" He kissed her long and hard. His big, warm hands cupped her ass. She could feel him hard against her belly.

Ready!

"That's definitely a yes from me." She nodded as he pulled back; she was probably looking like a crazy person.

Vortex gave her a feral grin. He was sexy when he was turned on.

"Okay then." There was the sound of a zipper going down. Then he gripped her thighs, his eyes on hers, and hoisted her up easily. "Put your legs around my waist." She hooked her ankles at his back, his cock flush up against her since he was commando. Why did she find that so hot?

She looked down between them, and his dick looked

even bigger somehow now that it was against her lace-clad pussy. Amy groaned in anticipation.

"That's it." He flashed a grin as she did as he asked. "I'm going to make you come so damned hard. I might break down this door and give the neighbors something to talk about." He held her up off the floor like it was nothing. Easy-peasy, fulfilling every darned fantasy and then some.

Holy mackerel. This was really happening.

"Can't wait to come inside that snug pussy." His gaze was there, at the junction of her thighs. Her throat closed hearing him talk like that. She liked it, though. She never thought she would, but lord help her, she did.

Dirty talk turned her on, and it seemed that Vortex was an expert.

His mouth closed on one of her nipples, then his hand was between them, and in one jolt, he tore the lace G-string away, putting her sex flush against him. Even that was sexy.

Amy licked her lips. Thankfully, she was really good at keeping things neat down there, even though she didn't have a sex life to speak of and hadn't for a good long time. There was a neat little landing strip; otherwise, she was bare.

"So pretty," he whispered, rubbing a thumb over her strip.

She groaned as the pad of his thumb found her clit. The tip of his cock was suddenly at her opening. Nudging its way in.

"You're big," she managed to choke out. Amy widened her eyes as he slid in further. His thumb continued to slip and slide over her clit. "Really huge."

"Yeah, and you're tight." He was frowning, a sheen of sweat on his brow. "Really fucking tight. But you'll fit me."

"Of course, I will. It was a compliment. I think I might be in love with your cock." She groaned. "He can stalk the hell out of my pussy anytime… and bareback, too. Ooooohhhh!" She squeezed her eyes shut. "I like bareback… Make that looove…"

Vortex chuckled, anchoring her against the door. His hand digging into her thigh just a little as he pulled out and then pushed back in. Easy, easy, inch by inch until he was finally flush against her. His thumb pressed against her clit, but he wasn't moving anymore. It felt maddeningly good. So stretched. So full. He was breathing deeply. His huge chest expanding and contracting against her, brushing up against her breasts. Her nipples were so tight that they hurt.

He kissed her neck, nipped at her ear, and she groaned.

"You feel good," he spoke against her lobe. "Fucking good." A low growl. "I knew you would. I've had a couple of fantasies of my own."

"You feel good too." She was appalled at how strangled her words were. Breathy and strangled and high-pitched. She wanted to ask him about the fantasies, but he didn't give her a chance.

"Hold on." It was all the warning he gave as the hand on her clit moved away to hold on to her thigh and hoist her further up him. Amy gripped his shoulders. His face became a mask of what could easily be misconstrued as fury as he pulled out of her. When all of those thick inches jackknifed back in, it had her mouth falling open and her back bowing.

Holy hell!

There was no other way to describe it but rough and primal. Vortex held her tight as he plowed into her from below. His knees were slightly bent, his jaw clenched tightly. Horrifying yet beautiful. There was a dull thud as her ass hit the door with each hard thrust. Her breasts jerked between them. None of it mattered because she was about to come again. Harder this time; she could feel it. It was right there. Her orgasm. Pulling, kneading, coiling, growing. Her cries were insistent. Amy was as loud as he was silent.

"Fuck! Fuck! Fuck!" she yelled every time he hit her g-spot, which was every darned time. "Jesus! Jesus!" she screamed. Then she was coming apart. The orgasm that tore through her wrung a long, deep wail from her. It had her clenching her eyes tight. It had her bucking against him. It felt like a tornado of pleasure ripping right through her. Like it might just rip her apart if she wasn't careful. It consumed all of her, not just one part or area, all of her. Every nerve, every cell, every single one, and all at once.

Vortex groaned her name; his head was buried in the crook of her neck. He grunted once, really softly as he jerked against her, hard. His thrusts were just as insistent, but not as controlled for a few beats. Then he slowed up. Moving less and less until he finally stopped altogether.

Amy slumped against him; she felt boneless. They were both breathing heavily. She was shaking a little. Or was it him? Maybe both of them. It was that good. It was magical. She'd had great sex before, but this was something else.

They both remained there, clinging to each other. She could still feel him inside her.

"Okay, so we might do that again after we eat." Vortex was breathing heavily.

"I have this fantasy that involves my coffee table," she panted the words out.

He chuckled, slowly lowering her, but before he put her down, it started up.

"Fuck! Fuck! Fuck!" Jake squawked, sounding distinctly feminine. Then there were a few moments of silence before that asshole of a bird went. "Jesus! Jesus!" Louder this time, followed by a long, drawn-out wail. There was no agony involved.

They locked eyes, and Vortex cracked up. "I love Jake."

"Nooooooo!" She couldn't help but laugh as well. "What's wrong with him? I definitely can't have anyone over ever again."

"One thing is for sure; he's a soprano."

They both laughed. Then her stomach rumbled... loudly.

"Let me clean you up and then feed you," Vortex said, brushing his lips over hers. It felt good. It felt like a whole lot of fun. It also felt like more. At least it did to her... and that was a worry.

I can't make any promises.

Vortex had been clear about that. Clear as day.

CHAPTER 23

The next day…

VORTEX HATED TYPING UP REPORTS. It was the shitty part of his job. It had to be done, so he worked as fast as he could… with a goofy smile on his face.

It couldn't be helped. Amy was just as amazing as he thought she would be. They'd eaten the pizza… and then fucked again. Amy with her back on the coffee table and her legs over his shoulders. It had been sublime. The word mind-blowing came to mind. Almost better than the first time. Almost!

She was sweet, beautiful, so receptive it was crazy, and she didn't take any shit. Not from him or anyone else, for that matter.

Vortex grabbed his phone and typed, *I miss you*. He almost pressed send and then thought better of it.

I miss having fun with you, he retyped and pushed send.

Straight up "I miss you" was a bit sappy. It leaned towards relationship status, and he needed to be careful of going there. This was casual, live-in-the-moment fun. Nothing more and nothing less. He liked Amy a whole hell of a lot and didn't want to see her get hurt when this ended.

His phone beeped, alerting him to a message. Vortex picked it up and smiled.

> I miss having fun with you too. Although I'm a little sore this morning, I won't lie.

He chuckled softly.

> Wish I could kiss you all better. (Tongue emoji)

He pushed send. The little dots appeared, telling him that she was replying. He sat there, phone in hand, waiting. Eyes glued to the screen like a pussy, but he didn't care.

> I don't know... the pain is pretty deep.

He choked out a laugh.

> Like right up there.

She added, and he chuckled some more.

> Wish your stalker dick could kiss it all better. (Eggplant emoji)

Vortex all-out laughed.

"Do me a fucking favor!" Cyclone snarled. "Can you keep your happiness levels to an 'I hate my life' level, please? I'm trying to work here."

Vortex turned, and sure enough, the male was at his desk, his two fingers at the ready. His deep blue eyes were even more blue than normal. They were sparkly and bright, which was the only thing sparkly and bright about him. Everything else was dark and spelled death.

Yet again, Vortex had been so wrapped up in his own shit he hadn't even noticed the male arriving. For someone so massive, he was surprisingly light on his feet. Vortex ignored the male.

> If only! My dick would like nothing better than to kiss your g-spot better. How is my favorite parrot, BTW?

The dots appeared. It took about 10 seconds for his phone to beep. Vortex put the thing on silent before Cyclone declared war.

> OMG! Still shouting my orgasm at the top of his lungs every chance he gets.

Vortex held back a snigger. He couldn't contain the smirk, though. No way was that possible.

> Please tell Jake that I love him. I'm thinking of adopting him just so that I can hear him do a rendition of you screaming in ecstasy on the regular. My kind of soprano.

It didn't take long for her message to come through.

> You really are a freak!

He gave an air chuckle through his nose, being as quiet as possible. There were more dots, followed by:

> Good thing I like freaks. (Hug emoji)

Vortex smiled.

> Can't wait to rip your panties off.

> (Blushing emoji) Next time I won't wear panties.

Holy fuck, he was getting hard. More dots. He held his breath.

> Next time, I'll answer the door naked.

He groaned.

"Holy fucking shit, asshole!" Cyclone pushed out. "If I have to listen to you snigger one more time, I'm putting my fist in your face."

"Sorry!" he mumbled, knowing he was out of line. This was a shared office, and he was being annoying.

"You smell fucking nauseating right now. Human female, sanitizer – a truckload of the stuff – then there's arousal, sunshine, and fucking happiness. I hate it! Fucking stop!" Cyclone growled. "I'm almost sorry I told you to call her. What's her name? Mrs. Winters?" He snorted. "*Mrs,* my ass."

"What? Um… no! You have it all wrong," he spluttered. How did Cyclone know it was Amy? If a dragon scented Amy now, they'd pick up his scent in a heartbeat but not the other way around. Not after cleaning up so carefully. Not after just two ruts. How? *Fuck!*

"I have it all wrong? Like hell I do." Cyclone turned towards him. "That female isn't mated. No fucking way is she mated. You weren't with some random human, either."

"Her mate is on tour. That's why she doesn't scent of—"

"It isn't her scent that's the giveaway." Cyclone shook his head. "It's the way the two of you looked at each other. How *you* looked at *her*. I got the vibe."

Shit! Was it that obvious?

"You can cool your tits," Cyclone went on. "No one else would've picked it up. I can't smell her specific scent on you either. The hints were subtle. You were discreet. I'm just that observant. I think it's fantastic that you're finally getting some. Blue balls did not look good on you. However, tone it the fuck down… at least while I'm in the same room. It's pissing me off."

"Perhaps you should take care of your own blue balls." Since they were sharing, Vortex thought that he would try to return the favor.

Cyclone growled and muttered something that sounded very much like, "Mind your own fucking business." Then he went back to typing.

Okay, then.

Vortex looked at the screen of his computer. He'd finish these reports, and then he'd respond to Amy. He needed to let her know that he was going to visit her again in two weeks. He'd asked for three days' leave, expecting Storm to turn him down, but the male had tapped him on the arm, saying that he was glad Vortex was taking a break. Storm himself would cover for Vortex. There was no fucking way Amy was going to that seedy pick-up joint. Not a chance. *Bottoms Up?* Hell, yeah! It would be Amy's bottom that would be up while he rutted her himself. He'd be her fill-in mate for the weekend. Hell, they could even go glamping in the Rocky Mountains.

Storm had a meeting scheduled with the goblin queen in a couple of days. A group of 16 vigilante males had been captured just that morning by their own people. They would apparently stand trial for their crimes. It was expected that adverse goblin activity would die down as a result. It remained to be seen. There was a small part of him that wanted to allow hope to take residence. The logical side of him wouldn't allow it.

Later that day…

LISA TOOK A STEP BACK, looking worried. "Is everything okay?" She clutched her chest with one hand, holding Christopher in her other arm.

"I thought I would pop by for a visit." Amy held up a bag. "I brought all the ingredients to make us a couple of French 75s." She jiggled the bag. "It's actual champagne this time since I not only got my job back but got a promotion too."

"I'm so proud of you."

"You can stop saying that. Wait just a minute." Lisa looked at her watch. You… here… now? It's only just past five."

"Exactly! It's time for a drink."

"It's a work night, though. Tomorrow is a workday? You're in management yourself now. Are you sure you're okay? Is everything is okay?" Lisa looked at her skeptically. "This isn't like you at all. You never go out during the week. You hardly ever go out on the weekends, either."

"I'm sure I want to be here, and yes, everything is just great. I have staff who know what they need to do. Besides, I decided that I spend too much time working and not enough time on the things that count. Like family and my newest nephew." Amy glanced down at the baby in question. He was so freaking cute. Christopher had big brown eyes and looked so much like his mom it was scary. He was sucking on his pacifier like it was a lifeline. She felt everything inside her melt just looking at him.

"Okay! Who are you, and what have you done with my sister?"

"I mean it, Lisa. I've changed." Amy shrugged. She felt

different inside. "I… I think I might be falling for someone. It might be a mistake, though." She chewed on her lip.

Lisa shrieked, scaring the baby. She soothed poor Chris while inviting Amy in using one-handed gestures.

"This is great. Oh, my gosh! I can't believe it. You? Nooooo! I'm going to lose on a long-running bet."

"What bet?" Amy frowned, walking into Sean and Lisa's home.

"Jen, Ingrid, Mom, and I might have this bet going." She made a face.

"What the hell, Lisa!" Amy feigned anger. "You bet *against* me ever finding love? You, who's always pushing me in that direction?"

"Ummmmm… can I plead the fifth?"

Amy gave her a dirty look. "Should I go and see Ingrid or Jen instead? Which one of them voted that I would find love? I'm at the wrong sister's house."

"Forget about the stupid bet. As much as I hate losing a thousand dollars, I—"

Amy gasped. "The bet was for a thousand freaking dollars?" She tried to keep her voice down, not wanting to scare the baby all over again. "What the heck!"

Lisa shrugged. "You've been pretty bad in that department. Shall I get some cocktail glasses? I only have time for one, then Christopher will have to bathe and go to bed." Her whole voice changed as she looked down at the little munchkin in her arms.

"I want that!" Amy blurted.

"Want what?" Lisa looked confused.

"Love. A baby. I want a baby, Lisa. I want all of it." Amy chewed down on her lip. *Shit!* Now she was scaring herself. It was true, though.

"Crap!" Lisa rolled her eyes. "A baby too?"

"What's wrong with that?" Amy frowned. "Of course, I want a baby. I'm turning 30 in two months' time."

"Darn it!" Lisa scrunched up her nose. "I stand to lose another five hundred and fifty bucks."

Amy's mouth fell open. "Really? You thought I would be a spinster for the rest of my life. A spinster with cats?"

Lisa laughed, putting two cocktail glasses down on the table. "No cats, just Jake. No self-respecting cat would live in your house with that bird."

Amy tried to hold it in, but she ended up laughing too.

"So, who is he?" Lisa asked as Amy started unpacking the French 75 ingredients. Her eyes widened as realization dawned. "It's your client. The one you were telling me about. What happened?" Then her eyes went wider. "Oh, my god! You had sex with him."

Amy smiled. No! Make that beamed. Amy beamed. It felt like a light was shining from inside of her. A bright light.

"Um… maybe."

"Holy shi… shenanigans!" She widened her eyes. "That was close." She brushed a kiss on her son's forehead. "It was good, wasn't it? I'm getting the feeling that it was great." She cackled like a witch next to a bonfire at midnight.

"More than good." Amy sobered up. "Better than great. Off the charts." She was grinning like a loon.

"There's a *but* coming up."

"He doesn't want a relationship right now. He's too focused on his career. He's me a couple of years ago, only worse. Hell, he's me a month ago… only much worse."

Lisa reached out and touched her on the side of her arm. "Oh! That is bad."

"Thanks! I knew that already. What I really need is some advice? I've never been in love. I've never wanted the whole nine yards with a guy before."

"Wow!" Lisa giggled. "That got serious fast. I know it's a bit of a cliché, but if it's meant to be, it will be."

"What if it's not meant to be? What if I want him more than he wants me?"

"That's how it goes. It's the beauty of love. That's why it's so amazing."

"I could get hurt."

"You could, but maybe you'll find love right back. This guy could be your soulmate. The one! How will you ever know if you don't try?"

"We've agreed not to think about tomorrow or next week. Not to overthink things in general, and to just have fun. To keep it casual. It's gone beyond casual for me already." She sighed. "Thing is, I think he really likes me right back."

"There you go. It's early days. It sounds like a plan." Lisa smiled. "That's how these things work. Who knows what will come of it? Could be amazing. Go with it."

"I could get my heart ripped out of my chest and torn into a thousand pieces."

Lisa's whole demeanor softened. "We'll be here for you. Your whole family. You're not alone. I say that you should go for it. You don't want to be left with nagging doubts of what could have been just because you were too afraid to leap."

"You might be right."

"I know I am." Lisa grinned. "If it doesn't work out, at least you know what you want now. There are more guys out there."

Not like Vortex.

"You're still young, sis. You'll land on your feet. You always do." Lisa gave her a playful nudge with her elbow. "What are you waiting for? Pour us some drinks. I feel a toast coming on."

"What are we toasting?"

"Let's toast to…" Lisa seemed to think on it for a while. "Amazing sex." She giggled. "To plenty of amazing sex. There's nothing better than that feeling in the pit of your stomach at the start of a new relationship. We'll toast to not being able to keep your hands off each other. Next time you come to my house at five in the evening, we'll toast to long walks on the beach and candlelit dinners."

"Let's make that long walks in the forest and s'mores over a campfire."

Lisa cocked her head. "How so?"

"We're going camping in the Rocky Mountains in two weeks."

Lisa did this bouncy thing on her feet, grinning from ear to ear. "Sounds amazing. I hope your tent collapses and that your air mattress pops." She laughed. "Where's my drink already?"

Amy snort-laughed. "I'm making them! I'm making them!" She couldn't keep the grin off her face if she tried. Glamping with Vortex in the mountains. She couldn't wait!

CHAPTER 24

Two weeks later…

Vortex eased into the parking space.

"I still can't believe it." Amy cringed as she undid her safety belt.

He laughed. "What I can't believe is that you're still blushing. We left the campsite almost half an hour ago, and your cheeks are just as red."

"It's so embarrassing." She covered her face and groaned. "They kicked us out. I've never heard of anyone being evicted from a camping site. Not ever!"

Vortex laughed harder. "In their defense, you are very loud and demanding in bed." He laughed some more. "It's a trait of yours I happen to seriously like." He leaned over and kissed her softly. "One of my favorites, actually. I definitely know where my boy Jake gets it from."

"Stop!" She couldn't help but smile.

"Vortex! Vortex! Yes, there! Right there!" he mimicked her.

She slapped him on the side of his arm, feeling her cheeks heat all over again.

"Stop that!"

"And then, of course, there's the cussing when you're getting close. 'Fuck! Fuck! Fuck!'"

She slapped him harder. "Stop it already!" Still smiling, even though she wanted to die from embarrassment. "I tried to keep it down. I really, really tried."

"It didn't work. You're super loud during sex." Vortex let his head fall back against the seat of the car and laughed… hard.

Amy would have noticed how cute he looked. How relaxed. How happy… if she wasn't dying… freaking *dying* right now. She'd never packed up a campsite so quickly. In fact, they hauled down the tent and tossed it in the back of the SUV without actually rolling it up and packing it away.

"Okay. In hindsight, I might have been a little loud," she conceded, remembering how sore her throat had been after round two last night.

"A *little* loud?" He turned and locked eyes with her.

"We set up camp on the other side of the grounds, far away from everyone. I tried to be quiet, I swear."

"Yeah…" He grinned. "Not far enough away. And don't try to be quiet in the future. You just get noisier at the end if you hold back. I think it's awesome you're so vocal."

She winced and rubbed a hand over her face. "You're just that good. We're good together. I mean in *that* way…

sexually." *Crap!* She didn't want to push him. Lisa had warned her against that. Pushing too soon resulted in pushing a guy away.

"I know what you meant." Vortex nodded.

"Like mind-blowing. Maybe it's a dragon thing? Is it always that good for you?" Then she chuckled. "Don't answer that. We're having fun here, not bringing up previous partners."

His demeanor stiffened, and his jaw tightened. "It's not always like that. We're just really compatible… in bed." Tension crept in, and it started to feel weird between them.

"Even if said bed is a blowup mattress." She pushed out a laugh.

Vortex chuckled, and just like that, the tension cleared. "A blowup mattress that squeaks during sex."

"Oh, lordy! Please don't remind me." She covered her face with her hand again. "Even the squeaks were loud, weren't they?"

"Don't worry about it. It's not like we'll see any of those people again. I can safely say that this is the most fun I've had in a long time. Besides, we get to stay in this lovely-looking B&B tonight."

"Solid walls and a regular bed… bliss!" She giggled.

"Let's go inside and christen the bed?" Vortex got that look. The horny-as-hell one. She loved that he was so insatiable. He couldn't seem to get enough of her. "Your 'husband' is in town for a short while only. Your scent needs to say 'off-limits.' Plus, we still have eight condoms left. We said we would try to finish them all." He grinned at her.

"I wish we didn't have to use those things," she said as she got out of the vehicle.

"Me too, but I can't get my scent on you. You're back at the lair in just under a week. This way you'll smell strongly of rubber. Otherwise, they'll scent it was a dragon. They might even scent me specifically. That would be a royal fuck-up," he said as he opened the door.

"Yes, it would." She sighed, getting out of the car.

Would it be such a fuck-up, though?

Amy didn't care anymore if everyone knew. She didn't care if they all found out that she wasn't married. She didn't care about losing her job. Realistically, she knew that thinking along these lines was crazy. It was too soon. They were having fun! Just having some fun!

"You just got serious on me. You have this look on your face." Vortex was scrutinizing her from the other side of the car.

"Nothing… I'm—"

His phone beeped with an incoming message.

"Must be work," he said, fishing the thing out of his pocket as he walked to the back of the vehicle, reading the message. "Oh, fuck! Shit just got real back at home."

"What? Is everything okay? Did the war start? Do you have to go?" she said in a rush.

"Nothing quite so drastic, but it does concern the goblins. Remember I told you about those 16 males who were captured by their own people?"

"Yep. One of the vigilante groups?"

He nodded.

"You said that the goblins were going to hold a trial."

He pushed a button to pop the trunk. "Yeah, well, they were executed this morning."

She gasped. "So Dommak was serious when she said that the queen planned on tackling this with an iron fist."

"Clearly serious as fuck! Her favorite male," Vortex widened his eyes, "whatever the hell that means, was among those put to death. Their bodies have been put up on spikes outside the entrance to the mine to serve as a warning."

"That's… that's…" She was at a loss for words.

"Barbaric? Chilling? Fucking insane?"

"Yep, I'll go with all three of those options." Her eyes were wide. "Put to death," she whispered.

"Sends one hell of a message to the others," Vortex said as he took out their bags. "Gives me confidence that perhaps Dommak was telling the truth after all." His phone beeped again. Vortex checked the message. "Storm is content with how this was handled." Vortex looked deep in thought. "He's given Shrakka permission to send more patrols into our area." He shook his head, his eyes blazed. "I don't like it. I know it's a step in the right direction, but…" He let the sentence die.

"If you want to go back, to cut our weekend short, I will understand."

"No!" Vortex put his arms around her. "They have it under control. There have been no vigilante groups spotted since the 16 males were captured. Perhaps this will do the trick." She could see worry clouding his eyes.

Amy reached up, managing to just plant a kiss on his lips.

"Let's go and christen that bed. Since we don't need the tent anymore, we can use those ropes. I might just let you tie me to the bed."

Vortex groaned. "Tie you up? Now, who's the freak in this relationship?" He leaned down and kissed her until her toes curled in her hiking boots. All the while, she tried extra hard not to read into what he had just said. He didn't mean it. Vortex didn't realize he'd even said it. A relationship? Nope. As much as she hoped otherwise, it wasn't one.

Amy unlocked their garden suite, opening the door. They'd asked for the most private unit on the property. It was a walk getting there, but at least Amy would be able to have at it. Vortex smiled. He couldn't stop smiling. They were having the best time. Hikes, s'mores, campfires, and squeaky mattresses. Now they'd have pretty rose gardens, a candlelit dinner, and a huge four-poster bed.

"Wow! That's some bed," Amy murmured as she walked in behind him.

Vortex put down the bags. "Are you tired… hungry? Do you want to freshen up? Go explore?"

She shook her head, a naughty little smile on her full lips.

Vortex grinned. "Me neither."

"I was thinking more along the lines of…" She rummaged in her tote, which was wider than normal on account of the rope that was inside. Amy pulled it out. "Of tying me up and having your wicked way with me on that bed… which had to have been made for sex."

He chuckled. "Only on one condition."

"What would that be?" She licked her lips.

"That you don't hold back."

She laughed. "That's not even possible with you."

It was true. He'd never been more compatible with a female. It was like sparks and dynamite. Explosive.

Then she was in his arms, her legs wrapping around

his waist. Their mouths came together in a clash as he walked to the bed.

Vortex put her on her back on the soft mattress. One by one, he pulled off her boots and socks.

Amy unbuttoned and unzipped her jeans. Vortex slid them from her thighs. He growled when he realized that she wasn't wearing underwear.

"I didn't see the need." Amy opened her legs.

He didn't think he'd ever tire of looking between those lush thighs at the slice of heaven nestled there.

He groaned. "Take it all off." He gestured to her top. She had the ripest little tits. They bounced just right and fit in his mouth like they had been made just for him.

Vortex pulled his own shirt over his head and toed off his boots before yanking down his jeans. By the time he was done getting naked and grabbing a couple of condoms, Amy was spread out before him like an all-you-can-eat buffet.

"Holy fuck!" he growled as he crawled over her. He took the rope, which was actually several shorter pieces rolled into a loop. "Am I tying just your arms, or your legs as well?"

"I like it when you lift my legs and go really deep."

His balls tightened up, and his cock dribbled some pre-cum. Amy had such a dirty mouth, and he fucking loved it. He kissed her quick and hard. Then he went to work tying her arms, one to each post. He took his time kissing her hands, her arms… her lush tits. She was spectacular.

"I want to taste you," he said as he looked down at her slit.

Pink is my new favorite color, he thought to himself. He

growled, watching as his little minx opened her legs even wider for him. She was already so turned on. It wouldn't take much. So sensitive. So receptive to him.

She nodded, eyeing him. Next time, he'd blindfold her as well. It would heighten the experience.

Next time.

Vortex had no idea when that would be. *Fuck!* He wasn't thinking about that now. He had better things to concentrate on. His eyes zoned in on the feast nestled between her thighs.

"So pretty," he said as his fingers trailed over her soft mound.

Strip of fur. Pink. Glistening. So beautiful.

Vortex's nostrils flared as he inhaled her delicious cherry scent. She whimpered as he closed his mouth over her clit. Amy threw her head back, her mouth open. Her back bowed off the bed as he gave her throbbing nub another suck.

A low moan filled the quiet space as he laved over her sensitive knot of nerves. Alternating between sucking, nipping softly, and licking. It wasn't long before she clawed at the sheets, panting heavily.

"Oh god! You're so good at this. Don't stop! Don't you dare stop."

Amy pulled against her rope binds. Her hips rocked in time with his thrusting tongue, so responsive, so sensitive. Vortex inserted a finger into her tight, wet sheath. Amy moaned, thrashing her head from side to side.

"Good! Yes! Holy shit!"

He pulled away.

"Why are you stopping?" She was so demanding. So

clear about what she wanted and how she wanted it. Vortex loved it. He used his teeth to tear open a foil package.

"I'm going to fuck you. You'll come twice in quick succession, on the end of my dick and you'll fucking love it," he said as he slid the condom over his throbbing cock.

"So damned arrogant."

"And you love it." He smiled while moving over her, careful to ensure that his weight was distributed on his arms, which he anchored on either side of her face. "Put your legs around me, sexy." She did as he said, locking her ankles at his back. Vortex thrust into her welcoming pussy, swallowing her cry with his mouth. Well, mostly. She was noisy as fuck.

He waited a few beats for her to stretch a little before sliding a little further into her wet heat.

"So big!" she groaned. "Love your cock."

He laughed. It was choked and tense sounding, but his dick was balls-deep, so he cut himself some slack. He pumped in and out of her a couple of times, groaning at how amazing she felt. How perfect.

He looked down at her, her arms wide and tethered. Her breasts mashed up against his chest. Her eyes closed, and her mouth slack.

Amy pulled her legs up higher. Vortex groaned as his cock slid deeper into her tight sheath. Already, he could feel his balls pulling up in anticipation.

Using slow, easy strokes, he moved within her. Loving the way they fit so perfectly together. Vortex cupped her chin, taking back her lips. She rocked her hips in time with him.

It wasn't long before she was yelling with every thrust.

"Yes! Oh! There! Right there! Fuck!" He felt her quiver beneath him with each thrust.

Vortex was grunting hard, too.

Her sheath tightened around him. Vortex thrust deeper, picking up the pace as she shuddered beneath him, her pussy clamping down hard, sucking on him greedily.

"Jesus!" she groaned, burying her face in his neck. Her pussy became a tight velvet vise around him as she wailed.

Just as she was coming down, Vortex clamped his mouth down softly at the base of her neck.

"Holy fuuuuuuck!" She jerked hard against him, yelling his name. The coiling inside him gave way to a rush of pleasure. It almost came as a shock; it hit him so damned hard and all at once. He also yelled. It might have been her name, or a cuss; he wasn't certain. He released her neck as he continued to grind into her tight heat. His body shook, and he roared loudly.

So damned good. Damned perfect. Both were covered in a sheen of sweat. Both panting heavily. Vortex was still careful to keep his full weight off of her. He rested his head between her breasts.

Shit! He hadn't meant to bite her. It wasn't an actual bite, but still. Maybe his instincts had been aroused because she was tied and unable to move much. That might have done it. Maybe it was how he seemed to get lost when inside her. Whatever the reasons behind it, it was bad. Such behavior was reserved for mates.

He carefully undid the knots and massaged her wrists, which were a touch red.

"I'm just going to," he got up, removing the condom and heading to the bathroom, "clean up."

"I think you blew my mind," she whispered when he returned. "I'm still shaking. I think that second orgasm was about three orgasms all on its own. Sheesh!" Her eyes were closed. When she tried to open them, they looked heavy. She was still lying in the same position he had left her in.

Vortex got into bed and pulled her against him. "We won't be able to do this when you're on dragon territory."

"I know," she whispered.

"The installation will take several weeks."

"I know." She nodded. "I thought we weren't going to think about things like that. We're having fun, remember?"

She was right. "I know. We are." He kissed her forehead. "It's going to be difficult to see you every day and not be able to touch you... that's all. I don't know when this would be able to happen again."

"I know, and it's fine."

"It might be better if we..." He pushed out a breath. Fuck, this was hard. "It might be better if we went back to being business associates after this."

She went up on her elbows. He half expected her to look hurt or angry, but she didn't; she was smiling. "I thought we agreed that it wouldn't be possible. Colleagues? Friends? Nope, and nope. Not happening. Let's just enjoy our weekend, and if we get together again in the future, so be it. If not... then that's okay as well." Her smile wavered for a second, but then it was back, bright as ever.

Vortex could get used to this. To her. To them. The danger was real. He might hurt her. What was he saying? He *would* hurt her.

"That's a great idea. Let's do that." He didn't mean it. "If it happens, it happens."

Cool.

Casual.

Fuck!

It wasn't going to happen. Couldn't! As much as he hated the idea, this was the last night they would spend together. It had to be that way. Vortex was becoming too attached. As much as Amy pretended to the contrary, he could see that she was falling for him. He could see it in her eyes and feel it in her kisses. Once the installation was done, she needed to go back home to where it was safe. He would be the most selfish bastard on earth if he kept her for himself and, in so doing, put her in harm's way. Deep down inside, Vortex still believed that war was coming.

CHAPTER 25

The next day...

"Come in and have a drink before you go." Amy grabbed his hand, squeezing it.

"I'm sorry I can't." Vortex's eyes clouded for a moment. "I've really got to get back."

Jake squawked from inside the house. The front door was open. Vortex had deposited her bags on the front step of her house.

He'd had been acting strangely ever since he'd given her that little love bite yesterday. She didn't know what had changed. He'd just seemed more reserved. Like he was holding back. This was especially true on the sex front. So much for using all eight condoms. They'd had sex after getting back to the B&B after dinner last night and again this morning, and it was really good. It just felt careful, like he didn't want to break her… like he was holding back. It wasn't just the sex; it was everything. He felt more distant.

It wasn't something she could talk to him about, since they were technically just fooling around. She wanted to, though. Even now, looking into his eyes, preparing to say goodbye, she wanted to ask him what had happened. What had changed?

Why?

Instead, she bit her tongue. She held back all the questions and put her arms around him instead. She told herself that the reason might have nothing to do with her, even though deep inside, she knew it did.

"I'll see you in a week," she told him. "For the installation."

He smiled down at her. Even that was a little pinched… a little too serious. Like he had been before they started sleeping together.

Jake squawked again, louder this time.

"He can hear that I'm home. He's wondering why I'm not going inside."

Vortex's eyes softened. His Adam's apple worked as his hand moved up and down her back.

"I had a great time."

"Me too." *I'm going to miss you.* It was right there on the end of her tongue, but she swallowed it back. It wasn't like that between them.

"So, you'll send me all of the information concerning the delivery of the equipment?" he said.

"No."

"No!" He narrowed his eyes.

"We're not doing that now. I'll email you tomorrow. You can contact me then. Right now, I'm going to thank you for an amazing weekend. Then you're going to kiss me like there's no tomorrow. I'm not talking business with you right now."

"Like there's no tomorrow," he repeated. "That I can do."

"Thank you. I had the best time."

Vortex cupped her face in his huge hands, and he kissed her. It was the best and the worst kiss she had ever had. It burned her up from the inside. It made her, and it broke her. It felt like goodbye. It was too soon for goodbye. There was never supposed to even be a goodbye. She was supposed to slowly work her way into his heart until one day he'd wake up unable to live without her, and they'd be together. The end! Only, he was saying goodbye early. There was no way she was in his heart yet. It just wasn't possible. It was too soon.

Amy felt pathetic. She *was* pathetic.

Why did the one guy she finally wanted, the one guy she finally fell for... why did he have to be unavailable? It made no sense, and it wasn't fair.

Vortex pulled away, brushing his mouth against hers one last time.

Amy still held onto him. He still held onto her. Their eyes stayed locked together; everything seemed to go still. Even her heart felt like it stuttered. This felt like love. It couldn't be, though. It was too soon, and she was being pathetic all over again.

So what if her younger sister had a baby before she did? So what? Now the sound of that ticking clock had gotten into her head and was turning it into a fuzzy mess.

She was not in love with Vortex… a guy she hardly knew. It couldn't possibly be. She was a logical person; she needed to be logical about this too.

First thing tomorrow, she was making an appointment with a shrink. She needed to sort herself out. Needed to get her head straight again. Everything she'd ever worked for was coming together. Amy was Regional Manager; next step was the corner office. Ron had called her in several times over the last two weeks to ask her opinion on a client, or an installation. She was being treated with respect.

Jake squawked, breaking the moment. Amy moved away.

"I'd better get inside." She used her thumb to point behind her. Then she pulled out the handle on her wheelie.

Vortex nodded.

"Have a safe journey home," she said.

He reached for her and kissed her one last time.

One.

Last.

Time.

Soft, sweet; that kiss felt like everything. She'd have to ask that shrink how to mend a broken heart. Amy watched him walk to the SUV. She watched him climb in. He waved once, and then he drove away. To rub salt into the wound, Jake started up an excellent rendition of her orgasm. Her life was officially in the toilet.

Later that day…

"WHOAAAA!" ICE FLASHED HIM A look. "Where the hell have you been?"

"I had some things to take care of on human soil." Vortex had hoped to make it to his apartment before running into anyone. It was not to be.

"And by some things to take care of, you mean a female? Who is she?" Ice chuckled. "Had to be good because you stink of condoms and," the male sniffed, "cherries." He wrinkled his nose. "Not a great combination."

"Stop smelling me already. It's fucking rude," Vortex growled, fear taking hold of him. *Cherries.* Did he scent of Amy? Probably, he'd slept with her wrapped around him. He'd lived between her thighs. Otherwise, they'd touched or kissed every waking moment. *Fuck!* This was bad. He'd lost his ever-loving mind. Being that cozy had never been his plan. It had just happened. It was what they had slipped into. It felt right, which was fucking wrong! He needed to get home and to get scrubbed up. Probably didn't have enough sanitizer in his apartment.

"Who is she?"

"Nobody." He had to fight a reaction to saying that. Had to fight the words that were right there, wanting to correct what he had just said, because Amy wasn't nobody. She was so much more, and he hated lying.

"You had an itch to scratch. I get it." Ice was grinning. "Although you scratched the living shit out of that itch." He waved a hand in front of his face, grimacing. "She must have been some female."

Vortex nodded once, his mind going to Amy. Her

chocolate stare, those full lips that smiled so readily. How fucking bossy she was in bed, which he loved.

"Good thing Storm just opened up the Stag Runs again, or you'd get death stares from the rest of the males."

"He did what?" Vortex growled, eliciting curious looks from a couple of males across the room.

"Yep, only half the number of males per trip than before, though. We've seen neither hide nor hair of a goblin since that vigilante group was captured. We're expecting less trouble since they were put to death."

"I wouldn't be so quick to think that everything was hunky-dory… it's not." Vortex tried to keep the bite out of his voice and failed.

"What got up your ass?" Ice cocked his head and narrowed his eyes, scrutinizing him. "For someone who just came right after an epic dry spell, you're highly strung. Who is this female?"

"No one… I told you. I missed too much work. I had to hear via text about the goblins. Now I'm finding out about the Stag Runs. I'm behind and out of the loop, and that fucks me off."

"That does sound very much like you." Ice chuckled. "Today was my last working day." His eyes were bright.

"That's why you're so nauseatingly happy." Vortex felt a little like Cyclone, talking like this. Grumpy as fuck. Then he remembered Azure and the pregnancy. "Oh shit! Your female. How is she? She hasn't had the whelp yet?"

"Not yet. He's only due in two weeks. Although they sometimes come early. I'm going to make the most of our time in the meanwhile."

"I'm sure you will. Although isn't rutting difficult right now? Doesn't Azure's belly get in the way?"

"Rutting." Ice laughed. "I fucking wish." He shook his head. "Azure is," he looked around them, lowering his voice, "she's quite big – sexy as anything, but big. Her ankles are swollen. Her breasts… holy fuck! Nope, she doesn't feel much like fucking. I was talking about sleep, getting lots and lots of sleep. Maybe going to dinner at the restaurant. That and watching movies. Maybe even binging a couple of Netflix series."

"What the hell happened to us? Since when do we eat eggs and watch television?"

"What do eggs have to do with anything?" Ice frowned.

"Nothing at all. I'm a little sleep-deprived. You should try *The Matrix*. Have you heard of it?" Vortex smiled just thinking about his and Amy's afternoon together. It had been comfortable and fun.

"Can't say I have."

"It released over 20 years ago, but it's really good. I suggest you try it."

"Thanks for the tip."

"Enjoy your last few weeks of freedom," Vortex said.

"Freedom?" Ice got this goofy look. "I don't see it like that. I can't wait to meet my son. I don't think I've ever been this excited in my life. Not for anything. Maybe the day Azure agreed to mate me… that was also right up there." Using his fingers, he drew an imaginary mark up high in the air.

Hearing the male talk made him feel depressed. "Let me know if you need anything."

"Maybe once the baby is here." Ice got this panicked look.

"You'll do just fine. I'll bring a couple of home-cooked meals around to your place. It'll be my turn to repay the favor."

"Can you even cook?" Ice looked skeptical.

"Yes. Mostly just steak, but I do that really well."

Ice laughed. "Okay, then. I look forward to it. Now, if you'll excuse me, I have feet to rub. Oh, and the belly… I'm going to rub that too. Then there's my poor mate's back. I also need to tell her how gorgeous she is. I—"

"That's enough already. My ears are bleeding," Vortex growled. *Fuck!* He really was turning into a grumpy fuck. He smiled. "Enjoy your vacation." Then he slowly walked to his one-bedroom apartment. He needed to try to wash the scent of cherry off his skin. That made him feel… It made him feel like total shit.

CHAPTER 26

One week later…

VORTEX CAUGHT A SNOUTFUL OF her first. By all things scaly, she still smelled as fresh as an ocean breeze. Like the sun dancing on the waves. Like cherry with hints of chocolate. Sated and yet sad… *What the fuck?*

Sad?

Why the fuck was Amy sad? He hated that she was unhappy. Knew that it more than likely had something to do with him. Of course, it had to do with him. He hadn't messaged her once since he left her. She hadn't messaged him either.

Despite her scent, Amy was smiling broadly. She waved at one or two of the males she recognized, her wedding band glinting in the sun. Then she thanked Pervious for escorting her there. Vortex hadn't been part of the team who picked her up. Hell, he hadn't planned on coming here now, but found himself walking to the balcony instead of wherever it was he was going.

Fuck, but she was beautiful. Her hair bobbed in a high ponytail. Her navy pantsuit fit her just right, showcasing all her curves. She laughed, the sound carrying to him. Bright, breezy… He didn't get the sadness from her this time. Perhaps he'd imagined it.

"You need to lose the puppy dog eyes." Cyclone stepped in next to him. "You were cautious before. Right now, that look on your face is red-flashing-light shit. And you smell rancid." Cyclone scowled.

"I showered," Vortex said. "I'm not sure what bullshit you're on about."

"You smell depressed. It's irritating me. Do something about it."

"I'm not depressed! Mind your own fucking business." He was sure to keep his voice down.

"I have to work with you and share a damned office with you, bitch, so fix it."

"Who are you calling bitch?" Vortex turned, putting his chest against Cyclone's. He grated his molars so hard he was sure one cracked. Fucker was getting on his last damned nerve.

"Tell her how you feel already," the male said between clenched teeth. "I never thought I would say this, but I preferred you scenting of sunshine and," he made a disgusted sound, "happiness."

Vortex turned away from the male. It felt like the wind had been pulled from his sails. He felt like a pussy. This needed to stop. "You have it all wrong," he ground out.

Then he walked over to Amy. He'd say hello, and then he'd move on.

Cyclone grunted from somewhere behind him. Vortex ignored him. Any smart remarks like that again, and he'd flatten his face.

Bastard!

Fuck him!

The closer he got, the more her scent filled his nostrils. His dragon purred like a fucking cat. It was annoying. It was the sex. After being celibate for two years, the great sex had messed with his head. His dragon could get over it.

Her smile brightened up a whole lot more when she laid those gorgeous eyes on him. His dick threatened to harden up.

Down, motherfucker!

Down!

She took a step toward him, her hands moving forward like she was going to hug him.

"Mrs. Winters." Vortex folded his arms.

Her eyes clouded, but she quickly schooled her emotions.

"Vortex, it's good to see you. I'm glad all of the equipment arrived as promised."

"Most of it is already here or at the mine. The rest will be transported in the morning."

"Typhoon showed me the containers back at the house… human side." She winked.

His stomach knotted. Did she wink when she was talking with all her clients? It was sexy as fuck. He hated the idea of her doing it to anyone else. Detested it. That thought made him a prick, but it couldn't be helped.

"What time are we meeting tomorrow morning? Are you going to come by my apartment? You can make me some of that Ph.D. machine coffee before we head out?" She quirked a brow.

Amy was being overly familiar with him. Cyclone was right. Vortex was looking at her like she hung the moon and the stars one second, and then he was jealous as fuck the next. Amy had been about to hug him.

Hug!

An Overlord, and now she was inviting him to coffee at her place? This was a problem. What had Cyclone called it? *Red-flashing-light shit.* It was, and it had to stop now.

"I have a full agenda tomorrow, Mrs. Winters."

Again, her eyes clouded in disappointment before she plastered a bright smile on her face.

"My apologies," he added. "It would have been good to go over the particulars related to the installation."

"No problem whatsoever." She flapped a hand like she didn't have a care in the world. "I completely understand. You're really busy. I mean, you're an Overlord." She widened her eyes. "I sent you the details yesterday, so you have everything already."

"How is Jake?" He wasn't sure why he asked.

She gave a small smile. "He's really good."

"Still singing my favorite song?" He really shouldn't go down this road, but he couldn't help it.

Amy's smile lit up her face, and she giggled. "All the time."

"Tell him I said *hi* when you Facetime again."

"I will do that."

"Pervious," he called for the male, who was not too far away. Pervious ran over to them immediately.

"Yes, Overlord." He dipped his head to show respect.

"Please help Mrs. Winters to her apartment. I want you to fetch her at eight sharp tomorrow morning. I need you to assist with the installation."

"I will be there." He inclined his head in Amy's direction. "Let me get these." He picked up her bags, which were numerous and large.

She screwed up her face for a second. "I brought more gear this time… now that I know what I'm in for."

"Gust!" Vortex shouted to the male. "Help Pervious with Mrs. Winters' bags." He locked eyes with Amy and almost told the males to fuck off. They were large and so eager. So bright and beautiful, the air seized in his chest. "We will be in touch. I wish you a pleasant evening," he said instead.

"You, too," she said as they walked away. Amy glanced back at him over her shoulder, but he forced himself to turn. To walk away. He needed to be strong.

CHAPTER 27

Three days later...

AMY WALKED DOWN THE HALLWAY. She stared into each of the open areas as she passed them.

"It's lucky that we're having such great weather," Pervious said. "So incredibly lucky. It normally rains a lot at this time of year.

"Yes, you're right."

"Means we're ahead of schedule."

She nodded. "Which is great." It meant she could get back home sooner. Being here was depressing.

"One of the males we passed earlier mentioned that whitetail stew was on the cards for lunch." Pervious was trying so hard to make conversation. Bless him. He was such a sweet guy. "Stew with homemade bread and butter." He rubbed his abs. "It's one of my favs. You're going to love it."

"Sounds delicious." She nodded a few times. "I'm incredibly hungry." Her stomach rumbled. Stupid stomach. She was pissed. That and upset. So, therefore, she was also hungry. Or hangry. Or 'sangry'. However, she looked at it, it was bad. Terrible!

Her very brief greeting with Vortex the day she arrived was the only time she had seen him since she got here. *Very busy? Yeah, no.* She didn't buy it. He was avoiding her. He was a cowardly asshole. Did he think that she was going to say something? Do something? Lose it? Jump him? It wouldn't have happened. She had more respect for herself than that.

Jerk!

Yellow-bellied jerkface. He always did this. He pulled her in… had her letting her guard down, and then he ran. No, he'd never promised her anything, but it still hurt. It didn't help that Lisa insisted it was because he liked her. Really liked her. That he was afraid. She said that guys did stupid things when they were afraid.

"We can take a table near the window?" Pervious asked as they walked into the dining hall. "Unless you'd prefer—"

"The window would be great. I love the view," she added on a sigh. Although, today it felt like nothing would help brighten her spirits. She spotted a formation of about 10 dragons drawing nearer. She held her breath until they got close enough to see and then pushed it out in a rush when she realized that he wasn't among them.

Vortex.

Vortex.

Vortex.

He was driving her insane. Amy had gone to see a

therapist to sort out her emotions, and the woman had spent an entire hour asking about her childhood. They were apparently going to start there and work their way – over about million sessions – to the actual problem. Her heart. Her broken, crushed, and bleeding heart.

Her childhood.

Please!

"Hi… you're Mrs. Winters?"

Amy had been so busy staring outside at nothing that she hadn't realized that someone was standing so close to her. A very pregnant someone. In fact, why wasn't she in the hospital with her legs strapped up, pushing out a baby?

"I know, I know…" The same lady rubbed on her swollen stomach. "I look like a whale shifter." She snort-laughed. "My name is Azure. Azure the whale."

Amy smiled. "You do not look like a whale. You look pregnant. Ready to have that baby at any second. But not like a whale at all, I assure you. I'm Amy. Please drop the whole 'Mrs.' thing."

"I'm huge," Azure groaned. She had the most mesmerizing eyes Amy had ever seen on a person. "And it's really good to finally meet you."

"You have a pregnant belly. Everything else is normal-sized, and it's good to meet you too."

"Not my ankles." The woman smiled. "Those are ginormous as well."

"That's all normal for someone in their final days."

"Amen to that. I still have about a week to go, but it could be sooner." She crossed her fingers.

"You poor thing. Sit, please." Amy gestured to the table that Pervious had pointed out when they arrived.

She noted that he was chatting with someone at one of the other tables.

The lovely lady sat down with difficulty in the closest chair, sighing as she did.

"I'm waiting for my mate." She looked at the entrance. "He should be here any minute."

"What does he look like? I can help you keep an eye out." She sat across from the other woman.

"Sexy as anything." Azure smiled.

It instantly made her think of Vortex, which was annoying. Sexy and unavailable. She needed to focus on the latter.

"My mate's name is Ice. He's good friends with Vortex. I had hoped to meet you sooner."

"Oh." Amy nodded a few times, not sure what to say. How did this lady know her? Had Vortex mentioned her?

"I invited you to dinner when you were here last, but Vortex said you had to work. I had him deliver the elk roast."

"Oh, yes!"

Shit. That was the day Amy got to find out how good that asshole of a man was with his hands. "That was your cooking?" Amy smiled. "It was delicious. I'm a fan of venison now."

Azure laughed. "I'm so glad. Oh… here they are now." She looked over at the entrance. It was Vortex with a blond guy.

Vortex looked over at her. Their eyes locked for a second or two before he turned back to the other guy. He was shaking his head. The other guy was shaking his head, too. They looked like they were arguing about something.

"There's my sexy mate now. Vortex is trying to get out of lunch." Azure rolled her eyes. "That one. He works too hard."

"Here you go." Pervious put some drinks on the table. "I got a selection. I wasn't sure what you wanted."

"Thanks." Amy grabbed a water. Her mouth was suddenly feeling dry.

"I'll take the orange juice. Please take the sodas back before I drink one. They look so good." Azure let her hand trail over the cans, lingering on the Coca-Cola. "Caffeine and sugar aren't good for the baby."

"No problem." Pervious put the leftover drinks back onto a tray. "And as for lunch, what will it be? Whitetail all-round? They're serving it with slabs of bread," he told Azure.

"Yes, please," Azure said. "And bring some mustard as well. Sounds yummy."

"Mustard with whitetail stew?" The blond guy put his hand on Azure's shoulder and squeezed.

Vortex was next to him, looking uncomfortable.

"Hi, I'm Ice." He held out his hand to her.

She took it. "I'm Amy… please don't call me Mrs. Winters. That's my mother." *Oh shit!* "I kept my family's last name. It's a story for another day." *Shit!* Now she was coming across as rude.

"I look forward to hearing all about it," Ice said. "I'm so happy to see you, my gorgeous mate." He kissed Azure.

Vortex finally looked her way. Only because he had to. It would have been rude of him to ignore her any further.

"Hello, Mrs. Winters. How are you?" he asked cordially.

Cordial sucked!

"I'm doing great." She thought about asking him how he was or filling the silence with talk of the installation but did neither.

"Mrs. Winters?" Azure laughed. "You're still calling Amy that? You heard her. Mrs. Winters is her mother. Stop fooling around."

Fooling around? If only.

"I guess I'm used to it," Vortex shrugged. "Are you all set for the big day?" he asked Azure, his body angling away from her.

"Am I ready to push a watermelon through a keyhole? No." She shook her head hard. "Not at all."

"A keyhole, hon'?" Ice massaged her shoulders. "And a watermelon?" His mouth twitched, but he managed to refrain from smiling. "I'm hoping our sweet little baby doesn't have a head the size of a watermelon."

Azure's eyes narrowed. "What I'm trying to say is that it's going to hurt like a bitch, babe." She smiled sweetly at him. "I'm feeling a little nervous about the whole thing all of a sudden."

"Oh, sweetheart, you'll be fine." Ice nuzzled into her neck. "You're the strongest female I know. You're brave, and I love you so much." He kissed her cheek and then her mouth.

Vortex cleared his throat. "I'm not staying for lunch."

"You can stay for a quick meal. You have to eat. What the hell has gotten into you lately?" Ice asked.

Had Vortex been acting strangely? Maybe he cared after all. Would that change things? Probably not.

"Nothing has gotten into me," Vortex said, his voice hard and biting.

"Bullshit, ever since you—"

Her phone started ringing loudly. *Dammit!* She wanted to hear this, so she quickly declined the call. Her sister could call her back.

"Sorry," she mumbled.

Go back to what you were saying, she silently begged.

"Ever since you got back from—"

Her phone started blaring again. It was Lisa trying to reach her for a second time.

"You might want to get that." Vortex frowned.

"Is everything okay?" she asked Lisa as she answered.

"No!" Lisa sounded panicked. "Thank god you picked up. It's Jake! Oh my god, Jake!" Her sister screamed her bird's name.

"What's wrong with him?"

"I found him just lying there on his back. He's having some kind of seizure," her sister yelled.

Amy jumped up, her chair clattering onto the floor behind her.

"What should I do? Jake… no-no-no-no!" Lisa screamed. "Don't die on me! Please, Jake! You obnoxious little shit. Don't you dare! It's bad! Oh god… it's bad, sis."

"Calm down!" Amy instructed her. "Take a few deep breaths."

"Okay." Lisa was crying. Amy could hear it from the way she was breathing. From the little sniffing noises she was making.

"Get something to wrap him in and take him to get help. The details for the ani… for the hospital are on my fridge. Bottom right. It's only five minutes away. They'll know what to do."

"O-okay." More sniffing.

"I'm on my way. Go now!" she shouted.

Lisa ended the call, and Amy burst into tears. Her bird! Her Jake! He was like a child to her. He'd been Amy's only companion on so many nights and weekends. He was more than just a pet. He was… he was her boy. She'd hand-reared him almost as soon as he was hatched.

Vortex watched her hold it together, and then he watched her fall apart. And there was nothing he could do. He took a step towards her, wanting to wrap her up in his arms. Wanting to comfort her, but he couldn't.

"Oh, honey." Azure was lumbering to her feet.

"It's bad?" he said. It was a stupid thing to say. *Bad!* Of course it was fucking bad.

Amy nodded. "Jake." She locked her tear-soaked eyes with his. "I have to go to him. I have to be with him."

"Of course." Vortex nodded.

"He might not make it." Another tear rolled down her cheek, but she wiped it away with the back of her hand.

"He'll make it," Vortex growled. "He's a fighter."

"Have you met Amy's mate?" Ice asked, frowning hard. Vortex could hear the confusion laced in his voice. "Jake is your mate, right?"

"Not now," he said to Ice. "We have to get you home," he told Amy.

Not *we*. He couldn't go. Red-flashing-light shit! Yes! Huge red lights. Enormous!

"Pervious!" he roared.

"Yes, Overlord." The male was right behind him.

"Get the team together now!"

"Yes, Overlord."

"We'll meet you on the balcony in two," Vortex said. Poor Jake. He was such a good bird, and Amy loved him. If anything happened— No! It was no use thinking like that. It didn't help anything.

Pervious ran for the exit.

"I'll escort you," he told Amy. "Is there anything I can fetch for you? Anything you need?"

"No." She sounded bewildered. "I have my bag." She put her phone into the tote and put the strap across her shoulders, then zipped it shut.

"Can I call anyone?"

"You're not coming?" she sounded shocked.

"I can't. I'm sorry, but… it wouldn't look right. I'm an Overlord."

Overlord.

Right then, he hated the title. Hated the responsibility. Hated all of it. If he wasn't an Overlord, he could go with her now. Be with her. But he was. He had responsibilities to his tribe. It was more complicated. It was a fucking disaster.

She looked at him with big, teary eyes. "I understand." Her lip wobbled.

"I'm so fucking sorry, Amy. Please call me as soon as you know something… anything."

"Sure." She turned away.

"I'll take you to the balcony." He followed.

"No… don't worry about it." She glanced behind her. "I know you have responsibilities." Her jaw was set. Her eyes blazed with hurt and anger.

"Amy, I—"

"I get it, and it's fine. No promises, right?" Then she was walking away, and he was letting her. Everything inside him screamed to follow. To forsake everything for her, for love. But he couldn't. He was an Overlord.

A fucking Overlord.

Half a minute later and the formation was leaving.

"I heard the commotion and came to see what was going on," Cyclone said from beside him, his voice even for once.

"It's nothing." Vortex hated saying it. It cut him up. Made his scales scratch and wings push inside him. He wanted to shift. He wanted to go after her.

"Nothing, my fucking ass." There was the growl he knew and loved. *Not!* "Why was the human crying?" The male narrowed his eyes and took a step toward him.

"Her mate is sick. Might die," he said simply, hoping that Cyclone would go away. What was the male's problem getting up in his face lately?

"Mate? You and I both know that's bullshit!" the male said under his breath. "Why is she crying like that? Why did she leave?" Thank fuck he continued to keep his voice down. "Who is Jake? I thought he was made up, but he must be someone to her."

"A bird. A parrot. She fucking loves him." Vortex realized he was pacing. "Shit!" He grit his teeth. The bird was cute. Vortex had liked him instantly, probably because of how much his female loved the thing.

His female?

No!

Fuck!

"You let your female leave… on her own… upset? Am I understanding this correctly?"

"What the fuck am I supposed to do, bitch?" He got into Cyclone's face. Right up there.

"I know you're upset, so I'm going to let that slide just this once."

"Fuck you! Get out of my face and out of my business."

"No can do! I was you once," Cyclone said, his voice soft.

Those words had the fire in his veins dying down. Had the growl that threatened to loosen turn to a whine. A whine he worked to keep inside him. He didn't fucking whine. Dragons didn't make such sounds. Ever!

Cyclone backed down first. Probably sensing the change in him.

"I fucked up once," the male admitted, speaking so softly that Vortex had to strain to hear him. Cyclone snorted. "More than just fucked up. I fucked my whole life up. If I could turn back the clock, I would. What I wouldn't give for another chance. One more kiss, one more touch. I'd give anything. Her name was Angela. My Angie… my angel. Sugar and spice." It was weird seeing the big male like this. His face had softened. His eyes had clouded. "I'll be damned if I let you make the same mistake as I did."

"What mistake?"

"Don't be an asshole!"

Vortex gave Cyclone a shove. "Stop with the name-calling, or this is going to turn into a bloodbath," he snarled, fists clenched.

Cyclone breathed deeply for a few minutes before his stance relaxed just a smidgen. Vortex didn't move or blink.

"I let the love of my life walk away. I had her, and I lost her." His eyes darkened with hurt. "She was my other half. She was the piece of my soul that was missing. I'm broken without her."

What the fuck?

"What happened?" he asked, relaxing away from Cyclone.

"I was an ass. A dumb-as-fuck ass. I hadn't been in my position as Overlord for very long. I met a human. We weren't taking human mates yet. We hadn't even officially started mingling with them yet. I wasn't on any kind of mating list. I acted like a total jerk. Told myself I needed to lead by example. Told myself I couldn't have her, even though I wanted her. I strung her along. I asked her to wait… indefinitely. No…" he snorted. "That's not true. My arrogant-as-fuck ass demanded that she wait for me. I told her we could keep things casual in the meantime. That we could keep having fun."

That sounded familiar.

"I take it that it didn't go down well."

"It went on for some time. Then it took a whole month before I could get back to her, and she was gone."

"Gone where?"

"Fucked if I know! Someone else was living in her apartment. I looked for her for two years. I still look for her… in my dreams… my fucking nightmares. I let her slip through my fingers." He looked down at his hands. "I was selfish. Arrogant. Stupid. Everything you're being right now."

Vortex felt a snarl building in his throat, but he held it back. Cyclone was sharing… with him. The male was also right. Of course he was right, but it didn't change anything. Did it?

Big no!

"I live with regret every day of my life. Do you want the same for yourself?"

"It's not like that." Vortex tried hard to believe the words. He wished he could believe them. He couldn't do that to her.

"I know you've worked hard. Harder than anyone I know. You stand to lose so much. Storm told me about the probation period. You could lose your position. You won't be an Overlord. Big fucking deal. The loneliness, once it sinks into your bones…" He choked out a humorless laugh. "Trust me, you don't want it. Living with a hole in your chest is fucking shitty."

His chest did hurt. Every cell screamed at him to go to her and to do it now. That was insanity. It was!

"I know what you're telling yourself. You keep telling yourself that she'll give you another chance. That you'll call her, send her gifts. Fuck! I don't know what males do nowadays. Maybe you'll find a way to get into human territory tomorrow, next week. You're telling yourself that you'll make it right. You'll fix it."

It was true. Those thoughts were swirling around inside him. They were helping him keep it together. Helping to stop him from throwing it all away.

"That's the kind of bullshit I told myself all the time. It worked once or twice… It worked until it didn't. I saw your female's face just before she turned away from you. That was not the face of a female who would accept a gift or any kind of excuse. That was the face of someone who was done. If you don't go to her right now – and I mean this fucking second – it's over! It won't be long before you realize that what you have versus what you gave up is no comparison. You'll be filled with regret, and there won't be a damned thing you'll be able to do about it."

Vortex kept seeing Amy's tear-soaked eyes. Kept seeing how they blazed with anger. The determined set to her jaw. Cyclone was right. He could tell himself a thousand times over that she would forgive him for this, but she wouldn't. Couldn't. She needed him, and he was turning his back on her.

"Fuck!" He scrubbed a hand over his face. "I love her. I fucking love her. She needs me. I have to go to her." He couldn't stand the thought of losing her. He had to go to her, even if that made him the most selfish male alive.

"Finally! Took a fuckload of convincing! For the record, I'm doing this because I won't be able to stand hearing your sniveling day after day. We're *not* friends!" Cyclone growled.

"Um… who is it that you love?" Ice asked, frowning. "Not the mated female… surely?" He had his arm around Azure, whose eyes were huge.

Vortex had been so deep in thought that he hadn't noticed both Ice and Azure had walked up to them.

"The mated female who isn't mated at all." Azure suddenly grinned. Then she turned serious, narrowing her eyes on him. "She's upset. You let her leave. What the hell is wrong with you?"

"Wait a minute." Ice looked bewildered. "Can someone tell me what the fuck is going on?"

"Amy and I have been dating. We've been…" *Having fun! Fooling around!* All of those things were on the tip of his tongue. He didn't say any of them. "We've been falling in love."

"You can't fall in love with a mated female." Ice was frowning hard. "What about the female you…" His eyes brightened up. "That was her. Amy! Cherries… Shit!"

"*Mrs.* Winters." Azure giggled. "Amy isn't mated is she? I can't believe we didn't notice what was going on. Then again, the tension was so thick between the two of you back in the restaurant."

"I need to go to her." He started walking.

"Yes, you do!" Azure shouted after him, still grinning.

"What am I going to tell the royals?" Ice shouted after him. "We have to tell them something," he added.

Vortex kept walking.

"I'll think of something," Ice shouted.

"The truth," Vortex shouted back. "Tell them the truth." Whether Amy felt the same or not. Whether she would take him back or not, it didn't matter. He was done hiding. Done lying. If he lost his position as Overlord over this, then so be it. All he could think of was her.

Amy.

What the fuck had he done?

Please don't let it be too late.

Please.

There was a small part of him that prayed she would turn him away. It was a small part, his better part.

CHAPTER 28

THE VETERINARIAN WALKED THROUGH THE white door for a second time since she'd arrived a little earlier. Amy could hardly breathe watching him approach.

"You can see him, Miss Winters, but only for five minutes."

"Thank you, Doctor. Has there been any change?"

His whole stance softened. "No, I'm afraid not. I believe that he is comfortable. He is stable right now."

"You said that hypocalcemia has a good prognosis."

"It does. I'm not sure why the treatment isn't reviving him. There is a chance that the seizures had begun quite some time before your sister brought him in. There's a chance of… damage. The long-term kind."

"I'm so sorry," Lisa sobbed. Her sister hadn't stopped crying since Amy had arrived there 15 minutes before. Her sister rocked the stroller, trying to get the baby to sleep. It seemed like it might be working.

"It's not your fault." Amy turned to Lisa. "I mean that."

"You asked me to take care of him. I should've agreed to look after him at my house. This would never have happened if he was under my nose."

"Jake is noisy. You have a newborn. Stop beating yourself up. You heard what the doctor said; this kind of thing usually has a good prognosis." The tears were threatening to fall. It didn't look good, but she didn't want Lisa to have this hanging over her. It wasn't fair. Right now, she was forcing herself to believe that Jake would be okay. It was the only way she could hold it together.

"They also usually perk up after receiving treatment, and he hasn't," Lisa said, wiping her eyes. Jake had a condition called hypocalcemia. A shortage of calcium. It caused seizures and, on rare occasions, if treatment wasn't administered in time, death.

"Jake is a fighter. None of this is your fault."

"I forgot to give him his vitamins," Lisa added. "I—"

"Back to the part about you taking care of a newborn. I was wrong to ask you to look after Jake. This is on me."

Lisa's eyes moved to somewhere past her shoulder. They widened up a whole lot.

"Oh!" She made a breathless sound.

"What is it?"

Even the doctor did a double-take at whoever had just walked in.

Amy felt her back prickle. Her scalp too. It was awareness. Her body heated. Amy turned.

"Vortex?" she said as soon as her eyes met his.

Was she dreaming?

What was he doing here? He'd made his choice, and it hadn't been her.

"Oh! This is Vortex," she said to her sister.

Lisa held out her hand. "Hi! I'm Amy's sister, Lisa. You're her client? I've heard about you."

"Lisa!" She widened her eyes and shook her head. He was already an arrogant ass; he didn't need his ego inflated anymore.

"Good to meet you." Vortex didn't take his eyes off of Amy. He wore black jeans and a white t-shirt. His hair was mussed. He looked amazing, which irritated her to no end.

Lisa was gaping. All-out gaping. Amy couldn't blame her; he looked like he had just stepped out of the pages of a men's magazine. His sexiness wasn't going to sway her. *Nope! Forget it.*

"What are you doing here? I left you. You were busy. You palmed me off, remember?"

"Can we step outside, please?" Vortex asked, looking pained.

"Jake needs me."

"He's stable. I'll keep an eye on him," the irritating doctor said with an even more irritating smile.

"Fine. You have five minutes. Jake needs me."

She looked over at her sister, who gave her the double thumbs-up. Amy rolled her eyes.

They walked outside.

"How did you find me?"

"Don't get mad." He ran a hand through his hair, roughing it up some more. "I broke into your house and looked on your fridge... bottom right."

"You really are taking stalker behavior to a whole new level." She folded her arms. "I'm listening. Make it quick."

"I fucked up."

"Again," she deadpanned. "For the…" She started counting it out on her fingers.

"Okay, okay! Yes, again. I keep doing it. Apparently, I'm bad at this."

"You don't say." There was no way she was going easy on him. After the last couple of days, she really felt like she wanted to be done. Sure, she wouldn't smile the same way for a while, maybe ever, but at least she would recover… mostly. If she carried on, she'd get broken. Broken into a million tiny pieces. There was no coming back from that. Not ever.

He rubbed the back of his neck. "I bit you. It freaked me out."

"That tiny little nip?" What was he talking about? "That's what's put you into a tailspin?"

"It's mating behavior. It got me all rattled."

"Mating behavior?" She knew she was repeating what he had just said, but she couldn't help it.

"Yes, it's an instinctual thing. My dragon has started to see you as his. It freaked me out."

"You'd better have a little chat with him." She folded her arms. "Because we are over." She sucked in a breath. "Wait a minute, you can't be over unless you have something to begin with. Chat to your dragon; he's a little mixed up."

"I deserve that and more. I had hoped after the biting incident that putting some distance between us would fix it. I've been running scared."

"Because we can't take this further. Because you didn't promise me anything. I understand that. I get it. The problem is that your eyes promise me plenty, your kisses too. The way you touch me, there's so much promise there. All lies. I can't read you. I can't get a handle on you, Vortex. Just when I think there's something between us, you pull back. You run." Her voice was raised. "When are you going to run again?"

He tried to answer, but she didn't let him.

"What did you tell them back at the lair? What lie did you make up?"

"I'm not lying anymore. I told Storm myself before coming over here. He was… pissed. I'll fix it when I get back."

What?

"You could lose your position?" She hadn't wanted this either. "You're good at your job. Great at it. The lair needs you. Your people need you."

"What good will I be to them if my heart is gone?" He pulled in a breath. "I'm fucking afraid, Amy. I shouldn't be here."

"I get it. You're afraid of losing everything you ever worked for, of having your heart broken. Well, welcome to the club. You're not alone. I want us enough to look past all that. I want that enough to risk everything. I had hoped that you would too, eventually, but I don't think you can."

"I can't look past any kind of risk to you. Cyclone told me that I was lying to myself… and I was."

"Cyclone?" She raised her brows.

"It's a long story." His mouth twitched for a second, and then he was serious again. His features were more severe than she'd ever seen them. "I'm afraid of what will happen when war comes. And it *is* coming. I feel it here in the pit of my stomach. What then, Amy? What then?

Fuck!" He looked tortured. "I almost lost it when that goblin took you that day. What will happen when a whole horde of those fuckers storms our lair? What then? I couldn't take it. I'm so selfish to be here. I'm selfish to tell you that I love you. Selfish to beg you for more. For every tomorrow. I want to make every promise that there is to make. Only, I can't make the most important one… I can't promise to keep you safe."

"Stop!" She took his hand. "It's not for you to keep me safe. I am my own keeper."

"If you were mine… If you agreed to be mine, it would be my job… first and foremost. I would take the responsibility seriously."

She had to try hard not to smile. Vortex was freaking out, and it was the cutest thing she'd ever seen.

"I know you would. You can't, though. You can't be there every second of every day. You can't think of every eventuality. I could slip in the shower or walk in front of a bus."

"Don't say things like that." He frowned. *So damned sexy.*

"It's true. We have to live our lives. I know you've been conditioned to expect the worst. It's a part of your job, just like it's a part of mine, but we can't take that home with us."

"You're right. It's still a tough ask."

"I know it is. Now we need to go back just a little, to the part where you sort of told me that you loved me without telling me that you love me. You can't do that." She shook her head. *What was wrong with this man?*

Vortex gave her a half-smile. "I'm pretty sure I told you I loved you. No 'sort of' or 'kind of' about it." He got down on one knee.

Got.

Down.

Holy shit!

"I love you, Amy. I'm glad you saw it in my eyes and felt it in my touch because it's true. Don't be afraid when I tell you that my dragon has already decided you are his." Vortex rose to his feet. "So have I, if you'll have me, and I'm talking about forever here."

"You're not going to make me live here and commute?"

He chuckled. "No! I would need to be close to you."

"I accept both offers."

"Both?"

"I'll take the position of Security Manager at the lair, and I'll be your girlfriend."

"Security Manager?" He raised his brows.

"I told you that you would need one. It was in my presentation. Someone to manage both security and the maintenance of all of the equipment once it's in. I was going to train the person, but since I'm the most qualified for the job, I'd rather just run with it myself."

He chuckled. "I'm afraid the answer is no!" His voice sounded gruff.

"No?" She frowned. "To which part? I'm willing to negotiate."

"No negotiations. You'll be perfect for the Security Manager position, but we're waaaaaay beyond dating. Way beyond boyfriend-girlfriend bullshit."

"Agreed." She nodded, trying to bite back a grin. "You got down on your knees, so does that make us…?"

"We just have to choose the ring and decide whether we want a big wedding or something more intimate."

"You should kiss me now to seal the deal. I can't believe we're engaged."

Vortex grinned. Then he took her into his arms and kissed her like there would be a whole lot of tomorrows.

"Jake's awake!" Lisa shrieked. "Sorry to interrupt, but I thought you would want to know."

"Jake's awake!" she shouted at Vortex, who grinned.

Sure enough, from somewhere behind Lisa came the familiar sounds of an epic orgasm.

"He's definitely a keeper," Lisa whispered, grabbing Amy's arm as she tried to walk inside. "So, this is the reason for Jake bellowing all of that… You know what kinds of noises he's making. The naughty kind." Her sister blushed. "Good thing we toasted to amazing sex." She winked. "It worked."

Her veterinarian was hovering nearby. "The good news about hypocalcemia is that once a patient recovers, they can go home immediately. Thank god! That bird has a great set of vocals. I'll arrange for his meds to take home."

"Are you saying that he's going to be fine?" Amy asked.

The doctor smiled. "Yes, Jake will be fine."

"How soon until he can travel?" She turned to Vortex and smiled.

He put his arm around her and squeezed. "As soon as tomorrow?" Vortex asked.

"That should be fine." The doctor nodded.

Holy crap! This was happening. This was really happening.

CHAPTER 29

Two days later…

"THANK YOU FOR THE UPDATE, Mrs…" Storm sighed. "*Miss* Winters. It's going to take me a while to get used to that."

"Please call me Amy."

"Amy will be mated soon, and she will retain her last name since dragons don't have one, so don't get used to 'Miss,' Sire," Vortex interjected, feeling his chest warm. His whole body warmed at the thought of taking her as his mate.

"Or just call me Amy." She smiled… looking so beautiful.

"Your scent is agonizing," Cyclone growled. "Stop! We're in a work meeting." The male kicked his shin under the table.

Vortex gave the bastard a dirty look but left it at that. He didn't want to start a fight in the king's office, although he would if the male did that again.

"Enough." Storm sighed. "I'm glad we're well on track with the installation and that you have tendered your resignation at Trivector. I am officially announcing that Amy has been appointed as our Security Manager here at the lair. She'll start in a month."

"We hope that you will be very happy in your new role," Thunder added.

Cyclone grunted, looking fucked off at something, which meant he looked completely normal. "I suggest that you start training your replacement," the male grunted.

"I haven't even started in my new position yet. Why would I train someone to take over?" Amy made a face.

"I give you three months." Cyclone pushed his chair back. "If you'll excuse me..." he spoke to the royals.

"Three months until what?" Amy asked, not taking shit from the big asshole. Although, Vortex had a soft spot – nope, maybe "soft spot" was pushing it – for the male now that he knew his story.

"I give you three months before you're with whelp."

Amy smiled, and her eyes softened, then she straightened her shoulders.

"No." She shook her head, looking wistful. "Not that it's any of your business, but Vortex and I have decided to wait until the various potential threats are well and truly behind us."

"There has been no further vigilante activity from the goblins." Storm was frowning. "I mean, don't get me wrong, I speak for Thunder and myself when I say we don't particularly want our new Security Manager pregnant, but the goblins are not a valid excuse." Storm looked at Vortex. "Before you say anything, we will move forward with all of our precautions, every last one of them. Cyclone over here is meeting with an arms expert in a few minutes. He and a select group of males are going to receive training in arms and ammunition. I think you should receive training too," he told Vortex. "We're still going through with the full installation. An upgrade of our defenses was overdue. Having said that, I think that the goblin leaders have the situation under control. We're no longer doing this because of an imminent threat."

Vortex clenched his jaw to keep from arguing. It was a huge fucking mistake.

"Yes, we have relaxed some of the restrictions, and you can be fucking thankful for that." Storm looked from Vortex to Amy and back, his eyes narrowing.

It was the only thing, in all of this, that Vortex was thankful for. His name was on the mating list, and so the rest was a formality. He had been thoroughly dragged over the coals for lying about Amy's marital status. Storm had understood his reasoning in bringing her to the lair anyway. That was where the understanding had ended. In short, he was lucky to still have his position. Very lucky!

"I'm going to be late for my introductory meeting with the human who thinks he can teach me how to kill," Cyclone growled. Then he walked out.

"How was the move here, Amy?" Storm asked.

"Fine, thank you. I only brought the most important things. I need to sell my place. Then I'll move the rest of my stuff over."

"We are preparing a three-bedroom apartment on the far north section of the lair for you. I hear that your parrot, *Jake*. Strange name for a bird." He clenched his jaw. "Is noisy." It was clear that Storm was still pissed, and rightly so. As it stood, his prince was being very understanding. More understanding than he would have been.

"Yes, apologies." Amy's cheeks went a bright red. "And apologies for… for…" She looked down at the table.

"Lying," Storm said. "I believe that is the word you are looking for."

"Yes, I didn't enjoy it at all. It wasn't supposed to get that complicated. I feel terrible. At the same time, I would do it again. Perhaps don't make such demands on women in the future. Anyone should be able to work on dragon soil, whether they're married or not. As long as they understand the situation. As long as they are prepared, then it shouldn't be a problem." Amy was right, but she was also wrong. They weren't human. They were shifters. Part animal… Part *dragon*.

"I agree," Thunder said, surprising them. "That's why we have done away with that particular rule. Any person, male or female, can work on dragon soil. A female must be on birth control, and she must understand the type of environment she will find herself in."

"Surrounded by horny males," Vortex bit out. Horny males governed by their animal side.

"It won't be as bad now that there are Stag Runs again. If either of you lies to me again, there will be hell to pay." Storm's voice hardened.

"Understood," Vortex said.

"Of course." Thank fuck Amy agreed. He half expected her to argue further.

"In that case, congratulations. I wish you a wonderful future."

Vortex looked at his future mate, and she looked back at him. There was so much promise in her eyes. There had to be some fear in his. Fear of the future and what it would bring.

"Please excuse me. I need to get back to work." He had a lair to protect. A female who was everything to him. He leaned down and kissed her, then turned to the others. "My Lords."

"You should go and join Cyclone's meeting," Thunder said.

"Why?" He frowned. "It's just an introduction. Training starts tomorrow."

"The arms expert is a female. A human female. See, Amy," Thunder said, "we *are* making progress." Then he looked back at Vortex. "I'm told that she's been on several tours to Afghanistan. That she is strong and independent. But I'm afraid that Cyclone might terrify her before she trains a single person. She's only been on dragon soil for less than an hour." The king scrunched up his face. "It will be tough to find a replacement on such short notice. Like Amy here, Miss Stanger is a specialist in her field. We're talking automatic assault weapons and bombs. Not little handguns."

"Shit. I hoped she signed an NDA." Vortex winced. "I'd better go." Cyclone would eat this poor female for lunch. She'd never be the same after this.

The End

AUTHOR'S NOTE

Charlene Hartnady is a USA Today Bestselling author. She loves to write about all things paranormal including vampires, elves and shifters of all kinds. Charlene lives on a couple of acres in the country with her husband and three sons. They have an array of pets including a couple of horses.

She is lucky enough to be able to write full time, so most days you can find her at her computer writing up a storm. Charlene believes that it is the small things in life that truly matter, like that feeling you get when you start a new book, or a particularly beautiful sunset.

The Program Series (Vampire Novels)
Book 1 ~ A Mate for York
Book 2 ~ A Mate for Gideon
Book 3 ~ A Mate for Lazarus
Book 4 ~ A Mate for Griffin
Book 5 ~ A Mate for Lance
Book 6 ~ A Mate for Kai
Book 7 ~ A Mate for Titan

The Feral Series
Book 1 ~ Hunger Awakened
Book 2 ~ Power Awakened
Book 3: Hate Awakened
Book 4: Hope Awakened

The Earth Dragon Series
Book 1 ~ Dragon Guard
Book 2 ~ Savage Dragon
Book 3 ~ Dragon Whelps
Book 4 ~ Slave Dragon
Book 5 ~ Feral Dragon
Book 6 ~ Doctor Dragon

The Bride Hunt Series (Dragon Shifter Novels)
Book 1 ~ Royal Dragon
Book 2 ~ Water Dragon
Book 3 ~ Dragon King
Book 4 ~ Lightning Dragon
Book 5 ~ Forbidden Dragon
Book 6 ~ Dragon Prince

The Water Dragon Series
Book 1 ~ Dragon Hunt
Book 2 ~ Captured Dragons
Book 3 ~ Blood Dragon
Book 4 ~ Dragon Betrayal

Demon Chaser Series (No cliffhangers)
Book 1 ~ Omega
Book 2 ~ Alpha
Book 3 ~ Hybrid
Book 4 ~ Skin
Demon Chaser Boxed Set Book 1–3

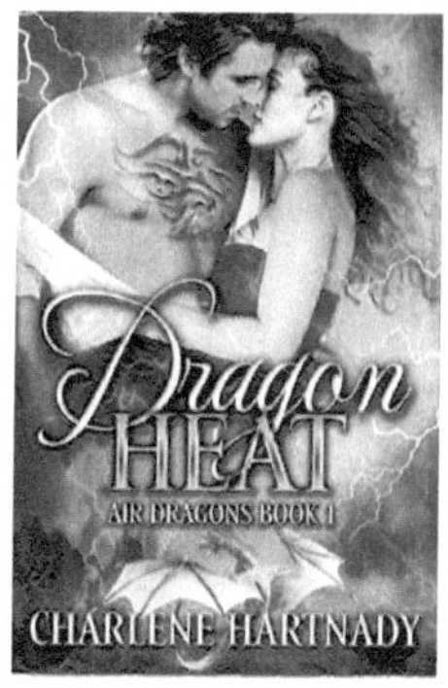

Air Dragon Series
Book 1 ~ Dragon Heat
Book 2 ~ Dragon Hunter
Book 3 ~ Dragon Avalanche
Book 4 ~ Dragon Overlord

PROLOGUE

Jaxon

BLOOD!

There's so much blood. It's everywhere I look. Splattering the grass around me. Soaking into the soil. I look down and my hands are covered in the stuff. I can scent the metallic tang. Can practically taste it on my tongue. I gag.

"Mom!" I shout. My voice is that of a very young boy. I can hear the fear etched into it. I can't stop looking at the blood. I gag again.

"Momma." My voice is soft and unsure. Fear unlike anything I've ever known has my mouth drying up and my blood rushing through my veins. I want to run and hide. I want to find my teddy bear and crawl into a small, safe place. I want my mommy so badly I whimper. I need to bury my head in her chest. I want this all to go away.

Red!

Red!

Red!

Everywhere I look is dripping red!

Then come the screams. Terrifying and pain-filled. There's snarling and growling, followed by more snarls. It's the screams that accompany each vicious, throaty snarl that make me sob even harder. He's coming for me next. He's coming for me! I just know it.

I have to be brave. I have to save her. *Please be okay, Momma!* On weak, little boy legs, I stumble forward, toward the terrifying noises. My lip is trembling so hard I can feel it. My teeth are chattering as well. I cover my face with my hands. I don't want to see. *I don't!* I have to. I have to save Momma. I have to try.

That's when I see him. He has his back to me. He's partially shifted. It's a mix of hair and skin. His ears are long with sharp tips that have tufts of hair growing off them. It's the dripping red claws that draw my attention. They're razor sharp. He snarls, slashing claws with another harsh snarl. Slashing, ripping, breaking. My mother is on the ground. She's… she's—

I scream.

The man turns around.

It's him!

No!

It can't be!

I sob even harder as his face is contorted with rage. Slightly more man than wolf. Somehow more terrifying because of it. His teeth are long and gleaming; they, too, are red-tinged. Blood drips down his chin… down his neck… down… down in never-ending rivulets.

I scream again. Or maybe I never stopped in the first place. His lip curls away from those razor-sharp teeth in a silent snarl. He rakes a claw across my chest in a vicious swipe that sends me flying backward.

I wake up. A scream trying to claw its way out of my throat. The sheets are tangled around my body; they're soaked with my sweat. My hand is on the scars across my chest. The nightmare is always the same, although, I haven't had these shitty dreams in a long time. *Why now?* I pull in a couple of deep breaths, trying to get my heart rate under control.

I know why. I can feel it. We all can. The power crackles in the air. It's time.

Fuck!

I scrub a hand over my face, trying to rid myself of the images. It was only a nightmare, I tell myself. But that isn't exactly true. It's all jumbled up. If only I could remember what actually fucking happened, it would be great. Maybe I could get over it. Who am I kidding? I'll never get over the murder of my mother. Not fucking happening. My biggest wish is for these nightmares to go away. At the very least, I wish it wasn't my father's face I saw on the wolf who killed my mom. The shifter who hurt me. It wasn't my dad who did any of it. It was *them.* I don't know what the actual murderer looks like. My crazy brain keeps muddling the details; too much time has passed. It pisses me off more than anything. One thing is for sure, I won't rest until the last Moone is taken down.

I'm sorry I couldn't save you, Momma.

CHAPTER 1

Jaxon

THE MOON IS THROWING FLICKERING rays of silver over our naked skin. We're standing in a clearing on pack lands. Three formidable figures dappled by light and dark.

"Tear out his throat!" my father snarls.

"He's still a human." I practically whisper, even though there is a part of me who wants to do just that.

"Not a human, you insolent fuck! A pre-wolf. There's a big difference and you know it." He pulls in a breath, "You'll do it then?" he says; his voice is deep, his eyes hard. As if he's giving me an option. I set my jaw, still resisting. What he's asking goes against my nature, even though I've been waiting for this day for a long time. I've played this moment in my mind a thousand times. It's always wolf on wolf.

"I'll kill the fucker as soon as he shifts," I growl. I'm not into killing humans, even if they deserve it. A pre-wolf may as well be a human. They can't shift. They're weak and have none of our strength. It will give me far more satisfaction to kill an equal. I'm not a murderer. Killing a human would be murder in the first fucking degree.

"He's strong. You can feel it… we all can."

"I'm strong, too," I insist. I am! I'm the son of a fucking alpha… the alpha of our pack.

"I've made up my mind! You'll do as I tell you." And there it is! His command.

I pull in a breath, shifting from one foot to the other. I'm seriously pissed. I'll do what, he wants but on my terms. It's not like I don't want vengeance. I do, just not like this.

"The Moones slaughtered your mother, boy. I took care of the parents. I killed them and made them pay, now it's your turn to do your part." His eyes drift to my scars, pausing on the one on my chest. On the claw mark. "Their unholy spawn walks this earth, remorseless, unpunished. I'd have thought you'd be itching to rip the bastard's throat out."

He's pulling all the right cards. My father knows exactly how to get to me. The wolves who assassinated our alpha leader almost twenty-five years ago had no qualms about leaving my mother dying in their wake. *Collateral damage.* I was just a pup then, but I can still remember her sweet face; eyes and gentle as a breeze on a moonlit night. I was there when it happened, but I can't remember a thing. All I have are strange nightmares that haunt me. "A pre-wolf is no match for me," I mutter. "Let me—"

"Exactly!" my father snarls. "That's why you find that thing and kill it now. You look it in the eyes, and you rip its throat out. Bring me the bastard's head."

"But—" I try again.

"Jaxon!" My father's deep voice pulls me back to the present. I resist for a moment before I raise my eyes. Silver meets silver. It's like looking into a mirror twenty years from now. My father's features are much like my own, except gray streaks his thick dark hair, and his nose is flanked by sharply etched lines around a cruel mouth that never smiles. Mine doesn't either. Not much to smile about when you're the son of the pack leader. Not much to smile about as his silver-gray eyes narrow on mine, thick brows lowered in a scowl. I flick my gaze down quickly; he may be my father, but that doesn't mean there won't be swift sanction for insolence. Don't challenge the alpha… it's a rule written in blood. Lately, it's a rule I've been itching to break.

"Warden," a voice halts the building tension between us, and I'm grateful for the intrusion as I look over at my uncle. Garret Skau could easily be as strong and powerful as my father and me—if it wasn't for the defect that has ailed him since birth. A twisted hip that left him with a permanent limp. Not completely debilitating, but there's never been a time he could keep up with the pack. And so, there's never been a time he'd be considered as alpha. That was my father's lot—yet he defers to his twin brother, for some reason. Probably the only man he's ever listened to. He's listening to him now. Almost.

"Warden," Garret continues, looking at me with the same silver eyes. His are softer… kinder. I feel myself relax instantly. "I think your kid may be right,"

Kid.

Hah!

I'm twenty-eight. Coming from Garret, I take it for

what it is. I can see a further softening in my uncle's eyes and for a moment I feel relief… an ally. "We don't need to kill the pre-wolf. We—"

"No!" my father barks out the word so violently I'm sure I can feel the sound rumbling in the earth. "We've felt the pull of its power growing daily. That soon-to-be-shifter is coming into its prime. That beast is destined to be an alpha. Could very well be a double-alpha. You know this as well as I do. A greater threat does not exist. Then take into account all they did to us… to Arken… to Jasmine… We're talking about the offspring of Jasmine's killers. If Jaxon had been any older, he probably would have been slain too." His voice vibrates in a low growl. "My mate was torn limb from limb… so much blood. The agony she must have felt… it took a long time for her to… to die." I watch his throat work. "Her eyes… her screams." He shakes his head. "Couldn't even string two words together. Shouting your name, Garret, in hopes that you could save her." He looks at my uncle, who drops his gaze to the ground. I think I might have seen a glint. I definitely saw shame and guilt.

Poor Garret! Such a burden for him to bear. We know he did everything he could to save her.

My father's clawed hands clench into fists. "I want that fucker dead. I want his head."

I grit my teeth when I hear my dad's words. My gut churns. What son wants to hear the details of his mother's gruesome death repeated over and over? I've blocked it from my memory and so my father never lets me forget it. At every opportunity, he reminds me of what happened the night that Callum and Ella Moone plotted to overthrow our leader and take over the pack.

A bloody coup that was thwarted. The perpetrators were thrown out of the pack for good. My father would have killed them then, if he'd had the chance, but Fate interceded. And now Fate has interceded again. The pair had a pup. A wolf born of two prime alphas. It rarely happens, but when it does… Even I can feel the pull the pre-wolf is giving off. This bastard is going to be strong as fuck should he be allowed to turn. Maybe my father is right.

No!

I'm not a murdering bastard. If I kill a pre-wolf, it will be outright murder. Like a lamb to the fucking slaughter. I won't do it! I fold my arms. I am strong enough to take him once he turns. I know I am.

My uncle steps forward. "Wait just a minute, Warden."

My father snarls. I see his face shifting. His teeth sharpen. His eyes narrow and brighten like shards of steel. Garret is still facing him. A lesser male would be cringing on the floor by now in a pool of piss. Garret's not a lesser male, he's as tough as my dad and my father is as badass as they come. That fleeting eye-contact earlier would normally have earned me fang-marks on my throat. At the very least, I'd be shaken viciously and taught a violent lesson. Although these "lessons" have been becoming fewer and fewer. It's no longer as easy for Warden to take me off my feet. I think he knows this as well as I do. It's only my respect for him that compels me to submit nowadays.

He's a hard man, but it's not his fault. Ruling a pack comes with responsibilities. And after the brutal start of his reign, he's always held onto his position with an iron fist. I know he cares for me; he just can't show it. Something broke inside him the day my mom died. Everything soft was whittled away, leaving him brittle and hard in its wake.

They're still in a standoff; my father's features are still half-turned. "Warden Skau!" my uncle says sharply, snapping his brother out of the onset of his blood-rage. "Calm down, brother," he continues, his tone gentler now. All over again, I am shocked at their dynamic. No one else would dare tell my father to calm down. My uncle goes on, "I have another solution. One I urge you to consider. You know it won't do well to call attention to the pack. A blood killing among the humans? We both know this could be disastrous. If they ever found out about our existence… " He doesn't elaborate. He doesn't have to. We all know what the consequences would be. Humans might be weak, but they outnumber us by a mile.

My father shakes his head… but he's listening. The bristling hackles that had risen along his bare spine are easing back beneath his skin. He's a broad, muscular man. Tall for a lupine… towering by human standards. Even in his bare human form, he's intimidating. I guess all of us are.

"Go on," my father says to Garret. His jaw is still tight, his eyes still narrowed.

"I've devised an antidote," he says simply. My uncle's disability may have diminished a lesser man, but Garret let it drive him to a different path. His considerable power has been channeled into nobler pursuits. He's been the pack's healer for as long as I can remember. I've seen him tend to scrapes and grazes… shattered limbs and torn bellies.

I think he started on this path in the hope of finding a cure for his own ailment. Or maybe I'm completely off base. He seems quite content with his life, even though it was he who should have been alpha. Just like me, Garret was the firstborn; only by minutes, but to us, it holds weight. Perhaps another reason for my father's lenience. My dad is staring at him now, slightly perplexed.

"An antidote?" he says. I can see he's not convinced. Not even close. Warden Skau wants to hear about blood and gore, especially when it comes to his enemies.

"A powerful curse," Garret rephrases. "A potion so potent it will strip every ounce of strength from the pre-wolf. By the time it's been administered, you'll be left with a mewling kitten instead of a burgeoning beast. Just think of it, Warden. Your legacy—not one of bloodshed, but of complete domination. You don't need to simply kill your enemies. You have the power to strip them of theirs. A wolf who can't shift. A wolf who is nothing. A shell of what they should be. It would be hell. A living hell is better than a swift death when it comes to this particular individual."

He's speaking my father's language now. I can see it on his face. Warden turns to me, a grin slowly spreading.

"Yes… a living hell." He barks out a laugh that's devoid of all humor. "I like it." He turns to me. "You'll do this for our pack, Jaxon. Find the pre-wolf, deliver the antidote. It will also offer us a degree of vengeance. Although, nothing can make up for what happened to your mother."

I nod. "How would this antidote affect a human?" I ask Garret. I need to have all the facts. They would be surrounded by humans, after all.

"That's an excellent question," my uncle says, rubbing his chin. "Administered to a pre-wolf, it will prevent the change from ever happening. It would turn a human into a bumbling idiot if given in sufficient quantities. It might even be enough to kill one. You would need to be very careful. Also, there would be a reaction in the pre-wolf. I suspect it would look similar to an epileptic fit. So, I don't suggest that you give the antidote anywhere in public, at least, not if humans are near. It's important to fly beneath the radar… subtlety is what is required on this mission. You administer the dose to the pre-wolf and make sure they consume the entire vial. Even better, you should inject it directly into a vein. You would need to do this without outing us or getting yourself arrested. It shouldn't be that difficult." He shrugs. "You are a shifter… a male in your prime." He pats my back.

No pressure!

I nod in agreement. It's by no means a simple task, but I sure as hell can get it done. With that, our meeting is concluded. I watch as their flesh sprouts fur. I feel my own transformation begin, feel the elongation of limbs and the tightening of muscles. When the moon flickers back through the trees, it glints off my charcoal pelt. I run, pushing hard; the soil is soft beneath the pads of my paws. If only that moon could lighten the burden I feel on my shoulders. I'm glad my father chose me. I need to do this for my mother… for my pack. There's a big part of me that needs to do this for myself, too. I will avenge the death of my beloved mother and keep the pack safe, even if it kills me.